I0824061

WATCH US CRACK

ALSO BY GABRIELLA LEPORE

Bad Like Us

The Last One to Fall

This Is Why We Lie

WATCH US CRACK

GABRIELLA LEPORE

STORYTIDE
An Imprint of HarperCollinsPublishers

This is a work of fiction. Names, characters, places, and incidents are products of the author's imagination or are used fictitiously and are not to be construed as real. Any resemblance to actual events, locales, organizations, or persons, living or dead, is entirely coincidental.

HarperCollins Children's Books,
a division of HarperCollins Publishers,
195 Broadway, New York, NY 10007

HarperCollins Publishers, Macken House,
39/40 Mayor Street Upper, Dublin 1, D01 C9W8, Ireland

Storytide is an imprint of HarperCollins Publishers.

Watch Us Crack.

harpercollins.com
Library of Congress Control Number: 2025937154
ISBN 978-1-335-01387-3
Typography by Laura Mock

25 26 27 28 29 LBC 5 4 3 2 1
First Edition

To Natalie, Rhodri, Emily, and Tom—
for all the fun!

Friday, January 31

MY HANDS ARE NUMB, AND *my jeans are rough and heavy, wet at the bottoms. I shake the snowflakes from my hair and find a spot at the back of the train, away from the others. The seat creaks beneath me.*

Sometimes they cancel the Metro service to Hailing when the weather gets this bad. But not tonight. Tonight, the train pulled into the platform as usual, and we all piled into the empty cars, snowflakes melting on coats and damp footprints in the aisle. The seats are full now, voices are loud, energy is buzzing.

We stayed late tonight, team bonding—sharing plates of fries and wings in the diner overlooking the ice rink, pretending we're a tight unit.

In the cram of bodies finding seats, she passes me. She hesitates in the aisle, her gaze wandering over my backpack propped on the seat beside me. I'm about to move my bag, to offer her a place to sit. But before I can speak, she slips something into the open front pocket, so subtle that I almost miss it. A folded piece of paper.

I frown at her from my seat, confused, but she doesn't look at me. She moves on, heading toward the compartment doors.

The train lurches forward, screeching on the tracks, and my heart gives a slow thud as I reach for the notepaper.

Friday, February 21

SADIE

THERE'S BLOOD ON THE FLOOR.

It's just a small speck on the worn rubber surface of the train car, barely visible. But I see it.

I shift in my seat and shuffle away from the window, retreating from the biting wind sweeping through the western region of New York State. Outside, the tiled platform arcs into a too-bright tunnel. Neon words flash on the live departure board. *HAILING SERVICE 11:20.*

An automated announcement grits out, "Doors closing, please stand back. Doors closing, please stand back." It repeats as the electric doors click and groan shut, trapping the cold air outside.

I exhale slowly.

The train starts lumbering along the tracks, and I untangle myself from my messenger bag. As we leave Arcadia behind, the luminous platform is replaced by the darkness outside and my own faded reflection caught in the window. I smooth down my hair, twisting it over my shoulder.

I missed the 9:30 service that I usually take after my Friday evening shift at Raleigh's Rec Center diner. The 9:30 is always busy, full of voices and life—people, bodies, company in the darkness. The 11:20, on the other hand, is a lot quieter.

But I'm not totally alone. There are a few girls seated at the back of the car. Every now and then, I hear them burst into fits of laughter.

I noticed them earlier, waiting at the platform. Three of them, a little older than me, college students. They were carrying bottles of beer hidden in paper bags, chatting and giggling.

One of them—a blonde with hoop earrings and full red lips—asked if I went to ACU, and I told her no, that I'm a junior in high school. We talked for a minute, passing the time. I could smell the alcohol on their breath, but I felt safer on the platform just knowing they were there—strangers, but allies in the night.

I hug my bag, resting my chin on the top.

Fortunately, Hailing Station is only fifteen minutes away, and it's pretty much right outside my house. If it wasn't, I don't think my dad would be down with me catching the last train home alone on a Friday night. Okay, so he didn't technically agree to the *last* train, and I don't intend on sharing that detail with him, either. Dad works the graveyard shift as a hotel security guard on weekends, and in this case, what he doesn't know won't hurt him.

The car's connecting door slides open, and just like that, I'm holding my breath.

A boy steps through the entry, broad and solid looking, wearing sweats and a blue-and-black hockey jacket, with a sports bag slung over his shoulder.

Cason Tano.

He plays for Hailing High School. Their team was out on the ice earlier this evening, sticks clashing as they battled for the puck. They use Raleigh's for their Friday night practices at the same time I work my shift at the diner, where a glass wall overlooks the gleaming rink.

I know the Hailing boys, kind of. We went to middle school together, but I transferred to Arcadia in freshman year. After my parents separated and my mom moved away, my dad thought Arcadia would be a fresh start for me. A new opportunity. Hailing High School doesn't exactly have the best reputation, unlike Arcadia, which is renowned for its academic excellence and wide-ranging extracurriculars—at least, that's what it states on the brochure.

Cason's gaze lands on mine, just for a second. "Hey, Sadie," he murmurs. His reddish-brown hair is mussed from the wind.

"Hey," I echo.

Then he's gone, walking right on past. Somewhere behind me, I hear his jacket rustle as he takes a seat.

I slip my phone from my coat pocket and open the last text thread, my most recent conversation with my best friend, Quinn.

Kai texted me, she'd written. He's meeting me at Hailing Station to talk. TALK?

Quinn called in sick tonight, and I covered for her. When I got the job at Raleigh's a few months ago, Quinn had begged me to convince the diner's manager, Maya, to hire her too. I spent hours pitching Quinn as a shining employee, an asset to our small team.

But my recommendation calls in sick more than she shows. And when she does show up, she takes way too many bathroom breaks.

Still, I wouldn't have it any other way. Quinn and I are the definition of codependency. I spent most of my summer surrounded by dust and spiders, helping Quinn organize her family's garage when she was going through her Marie Kondo phase. And when I moved to Arcadia High School, we'd convinced her parents to sign her transfer application before the end of the first semester.

I start typing. **How's it going with Kai? Are you back together yet?**

Quinn has been in love with Kai since sophomore year homecoming—he beguiled her with his chiseled features and sandy-blond curls. But they've been on a break for the past few weeks. The fact that he was even willing to cross the border into Hailing tonight had seemed like progress. I'm pretty sure Arcadia people can't comprehend why anyone would ever voluntarily hang out in Hailing, let alone *live* there like Quinn and I do.

Before I hit send, I add, **I missed the 9:30 train. But I'm on my way home now. Are you still at the platform?**

My gaze wanders to the opposite window, where the train is reflected over the backdrop of darkness rushing by outside.

Cason is a couple of rows behind me, one arm slung over the seat back, looking totally relaxed. I doubt he'll be so relaxed when he's face-to-face with Kai Harrison at the other end of this journey. The boys got into a huge fight after the Hailing versus Arcadia hockey game last month, and there's a ton of bad blood still lingering.

A shiver crawls down my spine. Maybe it's the emptiness of the night train, the jolts of the cars racing along the tracks. Or maybe it's the thought of that fight. Because I was there, and that kind of violence is hard to forget.

I bury the memory, then I close my conversation with Quinn and open a new text thread with someone else. My stomach knots as I type out the words, **Wanna hang out at my house?**

I wait, staring at my phone. And then the reply comes.

Yeah. You mean tonight?

The speaker in the train car's ceiling crackles, and my eyes snap up from my phone. "Last stop, Hailing. Please make sure you take all your personal belongings." The muffled words echo, and the train slows before coming to a standstill at the platform.

I haul my bag over my shoulder as the doors click open. A ticket machine is partially hidden by shadows, and a single streetlamp casts light on the brick wall covered in neon tags. But Quinn and Kai aren't here.

The college girls stumble onto the platform, shrieking with laughter as the brunette missteps. She clutches the blond girl's arm for support, but she's giggling. They all are. A concealed beer bottle is still sealed in her grasp, willowy arms exposed to the biting winter weather. They stay knotted together, oblivious to anything outside their bubble.

Above me, the roof creaks as I make my way toward the rusted railing leading to the stairwell. Without the light from the platform guiding my path, I descend into darkness. My shoes clang fast on the metal rungs.

I hear Quinn's voice before I see her. "Please, just think about this—"

"I already have." Kai cuts her off. "We've been doing this for too long. I'm done, Quinn."

"You can't do this to *me*," she chokes. "To us."

"I don't owe you anything. Not anymore."

I hurry down the last few steps and see them standing on the sidewalk. They stop short when they notice me.

Quinn's sleek auburn hair is pulled into a low ponytail, a few strands loosened by the wind. She dabs at her eyes with the sleeve of her oversized sweatshirt—*Kai's* hockey sweatshirt. The one he gave her at the end of last season, back when they were still together. Still going strong.

"Hi," I say, looking between them. "Is everything okay?"

Quinn folds her arms around herself, and the muscles in Kai's square jaw bulge.

"No," Quinn answers. "Not really." She sounds breathless, like she's barely keeping it together. But she won't look at me. Her focus stays trained on the pavement.

Footsteps and voices echo in the stairwell behind us, and we pause as the trio of girls emerges. Their shoes tap quickly on the pavement as they sidle past, walking arm in arm down the sidewalk. The blonde glances at us as they pass, whispering something to her friend before they stop to take a selfie by the rusty Hailing Station signpost.

Kai's wide-set stare goes back to Quinn. "We're done here," he says, catching her gaze. "It's done."

"You don't get to make that decision alone," she shoots back. "We need to talk about this, Kai. Please."

My heart sinks for her. "Kai," I jump in, lifting my hands in peace. "Please don't leave like this. She's clearly upset—"

He scoffs at that.

Quinn draws in a shaky breath. "Sadie, would you give us a minute?" She meets my eyes, communicating silently with a look.

"Okay," I murmur. "I'll be at home. Call if you need me."

"Yeah," she says, swallowing.

Leaving them on the sidewalk, I cross the street and head for my house. But I pause in the shadows. Where they're standing, Cason will have to pass them when he leaves the station, and that makes me uneasy.

I can still hear Quinn's hurried words as their voices drift faintly through the night, wrought with emotion.

"Please don't do this."

"This was you, Quinn. You did this to us."

Tall elms line the sidewalk, like sentries in the darkness. Their leaves have fallen, and the long, gnarled branches are reaching out into the road, casting shadows over Quinn and Kai. Their silhouettes are distorted in the bending lamplight. Quinn's slim arms are folded tightly, and Kai's hands are knotted through his hair.

Their voices are lost, stolen by the wind. And then it's over. Kai's walking away.

"You're making a mistake!" Quinn yells after him.

But he doesn't stop. His silhouette dissolves into the darkness. Alone on the street, Quinn scrubs at her face and brings her cell to her ear. ". . . Hey." Her voice cracks. "I tried to stop him, but he wouldn't listen. . . ."

"Quinn," I call to her as she steps onto the pavement. "What happened?"

Her eyes dart to me. "Emma, I'll call you back," she says into her cell. "I'm with Sadie." She lowers her phone. "Kai," she says, glancing over her shoulder as though she's looking for him, expecting him to be there. "He just . . ." Her voice breaks and shatters into a sob.

I rush to her and pull her into a hug. "I'm so sorry, Quinn."

"He left," she whispers, leaning into me. "He actually left."

Gently, I guide her toward my house.

Inside, the hallway is too quiet. Too dark. The wind is batting at the walls, tapping at the windows as we pad upstairs.

My bedroom is small, with just enough space to fit my bed, a dresser, and a flea-market desk that Mom and I painted purple on her last visit. String lights glow yellow and red above the mirror and curtain rail, blushing the arrangement of photos I've tacked to the wall: Quinn and me at a football game with our friend Emma, our faces striped green and yellow in Arcadia colors; last summer's beach trip with a few girls from my grade; and Mom, Dad, and me huddled together at the top of the Empire State Building.

Mom lives in Staten Island with her new boyfriend, Bryce. She runs an interior design business in the city. I miss her, and it's no secret that she wants me to move down there with her. When she signed the lease on her apartment, she made sure that there was a bedroom for me, with a walk-in closet and upcycled furniture that she spent forever choosing. But my life has always been here, with

Dad, with my friends. It was always going to be here.

Quinn crawls onto my bed and hugs a pillow to her chest.

"What happened?" I ask, joining her.

She works her lip between her teeth. "I don't even know. He's just so mad at me. I mean, he's mad because I've been talking to other people while we've been on a break. But he's been talking to other people too."

I huddle next to her. "Double standard. It's so unfair."

"The only person I was serious about was Kai. Surely he knows that."

"I'm sorry," I whisper, my throat tight. Because even if Kai doesn't know it, I do. And that makes it so much harder to hear.

Her gaze wanders to the window, and a tear rolls down her cheek. It's awhile before she speaks. "How could he do this to me?" she murmurs. "He just walked away."

I twist one of my rings restlessly. "You know you deserve better, Quinn."

She sniffs and wipes her eyes with her sleeve. "But I love him, Sadie. We were together for a year. It's just . . ." Her chest heaves. "None of this make sense." With trembling hands, she unlocks her phone and starts swiping. "Look at this. Read this." She angles the screen toward me, peach-polished nails scrolling back through her most recent chat with Kai.

I skim the texts. Kai's cryptic **We should talk** message, and Quinn's eager response. Clearly, she thought they were getting back together tonight.

"I just don't believe anything he says anymore," she snaps,

jabbing at her screen and the messages. “He’s a liar, and he’s been gaslighting me this whole time.”

“It seems like—” My sentence is cut short by the sound of tires screeching on the road. We both stop and turn toward the window. Outside, a car door thumps shut.

Quinn sits a little higher, trying to see out. “Is your dad back?”

I glance at the time displayed on her phone—12:10. “No. He won’t be home for hours.”

An engine rumbles on the street. And then nothing, just the lonely howl of the wind.

Quinn returns her attention to me. “He ended it,” she says weakly. “It’s really done this time, isn’t it?”

I can’t bring myself to respond.

But my silence is enough. Her eyes fill again, and she draws in a shaky breath. “Can I sleep over?”

“Of course.” I try not to think about my own situation, and the text message still awaiting a response.

Quinn has already wrapped the comforter around her shoulders. While she rearranges my pillows, I reach for my cell.

Yeah. You mean tonight?

Sorry, I type back. Something came up. Another time?

“Who are you texting?” Quinn asks, peering at me from across the bed.

“No one. Just letting my dad know that you’re here.” The lie escapes way too easily.

My phone pings. Yeah. No worries. Night Sadie.

Night, Cason, I reply. And I hit send.

Saturday, February 22

SADIE

THE JARRING SOUND OF MY alarm wakes me.

Morning light lances through a gap in the drapes. Quinn's gone. I don't remember her leaving, but when I stirred at the sound of my dad's footsteps thudding up the stairs at dawn, Quinn was still curled beneath the comforter on the other side of the bed.

I find my phone and silence the alarm, squinting at the background image of Quinn, Emma, and me. We're standing outside Raleigh's, all three of us mid-laugh, our attention fixed on something out of frame. Emma's curly black hair is pulled into a messy bun, and there's a golden shimmer on her skin. Quinn is wide-eyed and beaming, her rosy cheeks scattered with freckles. Sandwiched between them, my hair has fallen loose from my braid and my makeup is nonexistent, but I like this photo. It captures *us*, noses crinkled in laughter, barefaced and real. Quinn and Emma don't get the same warm-and-fuzzies when they look at this picture, though. When Emma borrowed my phone last week, she grimaced and said, "Why would you have this on your home screen? Trauma flashbacks."

Yeah. She has a point. A couple of hours after the photo was taken, the smiles and laughter disappeared. This was the night the fight broke out after the Hailing versus Arcadia hockey match. It got bad. The police showed up, and some of the boys ended up in the emergency room—Emma's brother, Brandon, was among them.

But everyone recovered. Physically, at least.

I haul myself out of bed and pull a chunky knit from my closet before peeling back the drapes.

My breath hitches.

Outside, there are three police officers standing at the foot of the steps leading to the platform. Two squad cars are parked along the pavement, and access to the road is blocked by cones and yellow tape.

I grab my phone and Google *News in Hailing, NY.*

Results spill down the page, but my eyes fix on the top one, and suddenly I can't breathe.

Incident at Hailing train station. In the early hours of Saturday, February 22 . . .

Today. That's today.

I press play on a video still of what looks like a news report, filmed with the Hailing Station signpost in the background. The video springs to life, and the reporter's voice fills my room. "Good morning, this is Suraya Sharma reporting live from Hailing." Her jet-black ponytail bobs in the morning breeze. The camera is focused on her, with police cars and uniformed officers blurred in the background as they stretch tape across the steps. ". . . forces arriving on the scene here at Hailing station, just a stone's throw from where I'm standing . . ."

Police are trying to block the camera's view, but in the corner of the shot, EMTs emerge from the lower tracks carrying a stretcher. A sheet has been draped over the shape of an unmoving body.

I sink onto my bed with my hand pressed to my mouth. The rest of the reporter's words turn fuzzy.

But I hear it.

". . . where the body of a teenager was found."

ONE MONTH EARLIER

Friday, January 24

CASON

BREATH LEAVES MY LUNGS FAST. My helmet cushions the blow to my head when I hit the ice, but I still feel the impact. The guy who shouldered into me whacks my leg with his hockey stick as he passes. He acts like it was an accident, that we just collided going after the puck. But it was obvious he was aiming for me.

The intermission whistle blows, and bright lights blur and bleed above me.

A hand reaches over me, and the next thing I know I'm back on my feet, my blades scraping the ice. I take off my helmet and pull off my gloves with my teeth, then drag a hand through my hair, damp with sweat.

Michel lifts his face shield. "That should have been a penalty. The ref should get him on misconduct."

"And slashing. Did you see what he did?" I nod across the rink to where the Arcadia team has assembled with their coach, an older guy with a bald head and thick neck.

"We're still killing them, though." A smile twitches Michel's lips, and I mirror it.

This isn't new to us. We've been on teams together since elementary school, and it shows on our faces. Michel's nose is crooked from a break; there's a scar cutting through his heavy eyebrow, and a chipped front tooth from last year's Hampton Hill game. I've been lucky, mostly. A couple of small scars on my face from falls or a rogue puck, and a few sprains, nothing lasting. But I figure my luck's got to run out eventually.

Not tonight, though.

The scoreboard is in our favor.

My eyes stay on the Arcadia guy—Number 19, Kai Harrison. I recognize him. He's got a thing going with Quinn McKinley, a girl I went to middle school with.

I know he doesn't like me. We've played them before, and I beat him clean in a face-off. He's still pressed about it and has been trying to take me down all night, looking for a way to outplay me.

Their team is at the far side now, talking strategy, trying to figure out how they're going to pull this back. Not going to happen.

People from their school have shown up to support them, waving banners and all that shit. They've got twice as many supporters as we've got—as we've ever had. Friends, teachers, family.

Nights like this always make me think of my mom, because a few years ago she would have been here, cheering and freezing her ass off. Sometimes those years feel like they've passed in a blink, and other times it feels like forever.

I've lived with my uncle, Alec, since I was thirteen, in the same house that he and my mom grew up in. There are still photos of her all around the place. Photos of them when they were my age, graduating high school or on vacation. After my grandparents died, Alec inherited the house, and after my mom died, he inherited me.

It's been four years now, and I've dealt with the grief. I'm okay. Sometimes.

Michel claps my shoulder over the padding. "We'll get him," he says, and he moves to join our team at the opposite edge.

Our coach, Larsen, is looking my way, checking that I'm back on my feet and not out for the game. Some of the other guys are watching too. Ruben Hernandez lifts his hand, waiting for my response. "You good?" he mouths, and I nod.

My attention goes back to Number 19. He's taken his helmet off. Wide jawed and jacked up, with a smirk on his face.

Above the bleachers, I check for another familiar face. A face from the past who's been looking down over the rink from the glass-walled diner where she works.

Sadie Morelli.

There have been a couple of times where I've noticed her around Raleigh's, or on the Arcadia platform waiting for the 9:30 train to Hailing. We don't talk, but I know she's there. I like that she's there.

I wait for her eyes to land on me, then I half smile. She notices me, gives me a small wave before looking away.

Contact. It was nothing, barely anything, but it's a shift, a door opening. It's what I've been waiting for.

Skates scrape behind me, and I turn to see Ruben and Finley come up.

"Everything okay?" Ruben asks. He's built stockier than Finley. But that isn't an advantage, necessarily—Fin might be wiry, but he's the fastest guy we've got. Quietest guy we've got too.

"Larsen's popping off at the ref," Ruben says, nodding toward the edge. "Nineteen's been coming after you all night. We need to get him out." His eyes narrow. One thing about Ruben is that he's always in my corner. And I'm always in his.

I glance over at Coach Larsen where he's standing at the barrier, mad as hell, signaling to the referee with a lanky arm. Number 19 is with his team across the ice, and their coach is looking twitchy.

Finley lifts his face shield, flushed, with dark hair plastered to his forehead. "They're probably going to pull him after that," he mutters, dragging a hand across his brow.

"Yeah," I say, watching the ref signal. "He's out."

I turn back to the long window above the bleachers, checking for Sadie. She's disappeared back into the diner.

But she'll be supporting her school tonight, not us. Not me. Tonight, we're on opposite sides, no matter how much it sucks.

I crick my neck.

Tonight, I've got more enemies than friends.

Friday, January 24

SADIE

". . . I'M RUNNING OUT OF TIME, *but I have some thoughts on the evidence found at the Olivia Campbell crime scene. I'm not convinced that this is cut-and-dried. Like for part two."*

"Who won?"

I look up with a start and slip my phone under the table, hiding it from my boss, Maya Bennett. Her deep brown eyes are trained on me, hair braided to her shoulders and colorful jewelry matching her outfit.

"Um . . ." I glance at the glass wall, a vista to the rink below. "Hailing, I think."

Maya folds her arms, one perfectly sculpted brow raised. "Right," she says. "So, you're watching? Because it seemed like you were on TikTok."

I attempt a smile. "I'm on break?"

She slides into the red plastic booth opposite. "Careful, you're starting to sound like Quinn."

I gasp in mock horror. "Ouch."

Quinn requested to take the evening off work so that she could support Kai from the stands. Fortunately, the rink's diner has been near empty all evening. But we're expecting the hockey crowd to swarm the place after the final whistle. I told Maya I was going to keep an eye on the game, let her know when it was coming to an end. And I did keep an eye on the game—at least until I got distracted by a notification. TIKTOK: *@WildeOnCrime has posted a new video.*

Maya peers down at the rink, where the post-game music and clamor of supporters vacating the stands is muffled by the glass. Her face falls. "Yeah, looks like Hailing won."

Maya graduated from Arcadia High School five years ago, and she's a proud alumna. Former dance captain and valedictorian, she enrolled in the local college and is getting her PhD in Africana studies, all alongside managing Raleigh's diner and chairing her former sorority.

"What were you watching, anyway?" she asks.

I place my phone on the table and angle the screen toward her as I tap play.

Darcy Wilde's voice drifts out. "Yesterday, I posted a video on the unsolved Olivia Campbell case, and I had a bunch of comments requesting advice relating to this. Seems like a lot of you want to know what to do if you find yourself in an unsafe situation . . ."

Maya's brows pull together. "What is this?"

". . . and I would suggest you stay calm, make noise, know your exits, and guys, if you're going into a potentially unsafe environment alone, just make sure you let people know where you are."

I pause the video. "Wilde on Crime," I tell Maya. "Darcy Wilde is a former crime scene technician and forensic expert—"

"Everyone on TikTok is an expert," Maya says, rolling her eyes.

"No, but it's true. She's my idol." I wave my phone, showing Darcy frozen on the screen in a formal buttoned shirt, proudly displaying her long, gray-streaked hair, with one finger raised. I've always dreamed of studying criminology at the University at Buffalo, where Darcy Wilde graduated top of her class twenty-something years ago. That's always been my plan, ever since I was a kid and my dad would come home from his security jobs with some new story that intrigued him—mysterious break-ins with no signs of forced entry, or crimes where the evidence just didn't add up. It's something Dad and I share, the fascination with the how and why.

Sometimes I spend hours in my room storyboarding cases I find online. I map out the crime scenes, analyze motives, and build my own theories—trying to solve the cases myself. It gives me something to focus on, a drive.

The diner's double doors swing open, and the post-game crowd starts to filter in. Maya springs to her feet and gestures for me to put my phone away.

I slide out of the booth and follow her to the ruby-red wraparound counter along the back wall. The red-and-white art deco backsplash tiles brighten the bar area, which leads to the kitchen where Joey, our chef, is stationed.

Bodies start to flood the place, standing at the high-top tables in the center or claiming the side booths overlooking the rink. I recognize a lot of them, some from Hailing and some from Arcadia. It almost feels as though I've lived two lifetimes, with two identities: who I was at Hailing, and who I try to be at Arcadia.

Quinn and Emma stride in, arm in arm, cheeks rosy from the cold arena. Emma's bulky digital camera is strapped over her shoulder. She's on the school paper and covers pretty much every sporting event Arcadia has. That camera is forever attached to her, poised and ready for yearbook photo ops.

The two of them make their way over to the bar and hop onto the metal stools.

Quinn gives way to an elaborate sigh. "We lost."

I purse my lips in a show of sympathy.

A couple of boys from our team pass the bar area, their hair damp and faces drawn. Emma's brother, Brandon, and his friend Jacob Ritter muster smiles as they walk by, and Jacob drums the counter with his knuckles. Emma tried to set Jacob and me up over the summer, but we fizzled out after a few stilted texts and one painfully awkward coffee date, where Jacob spent most of the time talking about Kai, low-key resenting him for landing the captain spot on the hockey team.

Only Kai lingers at the bar, and Quinn wraps an arm around his waist as I prepare their fountain drinks. I'm not really close with Kai and the hockey guys—we're more friends by association, ever since Emma pulled me into the group after she and I bonded over our mutual hatred of gym class in sophomore year. When Quinn and Kai started dating, I got to know him a little better, and I've seen his good side—but I didn't see it tonight.

I slide their drinks across the counter, and Emma pops a straw into hers.

"So what happened out there, Kai?" she asks. "You got sent to the penalty box?"

He exhales, running a hand through his damp hair. "It's not my fault. The ref overreacted, and their guy totally sold it. I barely touched him!"

Quinn leans into him, her fingers resting on his broad chest as he heaves a sigh. "Of course," she says softly.

"There were college scouts in the bleachers," he adds, his jaw tightening. "That game made me look bad."

Emma frowns. "Yes, and now our team's getting a reputation for fouling. It's not just about you, Kai."

His nostrils flare, but he stays silent, and Quinn drops her gaze.

"There'll be other games," I offer, attempting to breeze over the tension. "You'll get other chances to prove yourself." But I saw how Kai played. Everyone saw. He was deliberately targeting Hailing's players. There was nothing accidental about it.

"Yeah," he mutters, his voice tight. He nods toward the booth across the diner. "I'm going to sit with the guys," he says, grimacing as he walks away, head down, shoulders tense.

Quinn hops off her stool. "I should go with him, he needs support. Sadie, do you want a ride home later?"

"What time are you leaving?" I ask.

"I don't know. Whenever Kai is ready, I guess. He's coming over tonight."

The last time I'd agreed to wait around until Kai was ready

to leave, I missed curfew and had to endure a lecture from my dad about my subpar timekeeping. "Don't worry about me," I tell Quinn. "I'll catch the train."

"Okay."

I watch as she hurries across the diner to join the Arcadia team. She squeezes onto the bench seat and huddles close to Kai, and he half-heartedly slings an arm around her shoulders. Quinn's overly cheerful buoyancy stands out in a sea of gray.

"I should probably go join the pity party too," Emma says, pointing her soda straw toward their booth. "I hate Hailing." She pauses, presses her full lips together, then adds, "Sorry. No offense."

I shrug. "None taken. Everyone who isn't from Hailing hates Hailing."

"All right." She heaves herself off the bar stool. "I'm going. Here's to misery." She places her hand on her heart, and I smile.

"Here's to misery," I echo, miming raising a glass.

She wiggles her fingers in a wave before weaving through the crowd, curls bouncing.

I grab a cloth and wipe the countertop, clearing the ring marks from their sodas.

"Hey." The familiar voice makes me jump. I whirl around and find myself face-to-face with a blast from the past. Only he's a little older than my memory paints him.

Cason Tano. Tanned skin, perfectly proportioned features, tousled reddish-brown hair, and that lopsided smile—the same one I recognize from middle school.

"Oh." I scramble for words. "Hi. Cason. Hi."

"Hi," he says with a grin. "Long time, huh?"

"Yes." A burning heat rises to my cheeks. "Yeah, it's been awhile." *Cason. It's Cason.*

"I saw you here last week," he says. "Downstairs in the lobby. I meant to come say hi." His light brown eyes look almost golden in the diner's soft lighting. "How've you been, Sadie?"

I take a small breath. "Good. Great." My heart starts beating a little faster. "You?"

"Yeah. You know. How long has it been?"

I blow out a breath. "Middle school?"

He nods and drags a hand through his mussed hair. "You know, I thought I saw you at the gas station outside Hailing a couple of months back. The one by the intersection?"

I tilt my head like I can't remember. I *totally* remember. I was coming out of the 7-Eleven just as he was walking in. He held the door open for me, towering over me, and we glanced at each other. Just a glance, with a flicker of recognition. A flicker of a memory from another life. I climbed into my dad's car and held my breath, waiting for my pulse to normalize. Cason Tano, my middle school friend. My middle school crush. My only real crush. Ever.

"So when did you start working here?" he asks.

"Since September. I'm saving for college. That's the plan, anyway."

He smiles—that cute, dimpled, genuinely interested smile. "Nice."

"And congrats," I say, gesturing to him. "On the game, I mean.

You guys played well. You're really good."

"Thanks. Sorry about the, uh . . ."

"What? The demolishment of my school's team?"

He grins. "Yeah."

"It's okay. You earned the win." My gaze travels over his face. There's a cut on his forehead, and it looks pretty fresh. I point to it. "Is that a consequence of tonight's game?"

He frowns as he reaches up and touches his brow. "Oh. Yeah. Does your guy always play like that?"

Unfortunately, I know exactly who he's referring to. "You handled it with grace," I say.

"Thank you." He looks down at his sneakers, but he's still smiling. And now I'm smiling. His eyes come back to me, making my heart beat triple time.

I remind myself to speak. "So what have you—"

"Hey," someone yells, and I jump. A middle-aged guy in a New Jersey Devils ball cap snaps his fingers in my direction. "Are you taking orders or what? I've been waiting here for, like, ten minutes."

"I'll let you go," Cason says, tapping the counter. "I'll see you around. Maybe next time."

"Are you leaving?"

"Yeah. I don't think we're welcome here tonight." He says it with a laugh, but it falls flat.

I can't deny he's right. Ninety percent of the people here are from Arcadia, and the glares pointed his way speak volumes.

"Have a good night," he adds.

Just as I'm silently cursing ball-cap guy for the interruption, Cason says, "It's good to see you, Sadie. I've missed you."

A rush of butterflies makes my stomach flip. "You too. We should hang out sometime." My face is burning. I've never asked anyone to hang out before. Maybe it's the dim lighting, the cacophony of background noise tricking me into thinking I'm braver than I actually am.

For a second, Cason looks taken aback, and I'm pretty sure my racing heart stills. Flatlines.

But then he speaks. "Yeah. Yeah, I'd like that. Do you still have my number?"

I nod.

"Let me know when you're free," he says. And then he's gone.

Ball-cap guy hollers at me again, and I force myself to hide the euphoric smile tugging at my lips—only half listening as he reels off his order and critiques our poor service and faulty QR code.

Regardless, I stumble through, putting in a kitchen order for blue cheese wings and fries, and Ball Cap retreats to his table.

A camera flashes, dazzling me for a second.

I blink the spots from my vision and frown at Emma and the extended lens aimed in my direction. Another click and a flash.

"What are you doing? Why are you taking pictures of me?"

She lowers her camera. "Because I'm wondering why you've got that look on your face." She lines up another shot, adjusting the focus on the lens.

"What look?"

Click, flash. "Too happy."

I glance beyond her to the booth, where some of the guys are working on share plates of fries and sliders. Kai's seat is empty.

Across the diner, the Hailing team is finishing their drinks and shrugging into their blue-and-black jackets, getting ready to leave. Their coach, a youngish, lanky guy with curly brown hair, is chatting with Maya at the bar, talking about some mutual friend from ACU.

But Cason isn't with them.

A strange feeling settles in the pit of my stomach.

And then there's commotion, people running for the door, banging on the windows. And someone shouts, *"Fight!"*

Friday, January 24

CASON

THE SMACK TO THE BACK of my head makes me stoop forward. Pain shoot across my skull. The blow comes again, a hockey stick, and then I'm on the ground. This isn't the ice anymore, and I'm not in gear and a helmet. We're in the dark parking lot, on the asphalt.

Number 19 stands over me. He lifts the stick and brings it down on my leg. Once, twice . . .

I roll out of the way, but my head is spinning.

"Getting *me* pulled out of the game?" he spits.

The shadowed parking lot revolves around me. My head throbs, and the light coming from Raleigh's windows starts to bleed, streaking yellow through my vision.

It takes me a couple of seconds to figure out what's going on.

There are shouts, voices.

Across the lot, Michel sprints toward us and pulls Kai back. But there are more of them, the Arcadia guys. Three, four . . .

I stagger to my feet and blink fast. It's not just us anymore. His whole team is outside now.

And some of mine too. Michel, Ruben, Finley . . .

They're in front of me, shielding me, and the Arcadia guys are coming at them because of it. But they're not moving. They're not leaving me.

Something crawls down my face. I drag a hand over my cheek, smearing blood across my palm.

People are screaming. There's a group of girls knotted together, and I see her through the crowd. Sadie. She's in the doorway, and I recognize the look on her face. The fear.

She slips free from her friends and runs toward us.

Someone shouts, "Stop!"

I know I have to get to her.

But Number 19 comes at me again, so I take a swing at him.

And another.

And another.

ARCADIA NEWS ONLINE

Police were called to Raleigh's Recreation Center in downtown Arcadia on the evening of Friday, January 24, where rioting had been reported after a high school hockey event.

Following the incident, a joint statement has been released on behalf of the Arcadia and Hailing school coaches, Richard Johnson and Zach Larsen, respectively.

"As advocates for team sports and the spirit of friendly competition, we stand firmly against this conduct. The poor judgment and actions of a small minority of our athletes do not represent our schools and the majority of our teams. The students involved have been reprimanded and will be issuing an apology to all those affected by the incident."

Police have no reason to believe that there is a link between this incident and the west byway car accident reported in the early hours of Saturday, January 25.

Friday, January 31

SADIE

IT'S BEEN A WEEK. A week since that night. This is the first time I've been back to Raleigh's since, and I was so close to calling in sick today. Especially because I knew the Hailing team would be here, practicing on the other side of the glass wall. I just don't know what I'm supposed to say to Cason after last week. Everyone at school is talking about how he jumped Kai in the parking lot, and it turns my stomach just thinking about it.

I set my tray on the booth table and start stacking the discarded plates, trying not to glance at the window overlooking the rink below, where the sounds from Hailing's practice reverberate. Hollow shouts, and the scrape of skates on ice.

Quinn hops up onto the table and crosses her legs. "Kai hasn't replied to my text." Her phone is poised in her hand. "It's been two hours."

I drop my cleaning rag onto the tray before brushing aside some stray strands of hair with the back of my hand. Maya is at the counter, focused on her laptop as she runs through the accounts with her glasses reflecting the screen.

"Which text?" I ask Quinn.

She angles her cell toward me, showing her Miss you message left on read.

"Maybe he's busy."

She arches an eyebrow.

"Or maybe he thought he'd replied, but he forgot to press send. That happens sometimes."

"Should I text him again?" Quinn stares at me, head tilted, waiting for an answer.

"No."

She chews on her purple-painted thumbnail. "I could ask him what he's doing? Or is that too much?"

I turn my palms skyward, and she sighs to the ceiling.

"Help me, Sadie!" she exclaims. "I'm getting anxiety."

"Okay. If you want to message him that bad, just do it. He is your boyfriend, Quinn."

She laughs under her breath. "Is he, though?"

Kai has been acting off all week. At first I thought he was retreating to heal his bruises—bruised ego included. But at school on Monday, it became abundantly clear that the only person he's retreated from is *Quinn*. She's clinging to the threads of their relationship by her fingertips, and her determination only seems to be making him withdraw more.

Quinn thinks it's because of her connection to Hailing. She thinks Kai saw her talking to Ruben Hernandez as the players were coming off the ice last week, and now he's branded her a traitor.

Personally, I don't think the problem is Quinn. I think the problem is Kai. And his ego.

She fiddles with a strand of hair, wrapping it around her index finger. Her gaze moves to the glass wall, and she starts gnawing on her lip.

"That's time." Hailing's coach's voice reaches us, penetrating the glass barrier.

The neon wall clock above the bar reads 8:57. Maya is still stationed at the counter, absorbed in her laptop. Quinn and I are done with our shift at nine, but my stomach tightens at the thought of running into the Hailing boys at the train station, where their coach always chaperones them onto the same train Quinn and I take home.

"If I just—" Quinn stops talking when her phone pings. She checks the message and sucks in a sharp breath.

"What's wrong?"

Her eyes stay on her phone. "Oh my god."

"What?"

She starts breathing faster. "Hannah Sutton just texted me. She sent me a picture."

"Let me see."

She swings her screen to face me. The background of the picture is dark, and it's difficult to make out anything other than the figures in the center. Kai's arm is locked around the waist of a girl I don't recognize, and she's resting her head on his broad shoulder. Kai is holding a Miller bottle up to the camera and grinning, flashing perfectly straight teeth and a perfect red kiss mark on his throat.

My mouth falls open, and I scramble for something to say. Anything.

"He is . . . I can't believe he'd . . ." Words fail me.

Quinn's face pales. She looks like she's about to hurl.

"I'm sorry," I say, wincing.

Her teeth clench.

"Are you okay?"

"Mm-hmm." Her eyes fill, and she presses her lips together like she's trying not to cry.

"Oh, Quinn." I clamber onto the table and seal my arm around her shoulders. "I'm so sorry. He's unbelievable."

A single tear escapes and rolls down her cheek, leaving a black mascara track in its wake.

"Talk to me," I urge.

She draws in a deep, trembling breath. "Lipstick on his neck," she says through her teeth.

"Look, let's just go back to my house. You can sleep over. I've got Sponge Candy and three pints of ice cream in the freezer. We can find a new series to binge. We'll have the best time."

She chokes out a sound. I guess the *best* time is probably a stretch.

"I'm calling him." She fumbles with her phone, and I hear the dull ringing until it goes to voicemail. She tries again. And again.

I steal another glance at the clock. Beyond the glass wall, the rink is quiet now, meaning the Hailing boys are loose somewhere inside the building.

"Quinn." I touch her arm. "I think we should go; our train

leaves soon. The Hailing boys will be . . ."

Right on cue, the diner's doors swing open, and they troop in. All of them. They head for the booths across the room. Maya looks up from her laptop. She lifts her finger, signaling to them that she'll be right with them, but I catch the split-second grimace—the troublemakers are back.

As hard as I try to resist, my willpower crumbles, and my eyes land on Cason. Even from across the room, I can see the shadow of bruising along his jawline.

"Let's just go," I murmur to Quinn.

She straightens her shoulders. "I think we should stay awhile. The diner doesn't close until eleven."

I stare back at her, stunned.

She fixes me with an unnatural smile, teeth bared and eyes glassy. "We went to middle school with these boys. We have every right to hang out with them."

"They attacked our friends," I remind her tightly. "Clearly they're not the same people we grew up with."

But she isn't listening.

"Quinn," I hiss as she jumps down from the table.

"No one's forcing you to stay, Sadie," she says. "Just like no one's going to force me to leave."

And with that, she strides across the diner, beelining for the Hailing team.

Friday, January 31

CASON

SADIE SEES ME FROM ACROSS the diner, I know she does. But whenever I try to catch her eye, she looks away.

They were here when we came in. Sadie and Quinn. Just like they always were at school, names merged into one word, SadieandQuinn.

It's quiet in the diner tonight. The smell of fries and sweat is thick in the air, and beyond the long window, the empty rink below is glaring, white ice scuffed by our blades. Between us, we've taken three booths. Michel, Ruben, Finley, and me in one, with Adam, Seb, Ty, Kash, and Hudson in the booth right next to us. Coach Larsen is over at the counter, ordering a couple of share plates. Team-bonding shit. We all have to pretend like he isn't still pissed at us about the fight last week. Pretend like he doesn't think we started it, embarrassing him during his first season coaching. He singled out Michel, Ruben, Finley, and me, made us write some fake apology statement, groveling for forgiveness over something we never did.

Michel nudges me. "Look who's coming."

My eyes shoot across the room, expecting to see Sadie heading our way. But it's the other half. Quinn McKinley, chin raised and quick steps.

Sadie hasn't moved from their table. Her wavy brown hair is flipped to one side, like a curtain covering her face, a barrier from us.

"Hey," Quinn says, coming to a stop at our booth. "What's up?" There are dark smudges beneath her eyes, and her breezy smile looks ropy.

Michel stares blankly at her. "Hi," he says. It sounds like a question.

Across the table, Ruben comes to life. "Quinn McKinley." He slaps his hands to his face. "Love of my life." He says it with a wicked grin.

Next to him, Finley catches my eye and smirks.

Ruben's got a lot of loves of his life. He's had his heart broken by more people—guys and girls—than anyone else I know. He puts himself out there, all in. He isn't scared of rejection; he says what he thinks whenever he thinks it. Gotta respect that. Total opposite of someone like Finley. Fin keeps his guard up, plays it safe, analyzes. Knows how to shut his mouth and sail by under the radar.

I wish I could do that.

But Ruben's charm must have worked on Quinn, because she cracks a smile. A real smile this time. "Can I sit with you?" she asks.

Ruben shoves Finley along the bench. "All day, every day, Q. Tell us your troubles."

Quinn slides into the booth, and Ruben slings a jacked arm over the seat back.

At the bar, Larsen is looking our way, frowning. I don't think Quinn is welcome on our team-bonding night.

I lock my hands on the table. "What's up with Sadie? Why isn't she over here too?"

Quinn tears her attention away from Ruben. "Because of you," she says. "She's avoiding you."

My eyebrows shoot up, and Michel claps my shoulder. "Ouch," he says.

I shrug his hand away.

But he cuffs my shoulder again. "Don't worry, we all like you, buddy. Most of the time."

"Wait, wait, wait." Ruben raps the table with his scuffed knuckles. "Who doesn't like you?"

"Sadie," Michel says. "She doesn't like Cason."

Everyone's eyes are on me now. Because the joke is on me.

"I didn't say that," Quinn backtracks. "She just feels uncomfortable. Because of the fight that you started last week."

My jaw drops. "Hold up. The fight that *I* started?"

"Yeah." Her forehead crinkles. "But what do you care? You're not actually bothered about what some girl from forever ago thinks of you, are you?"

"I didn't start that fight."

Quinn's catlike stare stays on me. "We all know you did, Cason. Don't even deny it."

I choke out a laugh. "We all? You mean you and Sadie?"

Michel jumps to my defense. "It wasn't him. It was your boyfriend, Number Nineteen."

Her chin juts. "He's not my boyfriend anymore."

Ruben smiles bigger, top and bottom teeth on full display. "Good to know. You wanna watch out for guys like that, Q. He needs to work on his anger management."

Finley mutters something under his breath, and his fingers start tapping on the table. He gets twitchy whenever we talk about what happened last weekend, thin shoulders curling forward, pale mouth pressed. I see it and I get it. Fin doesn't talk about his past much, but I know his upbringing hasn't been easy, in and out of foster care since he was six years old, heavy stuff to deal with. The fight with Arcadia screwed with his head. The violence triggered him, I know it did.

I felt it too. After my mom died, the fragility of life hit home for me.

Maybe all four of us relate to that, because we've walked through the worst times together. That's why we get each other, watch out for each other. Don't leave each other when one of us gets jumped in a parking lot.

"Why don't you go over there?" Michel says, nodding toward Sadie's booth. "Go make friends." He's messing with me, grinning, showing off the chipped tooth he's been proudly rocking all year.

I think on it for a moment. Then I'm on my feet. "Okay. I will."

Michel laughs. "I was kidding, man."

"Well, I'm not."

Their stares stay on me as I climb out of the booth. They watch uncertainly, probably wondering if *I'm* messing with them now. But I'm not. I'm doing this.

Sadie notices me heading toward her. She presses her lips together, making her cheeks dimple. The reflection from the glass wall stripes rainbow light over the freckles on her nose.

I stop at her table. "Hi."

"Hi," she says slowly. Her deep-green eyes dart across the diner, like she's figuring out the best route to get away from me.

"Can we talk, please?" Then I add, "I'll leave if you want me to, but if you'll hear me out, this'll only take a minute."

She extends her hand, gesturing for me to speak.

"Just so you know . . ." I go straight in. "That fight wasn't my fault. Doesn't matter what you heard. I didn't want it."

She sighs and traces her fingers over her forehead. "That night . . ." She pauses for a second. "Okay, honestly, that night scared me."

I work my lip between my teeth. "I get it, Sadie. I'm sorry. It wasn't fun for me either."

"Then why did you start it?"

I press my hand to my chest. "*I* didn't." The words are raw because I'm feeling it. Turns out I do care about what some girl from forever ago thinks of me.

"Kai is saying you attacked him, unprovoked."

I laugh under my breath, and she frowns.

"Why would I do that?" I say in a breath. "You think I'd start something like that off the ice? Risk *my* future over—what? A game that *I* won?"

Her long eyelashes sweep down.

So I keep going. "I've got dreams. Plans. I want to get scouted; I want to get into the college leagues. And then I want to play in the NHL. Getting kicked off a high school team for fighting isn't in the plan." I'm talking fast, spilling words before I'm even thinking them through, telling her all the thoughts that I don't usually say out loud. "I would never start something like that. There's too much riding on this."

Her gaze wanders to the window.

"Okay, I defended myself." I accept it. "And it got out of hand. But I'm not taking the blame for something I didn't do."

She draws in a deep breath, then says, "Okay."

"I don't go after people like that. I don't do that."

"Okay," she says, lifting her hands. "Fine. I believe you."

Her words make me stop. "Oh."

"Oh?" she echoes with a small smile. "You sound disappointed."

"I had more to say."

"Sorry." She flutters her fingers. "Go ahead, I'm listening."

"Okay." I crick my neck. Nervous habit. "Well, it wasn't me. That's it."

She nods.

"You believe me?"

"Yes." She laces her fingers on the table, silver rings catching the overhead light.

"Okay, good." I stuff my hands into my pockets. "Thanks."

Her attention moves past me, straying across the room to my booth, where Ruben is drumrolling on the table. They've arranged a few cups into beer pong formation, minus the beer. Quinn lands her shot, and the guys cheer. Even Larsen, standing at the edge, manages a smile.

When he sees me, though, his expression changes, mouth

sharpening. He's giving me his best telepathy. *What are you doing over there? Your team is here.*

I wave my hand, like, *Yeah, yeah, I'll be right there.* I won't be right there.

Then Quinn lands another shot, and he's clapping and smiling again, just like everyone else.

"You haven't changed, Cason." Sadie's voice pulls me back. Her gaze is on me now, with a trace of amusement. "You were always like this, determined to get your point across, getting all fired up about it. And you still talk just as fast as ever."

I squint back at her. "Is that supposed to be a compliment or an insult?"

She just smiles. "I'm sorry we drifted apart. Life just got . . ."

"It wasn't all you," I say, scrubbing a hand through my hair. "I could have reached out more after you moved schools. I should have." Then I add, "No one else wants to talk about alternate realities with me anymore. Not like we used to."

She gasps. "Same!"

"Imagine a reality where you stayed at school in Hailing."

"Or you moved to Arcadia."

My lip curls. "Not in any reality is that happening, Sadie."

She laughs, and her eyes stay on mine for a long moment. "Are you okay?" she asks softly.

My heart moves faster. "Yeah," I say, ignoring the ache in my ribs. But I can't tell if she means after the fight, or in life. "Are you?"

"Yes." She floors me with a careful smile, her rosy lips lifting at the corners. "Start over?" She extends her hand, and I accept it, her fingers smooth and warm in mine.

"You can sit, if you want?" she says as she lets go.

So I do. I take the seat opposite her.

It's wild, being in this moment. It's like I'm not even here. I'm somewhere above my body, watching myself sitting across from Sadie. It's the same feeling I had around her back in middle school, only turbocharged. That feeling of wanting to be near her because her energy elevates me. I swear, I get high off it. She makes me laugh. She makes me think. She makes me happy.

I can't even hide it. I'm grinning too much. "Do you think your Arcadia people would mind if me and you started hanging out?"

"Yes," she says, dipping her gaze. "It wouldn't go down well after what happened last week."

"Quinn doesn't seem to care," I say, thumbing over my shoulder to the chants going on behind us.

Sadie quirks an eyebrow. "Quinn probably isn't planning on announcing this at school."

"Then you don't have to, either."

Her nose twitches. "What, you think we should keep this just between us? If we spend more time together, I mean?"

"Yeah." I nudge her foot under the table. "It's nobody else's business."

"Right," she agrees, biting her lip to suppress a smile. Her eyes flicker to the table across the room. Then she adds, "No one has to know."

Sunday, February 2

SADIE

I DON'T KNOW WHAT I was thinking when I suggested going ice skating with a hockey player. Considering I can barely stand up on the ice, this seems like a recipe for embarrassment.

Dad is in the kitchen when I come downstairs. He's at the breakfast bar listening to a podcast, and I catch some of the words. "Communication is an essential part of building a bond, and single fathers should make sure that their teen daughters feel—"

He pauses the episode.

"Really, Dad?" I arch an eyebrow. "Parenting podcasts?"

"Fascinating stuff, Sadie," he says with his wide smile.

"I'm sure."

"Essential listening, if you ask me." Dad has one of those friendly, cheerful faces, and if it weren't for the gray in his hair and the smile lines around his eyes, it'd be hard to place him at fifty. "I'm switching up my true crime playlist," he adds. "Although this series is turning out to be just as hair-raising."

"Sounds it," I say wryly.

"Are you going out?" His gaze lands on my like-new skates

poking out from the top of my bag. "At six o'clock?"

It's the way he says it, with a hint of shock, like he can't believe anyone would leave the house after sunset out of choice.

"I'm going to Arcadia," I remind him. "I thought I told you?"

"Yes, but I didn't realize you meant now." He glances at his watch.

I should just say it. *I'm meeting a boy. He plays hockey, and he's taking me skating.* But the words don't come out.

"Do you want me to drive you?"

I shake my head. "Thanks, but I'll take the train."

He presses his lips, considering it. "Okay," he says at last. Dad's a worrier at the best of times, but he's been extra vigilant lately. Last week, someone was killed in a hit-and-run on the byway close to where Dad works. It shook the community pretty bad, but especially Dad, since he was the one who found the man and, despite his efforts to save him, the poor guy didn't stand a chance. They still haven't found the driver, and Dad has a whole thing about the injustice and the dangers of the perpetrator still being loose on the roads.

"Are you meeting Quinn and Emma?" he asks.

I make a noncommittal noise. Not a yes or a no, and thankfully he doesn't press. "Don't forget it's a school night. Home by nine."

"Got it."

"Have fun," he adds.

"Thanks." My stomach flutters as I skip for the door. It isn't only Dad I'm evading on this topic. I haven't told anyone about my plans to meet Cason. It's just too complicated. Brandon was involved in the fight, so I doubt Emma's going to be celebrating my entanglement with the enemy. And even though I desperately want to share this with Quinn, I've held back. She's heartbroken over Kai's betrayal right now. Given what she's going through, it doesn't seem right to gush about my new . . . Cason.

A smile tugs at my mouth. Just thinking his name. And I get an extra buzz because for the first time in a really long while, I've got a secret, and it's thrilling.

I close the front door behind me and hurry across the street. The sun has set, the streetlamps are glowing softly, and everything is sleepy and quiet with Sunday slowness.

My shoes clang on the metal steps leading up to the platform. A flush of exhilaration creeps into my cheeks when I see him seated on the bench at the tagged wall.

I quicken my pace to reach him, and he stands, his broad shadow stretching over the tracks. The tousled strands of his hair stir in the evening breeze.

"Hey," he says, sounding surprised. "You showed up."

"What, you thought I'd ghost you?"

His lips twitch. "Maybe. It crossed my mind."

I gasp, feigning insult. "I would never." I don't add that's it him, specifically, I wouldn't ghost.

The rumble of the train approaches in the distance. When it reaches the platform, we climb aboard and claim two seats. The train is mostly empty, and the periodic rumbles fall on beat with my racing heart as we slink through the night toward Arcadia.

Fast words fall from our lips, as though we're catching up on everything we've missed over these past few years. We're throwing pointless questions back and forth, with scarcely a pause in-between. What kind of pizza topping do you like? What's your favorite movie? Would you swim with dolphins? Orcas?

I'm so engrossed in our world that I hardly notice the autopilot motion of getting off the train and crossing the street toward Raleigh's complex, where it's lost in its shadowy corner.

Inside, the ice is gilded by the gentle lighting above. The rink is empty. Even the stands are deserted.

"Not many people come here on Sunday nights," Cason says, following my gaze to the pristine ice. "It's always quiet."

A nervous excitement stirs in me—just the two of us here, the rink all to ourselves.

He tosses his bag onto a bench and starts lacing up his Bauers. I follow his lead.

In my blades, I edge toward the slick surface and grip the sideboard. "Did I mention it's been awhile since I last went skating?"

Cason grins. "You're okay. I won't let you fall." He carefully takes my hands and lets the ice carry him backward, guiding us smoothly in a loop of the rink. I hold his hands tighter as the cold air brushes my skin.

We drift quietly on the ice for a moment, and I find myself drawn to him. The way he moves—it feels so familiar.

"You're not that bad," he says, glancing down at my skates as we sail over the ice.

"Not *that* bad? Is that another way of saying *good*?"

His nose crinkles. "*Good* is optimistic."

I roll my eyes at him.

He picks up speed, gliding backward and steering me with him. When he slows to a stop, his blades create a dusting of snow that sprays onto my jeans.

There's playfulness in his eyes, something I recognize from a long time ago. "Sorry," he says, sounding not at all sorry.

"I was about to say you make an okay coach, but I think I take it back." My voice comes out strangely—faster, breathier. Maybe it's the rush of our movement, or our closeness. The addictive smell of the sports spray that he wears.

"Okay coaches are hard to come by," he jokes. "Although," he adds, "the coaches will tell you it's me. I'm the problem."

I laugh. "Oh, I know. We all heard Coach Collins yelling at you in PE every Tuesday afternoon."

"You think Collins was tough? You should meet Larsen."

"Aw," I say, exaggerating a sigh. "They just don't get you."

"Not many people do," he says.

In middle school Cason was always the loudest voice in class, talked *way* too much, and had the most infectious laugh. He changed a lot after his mom died, almost as though the fire in him had sizzled out. I moved schools not long after, and I always wondered who he became. Which version of him had landed.

An old sadness settles in the pit of my stomach.

"I'm glad we're doing this." His voice jolts me from my thoughts. "Hanging out again."

"Yeah, me too. It's been too long." I keep my tone light and easy, but there's depth behind my words, and I know he hears it.

"Remember when we used to hang out after school?" he says. "Down by the lake."

"Yeah. We had the weirdest conversations. Middle schoolers shouldn't know as many conspiracy theories as we did."

He laughs, then his thumb brushes mine, just a small, absent gesture. "I used to feel like I could talk to you about anything."

Warmth spreads through me, even in the cold rink. I nod, letting the silence linger for a moment before replying, "Same here." My gaze shifts to the rink. "By the way, whatever happened to that rope swing you were going to build near the water? Got it set up yet?"

He gives me a quick grin. "I'm working on it."

"Someday, right?"

"It's on my list. How about you?" he asks. "Catch me up. Is Arcadia everything you thought it'd be?"

I hesitate for a moment, lost in the past, in my memories. "I don't know. When I switched schools, everything changed. I had to start over. It was hard."

He nods. "I get that. Actually, I was surprised when you left. I thought you were happy in Hailing."

"I was," I say, and the admission feels heavy.

A wave of sympathy crosses his face. "At least you had Quinn with you, right?"

"True," I agree with a small laugh. "She's a permanent fixture in my life."

He smiles at that. "Maybe I am too. Because we're here again, just like it was before. . . ." His words trail off, and he looks at me almost uncertainly, as if waiting for an answer, or maybe just reassurance.

"Feels familiar," I say softly.

"Yeah, it does."

After all these years, I never thought I'd be back here, with Cason, holding his hands while we glide over the ice. We're older and different now, but somehow still the same.

There's this quiet moment between us, this pause.

Maybe I'm caught up in the moment, in the closeness, but before I have a chance to overthink it, I draw myself to him and my lips brush his, and the world stops for a minute. Everything else fades away, leaving only the coolness of his lips. He pulls me closer, and I feel his heart beating fast against me. My entire world reduces to this—this frozen snow globe moment, with a kiss that sends the best shiver over my skin.

It's just a moment, a kiss. But I know it right then, the way we both smile dizzily after, the charged energy buzzing between us. We have changed. We're not just old friends anymore, we're something new.

Tonight has been more than I expected—perfect, really. Beyond perfect.

Right up until we leave the building and step outside.

A Chevy four-by-four pulls into the dimly lit parking lot. The engine cuts.

In the darkness, my hand slips from Cason's. "Oh no," I murmur.

He frowns. "What's wrong?"

"I'll catch up with you," I tell him quickly, and I walk a few steps away from him.

Even in the sparse lamplight, I can see the confusion furrowing his brow, but he hesitantly walks on, heading for the train station, and I start toward the Chevy as the driver's door opens.

Kai gets out, and his eyes land on me.

I approach him with my arms folded. "Hey." I can't hide the edge to my voice, because I'm still mad at him for what he did to Quinn. Not to mention lying about Cason attacking him.

"Hey," he says, and for a fraction of a second, I almost feel sorry for him. He sounds broken. Looks broken. His big shoulders are hunched forward, mouth turned down.

But he doesn't deserve my sympathy.

"Can we talk, Sadie?" he says quietly.

"Sure. Did you have a good time on Friday night?" I ask. Passive-aggressiveness at its finest. When his pale eyebrows draw together, I peer at his throat and add, "Managed to get the lipstick off your neck, I see."

He runs his tongue over his teeth. "You talked to Quinn lately?"

"Yes, of course I've talked to her. She's my best friend."

The muscles in his jaw tic. "Right. She okay?"

"No. She's so far from okay, Kai."

"I still care about her."

I laugh at that. "You've got a funny way of showing it."

"I still love her. But . . ." He pauses and drags a hand over his mouth. "Did she tell you what happened?"

My blood rushes. "Yes. And if you keep saying that you *love* her, she's going to keep holding out for you. Keep coming back to you. What you're doing is cruel. I want to believe you're a better person than this, Kai."

He doesn't respond, but he's listening, jaw clenched.

"That's all I wanted to say," I finish. "Do with it what you will."

I've never been close with Kai, but we've always been good. He's shown his decent side from time to time—lending a hand when someone needs a favor or supporting Quinn's spontaneous ideas for elaborate theme nights. There's more to Kai than that picture. I hope.

"Just tell Quinn I'm sorry," he mutters.

"You need to tell her that yourself."

I cast a glance toward the train station. Cason is waiting across the lot, a silhouette in the darkness, tensed and on edge, like he's preparing to step in at any moment.

Kai follows my gaze. His eyes linger on the distant figure. His shoulders tighten. "Friend of yours?" he asks.

I know I've got to leave. I've got to get *Cason* to leave.

"Do better, Kai," I say as I walk away from him.

There's no reply, but I hear his slow footsteps heading in the opposite direction, walking toward Raleigh's.

I hurry to meet Cason at the edge of the lot.

"Everything okay?" he checks.

"Yeah." But my voice doesn't carry much conviction.

A sense of unease makes my stomach knot. Maybe this is about Quinn, worrying about how Kai's indecision will impact her.

Or maybe it's the two shadows in the darkness, Cason and Kai, and the palpable tension in the air as they stood on opposite ends of the same lot where they were pulled apart only a week earlier.

It's over, I remind myself.

The words sound good. Still, I can't help but feel like they're not true.

NOW

Saturday, February 22

SADIE

Quinn. Did you get home okay this morning?

SADIE

Quinn, check in. Something's happened right outside my house, at the train station. A body has been found and there are police everywhere. I'm worried about you. Check in.

Saturday, February 22

SADIE

ARE YOU OKAY? I send the message to Cason, and all I can do is stare at my phone, waiting for him to reply. Waiting for Quinn to reply.

I force myself to breathe deeply. There's no point in jumping to conclusions. I'm sure they're perfectly fine, at home, safely sleeping in their beds.

They have to be.

The sound of the doorbell chimes through the house. I toss my phone onto the bed and race downstairs, practically tripping over myself to get to the door.

Two figures are silhouetted behind the frosted-glass panel.

I flip the latch and swing the door open to the chilly morning air. Two police officers are standing on the stoop—a man in his fifties with a heavy mustache and thin lips chapped from the cold, and a younger woman, petite, with black hair twisted into a low bun.

"Good morning," the woman says. "My name is Detective Alanis." She flashes her badge. "And this is my colleague, Detective Sampson."

The man gives a stiff nod.

"Hi," I manage to speak.

"Can we get your name, please?" Detective Alanis prompts.

"Y-Yes," I stammer. "Sadie. Sadie Morelli." I've never had police standing on my doorstep before. A cold sweat breaks out on my skin. This must be standard procedure for a crime scene.

Unless it isn't.

Beyond them, the street is cordoned off with tape and cones, and access to the platform is blocked. A few passersby have gathered on the fringes, trying to peer past the obstructions. Two middle-aged women carrying pink pastry boxes are craning their necks to get a clearer view, and a man with a Labrador is lingering a few steps behind them, holding the leash tightly as he edges closer to join in the gawking. One of the officers on the scene is motioning for the trio to step back.

Detective Alanis catches my attention with a friendly smile. "Would it be all right if we come inside for a quick chat, Sadie?" she asks, her tone casual. "Informally."

"Uh, yeah. Sure." I open the door wider, glancing at the staircase behind me. "Should I wake my dad for this? He works nights and is still sleeping. If it's something serious, I should go get him, right?"

Before I can move, Alanis adds, "It's nothing official, just an informal conversation. You're fine."

I nod as they step inside, and before I know it, we're seated in the living room, facing each other on opposite couches. The bookshelf behind them is crammed with worn true crime books and

Dad's old psychology textbooks. I cross my arms tightly, trying to brace for whatever's coming.

A beat of silence passes, and the room feels smaller.

Just say it, I think. *Just tell me what's happened. Tell me who's been found.*

The man, Detective Sampson, runs a hand over his thick mustache. "We're investigating an incident that occurred on this street sometime during the early hours of this morning. The exact timings aren't clear yet."

I struggle to control my voice. "I saw the news report."

Sampson knots his rough hands and leans forward. "We're going door-to-door, checking if anyone saw or heard anything unusual last night."

I shake my head. It's all I can do.

Detective Alanis catches my gaze. "Sadly, there was a fatality in the area."

My stomach turns at the word *fatality*. "Who was found? Have they been identified—"

Sampson cuts me off, his voice gravelly. "We're unable to share any information at this stage. But anything you may have seen or heard could be crucial in our investigation." His sunken eyes hold mine over the coffee table. There's a coldness to his expression, a desensitized glaze.

But his stock response doesn't come as a surprise. I don't know why I expected anything different. I've been role-playing detective since I was a kid, preparing to study the nature of crime, make it into a career. I *want* to be desensitized, like Sampson is. I should be pulling out my notepad and learning from this experience.

But this isn't role-play. It's real.

And I know the drill. There's a whole list of reasons why a victim's name can't be released: next of kin needing to be notified, risk of compromising the investigation.

Suspicion of foul play.

My heart is in my throat.

"Any information you might have," Alanis says, taking over, "particularly regarding unusual activity in the area—" She halts her sentence at the sound of a door creaking upstairs and, a moment later, the thud of footsteps on the staircase.

Dad strides into the living room, his eyes still bleary from sleep and his graying hair rumpled. He double takes at the sight before him: me and two police officers gathered on the compact couches. I hug a cushion close to me as the detectives stand.

"What's going on?" Dad's voice is sharp now, alert. His eyes shoot to the window and the commotion on the street outside.

"I'm Detective Sampson, and this is my partner, Detective Alanis. A body was discovered at Hailing train station this morning," Sampson says in that same blunt tone, like he's spoken these words thousands of times before. Like they mean nothing. "Any information you have could be vital to our investigation."

Dad pales as he sinks into the spot next to me on the couch. "What kind of information? Why are you questioning my seventeen-year-old daughter? Do you have a warrant for this?"

My stomach knots as Detective Alanis's attention moves slowly, carefully, between us. She returns to her seat and purses her full lips. "This isn't an interrogation, Mr. . . . ?"

"Morelli."

"Mr. Morelli," she says with a nod. "But with your home so close to the scene, your perspective could help. We'll be talking to everyone in the neighborhood. This is purely confidential, and your names will not be released publicly."

Dad's shoulders loosen slightly. "I was working last night," he answers, running a hand over his mouth and the gray stubble on his chin. "Security outside the Wellington Hotel. I got home at around five a.m., and I didn't see or hear anything out of the ordinary." He turns to me, knitting his brow. "Sadie? Did you?"

I swallow. My throat feels like sandpaper. "I didn't hear anything either." The response is a reflex, though. Memories from last night somersault through my mind: stepping off the train into the blustery night, the shrieks of laughter from the college girls on the platform, Quinn and Kai's heated words on the sidewalk, Cason . . .

Where the body of a teenager was found. The reporter's words rebound, and my stomach lurches.

Detective Sampson lifts his bushy eyebrows. "Is there anything you'd like to disclose?" His stare is fixed on me as he no doubt reads my expression.

It's not just Detective Sampson—everyone's eyes are on me. We're in total silence, apart from the muffled sounds of the disturbance outside. A deep tone ordering, "Stand back from the cones, please, ma'am." And a woman's voice. "What's going on?"

I press my clammy palms together. My mind works fast, sifting through the information I should share. "I caught the last train home from Arcadia. The 11:20. I saw a few people when I arrived in Hailing, but that's all."

Next to me, Dad tenses, and Sampson and Alanis exchange a quick look.

I take a shaky breath. "Did someone fall?" A wave of nausea comes over me. Living so close to the train station, that's my biggest fear, to slip in the darkness, fall onto the tracks. . . .

Detective Alanis snaps me from my spiraling thoughts. "It's unclear what happened at this stage," she answers. "But you say you saw a few people? You mean, on the train, around the platform?"

"Yes. Both."

"Could you give us some descriptions, please?" she asks, and Detective Sampson reaches for his notepad and pen. "Anything that could be relevant." Detective Alanis is addressing me so gently, so patiently, but I can't help but feel like I'm the suspect. Like my every word is being scrutinized and condemned.

Or maybe it's me. Maybe I'm paranoid because *I* know I'm holding back. I just don't know why.

When I speak again, my voice sounds tinny and strangled. "I saw some people from my school, Arcadia High School. My friend Quinn McKinley, and her boyfriend, Kai Harrison. There were some girls leaving the train too, three of them, but I didn't know them. They were college students. One of them was blond, but I can't remember. . . ." I squeeze my eyes shut and shake my head.

The scratch of Detective Sampson's pen on paper sounds too loud, too frantic.

"It's okay, Sadie," Alanis says calmly. "Just take your time. What else can you tell us?"

I can't bring myself to look at Dad, but in my peripheral vision, I see him lean forward and press his thumbnail to his mouth.

"I'm sorry, I . . ."

Cason comes to the forefront of my mind. A clear snapshot. Chunky black headphones hanging around his neck as he maneuvered the train aisle with his head bowed, his hockey bag slung over his broad shoulder.

We acted like we didn't know each other, slipping into the roles we play whenever other people are around. It's become a quiet game between us, a private joke that's lasted for weeks. Knowing that Quinn and Kai were waiting at the other end, we played our parts, two strangers on a train.

But it's all a lie. I do know him. More than that, I know his history with Kai. They were both at the station last night, and now there's been an "incident." I should tell the police all of this, but the words aren't leaving my lips.

In my silence, the two detectives glance at each other, communicating something.

"Sadie." Alanis says my name carefully. "How would you feel if we moved this conversation to the precinct?"

AUDIO FILE_MP3

TITLE: CASE_339KH_SADIE MORELLI INTERVIEW

For the purpose of the tape, this is Detective J. Alanis conducting an interview with Sadie Morelli, with Mr. Leo Morelli and Detective P. Sampson present. The date is Saturday, February 22, and the time is approximately ten a.m. Sadie, thank you again for your cooperation in our investigation. We'd like to ask you some questions in relation to an incident that took place in Hailing this morning during the early hours. Does that sound okay?

Yes. Okay.

Sadie, you shared with us that you saw two of your friends at Hailing train station last night. Can you remind me of their names, please?

Quinn McKinley and Kai Harrison.

Thank you. And can you go into a little more detail on your movements last night, please?

Okay. I'd been at Raleigh's Rec Center, working at the diner until nine o'clock. Quinn was supposed to be there too, but she skipped her shift. I missed my usual train, so I hung around and took the eleven-twenty from Arcadia station. When I got back to Hailing, Quinn was on the street talking to Kai, her boyfriend—ex-boyfriend, I mean. They were on-off.

Both are Arcadia High School students. Is that correct?

Yes. Then Kai left, and Quinn came to my house. She slept over. The thing is, I'm worried about her, because she must have left my house at about five a.m. when my dad got home. I texted her this morning, checking in after I saw the news. She

hasn't replied. Can you just tell me, the person you've found, it isn't Quinn, is it? I'm scared for her.

Okay, I understand. Let's just circle back for a moment. You described their relationship as on-off. What did you mean by that?

They'd been on a break for a couple of weeks. Just to mention, Quinn lives on Cherry Oak Street. Number 221. Maybe someone could check on her?

Thank you for this information, Sadie. Why were Quinn and Kai taking a break from their relationship?

I don't really know. Is that important? Is it one of them?

Any information at this stage could be relevant. Tell me a little more about the other people you saw on the train or around the platform last night. You mentioned some girls?

Yes, there were three of them. But I didn't know them. They said they were ACU students.

Was there anyone else who caught your attention?

There were others on the train.

Anyone who stood out to you?

(PAUSE.)

Sadie? Are you feeling okay?

No. I mean, yes. I think that's everything.

Are you sure? Is there anything else you'd like to add?

No. No, I don't think so.

Saturday, February 22

CASON

I ROLL OVER IN BED and sling my arm over my eyes, blocking out the light streaming through the window. Last night comes back to me. Slowly.

The sting of the cold when I got off the train. The crunch of my sneakers over grit.

Kai and Quinn at the bottom of the steps.

It takes me a minute to come around. My limbs ache. I've been training hard these past couple of weeks. This is a big year for us, and every win counts. If I want to make it to the NHL, the work starts right here.

My phone is on the floor next to my bed. I reach for it, seeing a new message from Sadie, sent a couple of hours ago.

Are you okay?

Squinting, I write back, Yeah. You?

Sounds leak from somewhere else inside the house, a tap running, my uncle Alec's muffled voice. I force myself to get up, stepping over scattered hockey gear and clothes, and scrub my hands through my hair before leaving the room.

My footsteps thud on the floorboards as I pass framed photos hanging in the hallway of Alec and my mom when they were kids. A radio is playing in the kitchen, crackling background noise, reeling off last night's basketball scores. And Alec's voice.

"Cason?" For a second, I think he's talking to me, but then he carries on, "Yeah . . . no, all good."

I step into the kitchen, and he looks up from his cereal. His cell is jammed between his shoulder and ear, and he nods good morning to me. I mirror it.

"Yeah, yeah . . ." He gets back to his call. "No problem."

I lumber across the kitchen. Nothing's changed in here since my grandparents owned the place. The appliances are tired, and there's damp on the ceiling. An ancient portable stereo is balanced on the ledge where the window overlooks the small patch of front yard.

"So I'll see you tonight?" Alec says into the phone. "After work?" His HiVis jacket is draped over the back of a chair, and his muddy boots are at the side door.

I swing open a cabinet and start rooting, pushing aside a couple of out-of-date granola bars and creamers.

Alec speaks into his cell again. The ceiling light catches the spot on his head where his dark hair has started to thin. "You're staying over this weekend?"

I don't hear the response, but I can take a solid guess at who's on the other end of the call, and what her answer will be. Alec's girlfriend, Thalia, has been staying here most weekends lately. It's great for him, I'm happy for him. Back when I first moved here,

Alec would go out on dates sometimes, but never anything serious. Then he met Thalia when she started working at his construction company last year, and they've been going strong ever since.

I try to stay out the way when Thalia comes over, finding anywhere to be but here. No shade to Thalia, I like her, and I think she likes me, but I get the feeling she doesn't want her forty-five-year-old boyfriend to have a seventeen-year-old roommate.

"Okay," Alec says into the phone, his mouth quirking at the corner. "See you tonight." He ends the call and flips the leather case shut. His eyes land on me while I tear open a packet of Pop-Tarts with my teeth.

"You must have gotten home late from practice last night," he says. "I didn't hear you come in."

I keep my voice easy. "Yeah. I stayed late." It's not a lie. "With a friend." I bite into the cold Pop-Tart and chew. "How long have these been in here?" I grab the box from the counter and turn it over to find the expiration date. "Yeah, they're a couple of months out."

"Couple of months is fine. Don't tell Thalia I said that." Alec takes a slug of coffee from the only mug he'll ever drink out of. It's busted and chipped, and the print from his construction company logo has faded into mist. But he's too set in his ways to let it go. "What time did you get home?"

I take another bite of the Pop-Tart and shrug. "Midnight or something."

His thick eyebrows raise. "A text wouldn't have hurt, buddy. Practice finishes at nine."

I toss what's left of the Pop-Tart into the trash. "Yeah. Sorry. I didn't think."

"That's a nice shiner you've got."

I frown, and he gestures with his mug toward my face.

I touch the spot beneath my eye, and I feel it then. The ache of a bruise.

"Rough practice?" he asks.

"It always is."

I pretend not to see the skeptical look on his face, deep lines on his forehead. Ever since I came home from the Arcadia game last month in the back of a cop car, bloodied up with a few bruised ribs, he's been watching closer. I get the feeling Alec's waiting for it to happen again. I am too. But he backed me, fuming, threatening the parents, the school, talking about lawsuits and restraining orders—like we could afford a lawyer.

They won't get away with this, he'd said. But they did.

I grab a bottle of water from the fridge and pull out a chair at the table.

Alec leans back in his seat. "How's it all going? Hockey, I mean."

"Good." I start playing with the bottle cap, spinning it between my fingers. "Scouts are showing up, so we're training hard."

"Maybe I could come watch one of your games?"

"Yeah? You want to?"

"For sure. I want to see if you're any good." He grins, and for a second I almost see my mom. Her quick smile.

"What do you think of your new coach?" he asks.

"Larsen? Thinks he knows everything. Guy only qualified last year."

Alec squints. "You back-talk him?"

"Not always. Not as much as the last guy, anyway." Coach Taylor hated me even more than Larsen does. They say I don't listen. But I do.

Alec aims a finger at me. "Watch it. I don't want my kid getting a reputation for being a smart mouth."

I muster a smile. I'm not his kid. We both know it.

"Don't worry," I tell him. "I fall in line."

He slaps his calloused hands together. "Good. That's what I like to hear." He stops then, as though the conversation has triggered some thoughts for him too. He clears his throat. "You know, Adrianna's anniversary is coming up. I was thinking we could take a trip to the cemetery, lay some flowers."

"Yeah."

"Some of those roses she used to like," he adds. "The pink ones."

I don't tell him that I hate those roses. The smell of them makes my chest ache. Because it reminds me of her.

"She's been on my mind," he says, and his eyes move away from me. "Thinking about that damn hit-and-run." He stops, and his jaw works. "Brought up some stuff." His chair scrapes as he stands and carries his bowl to the sink.

It was all over the news when it happened a few weeks ago, the hit-and-run. My mom died in a car accident on that same stretch of road. The locals call it Lethal Bend. More fatalities happen on that byway than anywhere else in a fifty-mile radius.

"... early hours of this morning in Hailing ..."

The distant sound of the news report on the radio catches my attention. I stop fiddling with the bottle cap.

"... body of a teenager was discovered ..."

I swear, I turn to stone.

Alec must have caught the same words I did, because suddenly he's cranking up the volume on the stereo.

"The victim's name has not yet been released, but police are investigating the circumstances as suspicious and calling for anyone who might have been around Hailing train station last night to come forward."

My breath leaves my lungs too fast, and Alec looks at me.

"Did you catch the train home last night?" he asks.

"Yeah, but ... I didn't see anything."

"Cason?" Alec's tone is serious. "Are you sure you didn't see anything? Do we need to be calling the cops?"

"No," I answer, numb. "I don't know anything about it."

CASON
Look up Hailing news.

MICHEL
Oh shit.

MICHEL
I called Ruben last night. After I spoke to you.

CASON
I'll come by your place.

SADIE
Have you heard from Quinn this morning?

EMMA
No. Why?

SADIE
I'll call you when I can. I'm at the police station in Hailing.

EMMA
What??? Why??? Are you okay?

SADIE
Yes. I'll explain ASAP. Check the news.

Saturday, February 22

SADIE

DAD AND I LEAVE THE precinct through the tall, arched door. Dad is nursing a Styrofoam cup filled with black coffee that he hasn't touched. He looks sick and washed-out—just like how I feel.

Detective Alanis follows us outside. "Thank you for your cooperation this morning," she says.

I manage to nod.

But Dad hesitates in the doorway. "Sadie," he says hoarsely, "would you give me a moment to speak with Detective Alanis privately, please?"

"Sure," I murmur. I hug my coat tightly around myself as I leave them at the top of the wide stone steps and head for the street.

People are out this morning, strolling along the sidewalk with shopping bags, going in and out of the hardware depot or grocery store. A middle-aged couple, a woman carrying a baby, a group of older men. I watch them pass by, absorbed in their own lives. But surely they've heard the news, and if they haven't, it'll no doubt reach them soon. They'll mutter about Hailing's rising crime rates and out-of-control kids.

I check my phone, reading Cason's message for the dozenth time. He's responded to my text asking if he was okay.

Yeah. You?

That's all he said.

I almost feel guilty for the relief I felt when I first saw his name pop up on my screen. Because it wasn't Quinn.

A beige Mini pulls into a parking spot along the street. The engine cuts, and Emma jumps out of the driver's side and rushes toward me. Her curls are scraped into a ponytail, highlighting the panic sharpening her soft features.

She envelops me, almost bowling me over. "It's all over the news," she says. "Are you okay?" Her eyes dart to my dad, still standing at the entrance to the precinct, engrossed in conversation with Detective Alanis.

"I'm okay," I assure her. My voice comes out weakly, though. "Have you heard from Quinn or Kai this morning?"

"No." She pulls back from me. "Why, what's going on? You don't think it could be one of them, do you?"

Despite my best efforts, I can't seem to quell the fear. "I've been trying to call Quinn and text her all morning. This is so unlike her, right? She always has her phone on her."

Emma presses her hand to her mouth. Because she knows. Our group chat is often flooded with messages from Quinn before either of us has a chance to respond.

"I mean, I might be totally overreacting," I muddle on. "It's still early. She might just be sleeping." A strong wind makes me shiver, and I brace as the gale flurries my hair. "We could drive to her house, though. We could check on her?"

"Yes." Emma's grip tightens around her car keys. "Yeah, let's go. I'll drive."

I glance at Dad. Stress lines are creasing his brow as he listens to whatever Detective Alanis is saying. I can't hear their voices from here, but both their expressions are tense.

"I caught the late train home last night," I relay to Emma. "Quinn and Kai were out on the street when I got back. It was messy, and . . ." I rake my hands through my hair, catching the strands as the wind whips them back and forth. "When Kai walked off, Quinn came over to my place."

"Was she okay?" Emma presses.

"She was sad, but . . ." I check my phone for what must be the hundredth time this morning. My messages to Quinn are still unanswered. Still unread.

Emma stares at me, waiting for more. I start fidgeting with my phone case, restlessly peeling at the soft cover. "Quinn stayed over. She didn't say goodbye this morning, she just left." My gaze wanders back to the precinct. "And the police wouldn't confirm who was found, or what happened to them. But Quinn was really upset last night. You don't think she would have . . . done anything drastic?" I trail off because I can't bring myself to voice my concerns aloud.

"No. No, she wouldn't."

"I've got a really bad feeling, Emma." My breath falters in fear.

Fear of what might have happened to my best friend. "Someone died last night."

A police car pulls up outside the precinct, and Emma and I stop. Our attention stays on the vehicle as the engine cuts. An officer emerges from the driver's side and skirts around to open the back door, the faint glint of his badge catching the light as he moves aside.

My breath stalls as *Quinn* steps out onto the pavement.

"Quinn," Emma cries, and we rush toward her.

Suddenly there are police between us and Quinn, as if they've appeared from out of nowhere. They're keeping us apart, and somewhere in my peripheral vision I notice Dad racing down the steps toward us.

But I'm only focused on Quinn. Her face is ghostly pale and streaked with tear tracks.

"I told them we'd been fighting last night," she calls to me, her words coming out too quickly, separated by hiccupped breaths. "They were asking me questions, and I just told the truth. I told them we'd been fighting, and he broke up with me."

Her words sink in, but my voice fails me. Suddenly I can't breathe.

Farther along the street, Quinn's parents hurry from their car, and then police are ushering them all toward the precinct steps, and Quinn keeps looking back at me, frantic and panic-stricken.

Emma grips my arm, her fingers digging into my skin. "What's going on?" she cries. "Why won't they let us talk to her?"

In the jumble of people, Quinn is escorted into the building. My chest heaves because I realize what's happened.

The body on the stretcher. The sheet covering his face.

I choke out the words. "Kai is dead."

HAILING ONLINE NEWS

An investigation has been launched after a young male was found unresponsive at Hailing train station this morning, Saturday, February 22. Emergency services were called to the scene after the body was discovered by a passerby.

Despite the efforts of EMTs, seventeen-year-old Kai Harrison was pronounced dead at the scene. Police barricades remain in place around the station, blocking outbound access from Hailing.

Some services to the station have been canceled and will remain paused while the police continue their investigation.

Detective Julia Alanis from the Hailing Police Department has released the following statement: "Today our town is grieving the loss of a young life. While we are still in the early stages of our investigation, rest assured that we are doing our utmost to understand what transpired.

"Witnesses will be crucial in helping us piece together this tragic incident, and I would urge anyone who may have information to come forward.

"Please contact HPD by texting 1004 or calling the precinct directly and referencing case 339."

Saturday, February 22

SADIE

THE WIND FUNNELS DOWN THE street, bowing the trees along the sidewalk. Quinn is gone, marched into the precinct like a criminal.

"What the hell is going on?" Emma's eyes are fixed on me, her fingers pressed to her scarlet lips. "This can't be happening."

Words churn through my mind on a horrible loop.

Kai is dead. My best friend's boyfriend—the guy who used to give me a ride when it rained, who was always around, part of our conversations, part of our lives. He's gone.

It steals the air from my lungs. Nothing about this feels real. I'm trapped in a nightmare that I can't wake up from.

Emma grips my sleeve, shaking me. "Why did they take Quinn away like that? Did she kill—"

"No," I say breathlessly. "Of course not."

Emma cringes and holds my arm a little tighter.

Suddenly I feel painfully hot, even with the bitter breeze whipping at my skin. There are eyes on us. The passersby aren't just passersby anymore. They're spectators, an audience with iPhones.

My heart starts beating too fast.

Kai is dead.

And I lied to the police.

I didn't tell them that I saw Cason last night. Even though Cason could easily tell the police that he had seen me, and that we know each other. We *more* than know each other.

My chest constricts. I should tell Emma everything. I should ask her advice. Do I backtrack, change my statement now?

"Kai," she whispers, jolting me back. "There's just no way. This can't be . . ."

A lump forms in my throat. "How could this have happened? Was he on the platform, waiting for his train back to Arcadia? Or was he looking for Quinn, did he come back for her?"

Tears pool in Emma's eyes, and I reach for her hand.

But I feel sick. I feel sick at the thought that this happened right outside my house, and if we'd just looked out the window, listened for him, maybe we could have helped him. Did he fall? Was he calling for help, and we didn't hear him?

Or was there someone out there with him?

My stomach rolls. *No.* This must have been an accident.

I'm not ready to think about what it means if it wasn't.

AUDIO FILE_MP3

TITLE: CASE_339KH_QUINN MCKINLEY INTERVIEW

Good morning, Quinn. I understand this has been traumatic for you, so please take your time. We're in no rush. Why don't you tell me a little about your relationship with Kai? Tell me about him?

He was my boyfriend and I loved him. What do you expect me to say?

Kai's family has told us that he was in Hailing visiting you last night. They've shared that you and Kai were romantically involved for some time but had gone your separate ways in recent weeks. He was in Hailing because he planned to end the relationship. Is that what happened last night, Quinn?

Yes. Yes, we ended things.

I can see how upsetting this is for you to discuss.

It is upsetting.

Was the decision to split up mutual?

No.

You didn't want the relationship to end? That must have been difficult to accept.

Of course. But it wasn't . . . you're making it sound like I did something to him. I would never.

That isn't what I'm trying to do here, Quinn. I'm just trying to understand what happened last night.

But you wouldn't let me speak to my friends outside. You're asking me questions as if you think I did something to him.

We need to understand Kai's movements and the moments that led to his death. Nothing about this is going to be easy, but it's important. Just take some breaths. Take your time.

Okay. We got into a fight. I wanted to make our relationship work, but he didn't feel the same. He wouldn't even give me a chance, he just walked away.

At what time did you part ways?

I don't know. Around midnight. A little before.

And where were you at this point? Because your parents can't vouch for your whereabouts last night. When we spoke to them this morning, they said you'd stayed at Kai's house in Arcadia, but Kai's parents claim they haven't seen you in weeks, and that they believed him to be with you in Hailing last night. You weren't at your house, I presume?

I told my parents I was meeting Kai. But I didn't know he was only meeting to break up with me. After he left, I went to my friend Sadie's house, and I stayed there. And then I woke up when the sun was rising, and I couldn't get back to sleep, so I walked home.

I see. Was there anyone else at Sadie's house last night, or anyone who can verify your story?

What do you mean? I just said I was with Sadie.

Anyone else who can confirm that you and Sadie were together in her house for the entire night?

No, but . . . we were. We're not lying. We wouldn't lie to the police. Please, you have to believe me. I didn't do anything to Kai. Neither did Sadie.

Of course not. This is just a conversation, Quinn.

TIKTOK

DARCY WILDE

@WILDEONCRIME

Season 19, Episode 1 #truecrime #forensic #fyp #HailingNY #JusticeforKai

So I woke up to some disturbing news this morning regarding a fatal incident involving a boy from Hailing. Guys, this is hitting a little close to home for me, literally, because Hailing is only a couple of towns over. Let me tell you, I'm going to be following this case closely.

Although the details of the death have not been released, the circumstances *are* suspicious, and police are investigating. One of my former colleagues was on the first response team and has indicated that there was blunt force head trauma. Now, to be clear, that could have resulted from a fall or a blow to the head, and these do present differently. Given what my source has told me, my instinct is that this trauma happened *prior* to a fall, and it's likely to have happened sometime between midnight and one a.m.

I've done a quick internet search on Kai Harrison to see what comes up in the preliminary, and I found a lot around his stats in high school hockey. From what I can gather, this boy was on track for big things.

Now, we still don't know if this death is accidental, homicide, or suicide, and those details are probably going to be held back for a while. In the meantime, I'm going to see what other information I can track down on this.

As I said, I'm going to be following this case closely, so like for part two.

Saturday, February 22

CASON

THE NEWS IS BLOWING UP.

It hasn't even been twenty-four hours and his name's already been leaked on social media. Kai Harrison. Seventeen. High school junior from Arcadia.

Alec is in the living room, half watching ESPN. His eyes keep coming to me, but he isn't talking. I can't tell if he's made the connection between the fight that broke out last month with us and Arcadia. Us and the kid who's all over the news.

A draft is leaking through the house, making one of the doors creak like someone's walking around in here with us.

I drag my hands over my face and stand. "I'm going to Michel's place."

Alec pauses the TV and frowns at me. "Right now?"

"Yeah. Is that all right?"

"Sure." But he doesn't sound sure. He drums the remote on the arm of his recliner. "Just let me know if you're not going to be home for dinner, okay? Keep your cell on."

"Yeah."

I leave fast before Alec can ask me any more questions. Michel's house is only across the street. It looks just like ours, a small single-story with a patch of lawn fronting it. But their lawn looks neater, the grass is cut, and there are hanging baskets with legit flowers growing in them.

I tap on the door, and Michel's mom answers. Her hair is pulled back, and she's wiping her hands on a dish towel, the scent of herbs lingering behind her.

"Cason," she says with a wide smile. "Hello." There's something about the tone of voice she uses when she talks to me. She's real with me, genuine. When she smiles, she means it.

Michel's dad is the same way, always making me feel like he's got time for me. Always looking out for me. The Konans have been good to us. After my mom died, Mrs. Konan brought home-cooked meals to Alec's place a couple of times a week. Attiéké and traditional dishes that she says she was raised on in Ivory Coast. She still picks up groceries for us sometimes too. She's that type of person, gives more than she takes.

Over the last few years, I've grown taller, and she's stayed the same. I'm head and shoulders above her now.

"Hi, Mrs. Konan. How are you?"

"I'm well, thank you, Cason. Busy, as usual." Somewhere behind her, inside the house, I pick up the familiar sound of girls arguing—Michel's nine-year-old twin sisters, Therese and Cisse. "And how about you?" she returns the question, tilting her head, warm brown eyes shining. "How's school?"

The fact that she's asking about school makes me think she

hasn't switched on the news this morning.

"Good," I answer. "Yeah, all good."

She nods, pleased with my response. "Michel's in his room. Are you coming in, or do you want me to call him?"

"Can I come in?"

"Sure, sure." She beckons me into the house and pats my arm as I pass. "You tell Michel to get you a snack," she adds before disappearing into the family room, probably gearing up to diffuse whatever the twins are fighting about.

I head for Michel's room, passing the canvases and family photos on the wall. There are potted plants on the side tables, with long leaves draping over the edges, and a faint smell of mint coming from the kitchen.

Michel's bedroom is at the end of the corridor, and his door is already ajar. "Hey," I call, rapping on the wood. "It's me."

"Come in!" he hollers.

I duck into the room and close the door behind me. Michel's on his bed, head propped up with pillows and headphones weighing down his thick black hair. He slips them around his neck, and tension tightens his jaw.

I slump onto a beanbag. "It's all over the news. Number Nineteen."

Michel sucks in his top lip. "Do they know what happened to him?"

I rub the nape of my neck. "No idea."

He reaches for his phone, and I watch his eyes dart from left to right as he scans whatever article he's reading on the screen.

"Okay." He sits up straighter. "Yeah, it's right here. His name's out. Seventeen-year-old high school student Kai Harrison found in the early hours of Saturday, February 22, at Hailing train station. Police are requesting that anyone with information come forward." His eyes land on me.

"I'm going to tell the cops I was around there last night."

There's a beat of silence. "What exactly are you going to tell them?"

"Just that I walked past him, and he was arguing with Quinn McKinley. Then I left. Probably just the stuff they're going to know anyway."

"Okay." He runs a hand over his mouth. "Shit," he mutters.

"So that's all. That's all there is to it."

He lowers his voice. "Okay, but what if they check your phone and ask why you called me at midnight last night?"

"You're my friend, I call you all the time. What makes last night any different, right?"

"Yeah. No, yeah. Exactly." But his hands twitch. "I called Ruben right after I spoke to you. Then Ruben called Fin."

"It passed between the four of us?"

"Yeah."

"No one else?"

He shrugs. "Just the four of us, I think."

The four of us. A memory comes back to me. At my mom's funeral, I sat in the front row, numb, staring at the same spot on the wall, trying to forget where I was. Michel, Ruben, and Finley stood at the back. I never asked them to come. I didn't even know they were there until it was over—until I walked out, and they fell in step beside me. None of us spoke. But they walked with me.

They don't know it, but they saved me that day. From everything. From the sad faces, the adults hovering, waiting for a chance to tell me how sorry they were.

No one could get to me.

Since then, it's always been the four of us.

"Don't worry," I say to Michel, drumming my knuckles on my mouth. "It's just a couple of phone calls. No one's checking on that."

"No. No, you're right." A pause. "You're probably right."

"Yeah. So I'll do that, then. I'll tell the cops I saw Kai arguing with Quinn, and I'll leave it at that. Because there's nothing more to tell."

His eyes stay on mine. He doesn't have to say it, and I know I don't either.

Silence is what we do best.

Saturday, February 22

CASON

THE POLICE STATION IS IN a brownstone building downtown, with a couple of steps leading up from the street.

"I'll wait for you out here," Michel says. He presses his lips before he adds, "Should I call Ruben and Fin? Tell them to get down here too?"

My chest tightens. "No. We'll talk later."

Michel nods, but the frown on his face lingers as I walk away, leaving him alone on the street.

Inside, the waiting room is a mash-up of voices, phones ringing, and the crackling sound of radios. It makes my head spin.

At the reception desk, there's an older woman seated behind a screen. Her glasses are hanging from a chain around her neck, and her head is bowed as she sorts through paperwork.

"Excuse me." My voice comes out rough, strained.

She looks up from her paperwork, eyeing me through the divide. "Yes?" A phone starts ringing behind her. "Can I help you?"

"Yeah. Hi." I clear my throat. "I'm here about the thing that happened last night. I was in the area, around the train station."

She stills. "Okay." She sets her pen down and sits straighter, thin shoulders tightening. "Hold on one moment, please." She reaches across the desk and types something fast on her keypad. When her attention comes back to me, her voice turns practiced like some AI bot. "I'm going to need to take a little more information. Name, please?"

"Cason Tano. T-A-N-O."

She types on the keypad again. "At what time were you around the train station area, please?"

"Eleven thirty, or just after. I saw him, the kid that died."

She takes a small breath, and I'm all in now.

"Yeah." I keep going. "I saw the news, and the appeal for people to come forward. So, yeah. Here I am."

"Right." Her voice sounds calm, but the twitch of tension in her pinched mouth gives away something else. "One moment, please." She reaches across the desk to pick up her phone, then presses a button. A couple of seconds later, she starts talking quietly into the receiver, murmuring code to whoever's on the other end of the line. She ends the call, and her beady eyes come back to me.

"Someone will be right with you," she says, gesturing to a row of metal chairs at the back of the room.

I nod thanks, and head for the seats beneath the leaded window.

People pass through the waiting room. No one's looking at me; everyone's too caught up in their own shit. The clock on the wall keeps ticking.

I reach for my phone and check my messages.

Are you okay?

I replied to Sadie before I heard the news. Yeah. You?

She's read it, but she hasn't answered. My sneaker starts tapping on the floor as I type out another message. Sadie you good?

"Cason Tano?" I look up at the sound of my name. A shorter woman with dark hair and a turtleneck shirt is heading toward me, shoes clicking fast. "Detective Alanis," she introduces herself. "We're ready to see you now."

AUDIO FILE_MP3

TITLE: CASE_339KH_CASON TANO INTERVIEW

Good afternoon. My name is Detective Alanis, and this is my colleague Detective Sampson. Can we take your name, please?

Cason Tano. T-A-N-O.

Thank you, Cason. I understand you were at Hailing train station last night, Friday, February 21. Is that correct?

Yeah. I caught the last train back from Arcadia.

For the purpose of the tape, I'm showing the interviewee an image of a young white male. Do you recognize this person?

Kai Harrison, right? He plays hockey for Arcadia High School. I play for Hailing, and we had a game about a month back.

You knew him?

Only through hockey. And he's dating a girl I went to middle school with too. Quinn McKinley.

And did you see the pair last night?

They were out on the street, standing at the bottom of the platform steps. I didn't talk to them, though. I just saw them.

Did you hear any words exchanged between them last night?

They were fighting about something.

Can you be more specific?

I don't know. Quinn was upset, asking him to give her a chance to talk, and that's all I got.

What happened after that?

I don't know. I walked home.

Okay. Did you notice anything else that might be relevant or important?

I wasn't paying that much attention. Hey, also, because I don't want to get pulled on this, their team and ours got into it after our game last month. But we're over all that now.

What do you mean when you say "got into it"?

We had a fight. Arcadia police showed up.

I see. Thank you for this information. And when you said, "We're over all that," do you mean there's no ill feeling from either side?

Yeah. We squashed it.

You're certain about that?

Yeah, yeah. It was a month ago. Trust me, no one's holding on to that.

Saturday, February 22

SADIE

THE SUN IS STARTING TO set, bronzing the pavement outside my house. All along the sidewalk, the streetlamps have come on, spotlighting the road.

Dad keeps offering me food, or suggesting I take a nap. But all I can do is stare out the living room window, frozen.

I pull a throw blanket around my shoulders. This room feels freezing today, and the violet walls my mom painted before she left are only adding to the coldness.

I huddle on the bay window seat and stare out at the street. I don't want to be here, but I can't bring myself to move. I can't tear my eyes away from the police team gathered across the road. The crime scene, that's what it is. The place where Kai Harrison's body was found.

Commuters are still using the station, disembarking from inbound services. I watch them tread down the steep steps, gawking at the police barricades as they pass.

Cason's last message is still unanswered on my phone. **Sadie you good?**

I want to reply. I want to call him, talk to him, hug him, tell him that I'm a long way from being *good*. But I'm scared. Because he was there last night, at the station. He and Kai have history. I didn't see Cason leave the platform when I was outside with Quinn and Kai. So I can't help but go there—what if he *didn't* leave? What if he was still on the platform when Kai went to catch the train home?

"Sadie." Dad's voice makes me jump, and my eyes shoot to him where he's standing in the doorway. "Bridget McKinley called," he says.

I sit up straighter. "Quinn's mom? Why?"

"She wants to know if you've spoken to Quinn this afternoon. Bridget says after they left the police station, Quinn ran off, and now she isn't answering her cell. They don't know where she is. They're worried."

I pounce on my phone and dial Quinn's number. My stomach lurches when it goes straight to voicemail.

Dad trails a hand over his stubbled jaw. "Right. I'd better call Bridget."

I follow him into the kitchen and stand anxiously at the breakfast bar while he lifts his cell to his ear.

"Hi," he says into the phone. "No . . . I will . . . of course. And let me know if . . ."

I hold my breath. When he ends the call, he turns to face me.

"What did Quinn's mom say?" I ask.

He presses his fist to his mouth. "She's worried, understandably. Quinn's taking this badly; she was upset when she left the precinct."

I sink onto a stool at the breakfast bar. "She didn't tell her parents where she was going?"

Dad shakes his head. "Let's hope she calls them soon, eh?" There's a pause, a tense silence, and then he says, "I'm going to put some coffee on. Do you want some?" He starts fussing with the machine, fumbling, and clattering around.

"Dad, are you okay?"

"Me? Oh. Uh . . ." He dodges the question, his attention fixed on the coffee maker. "How are you holding up? Can I get you anything? A sandwich or something? I think we've got some cold cuts." He doesn't wait for my response. He swings open the refrigerator door and starts rummaging through the compartments, knocking things over and cussing under his breath.

"Dad," I murmur. "Stop. I'm okay."

He closes the fridge with a soft thump. "I'll go to the store. Or we could get takeout. What do you feel like ordering?"

"It's okay. I'm not hungry."

The emptiness I'm feeling isn't hunger. It's something else.

My gaze wanders to the kitchen window, a frame to our backyard and the old maple tree with its tired branches. The sun is sinking, and what's left of the daylight is dull gray, threatening rain. The muted light amplifies the grimness surrounding us. I feel it attached to me, this heavy energy that I can't escape.

Dad heaves a sigh as he pulls out a stool at the breakfast bar. "Today has hit us all pretty hard, huh?"

"Yeah." Seeing Dad rattled makes me rattled. For years we talked about cases together. Examining crime, analyzing the impact—objectively, from the outside.

But this isn't some abstract story. It's Kai's story.

"Why were you on the eleven-twenty train, Sadie?" I can tell by the way he blurted it out that he's been holding on to that question all day. Honestly, I'm surprised it took him this long.

"My shift ran over." The words limp from my lips because I know I'm lying. And I know he can tell. *I've been meeting a boy.* That's what I should be saying. *I've been meeting a boy who might have been involved in a homicide last night. A boy that I forgot I knew when the police interviewed me this morning. Surprise!*

"I've always trusted you, Sadie," Dad says. "I expect a lot from you. Too much, maybe." He rubs his brow.

"It won't happen again."

"When you started this job at Raleigh's, we agreed, the nine-thirty train. Nine o'clock is your curfew, I already extended it." He laughs under his breath, but there's no humor there. "Coming home close to midnight when you know I'm at work and won't be here to catch you out? That's not okay."

I stare at the mottles in the breakfast bar, tracing the charcoal patterns with my gaze. Last night wasn't the first time that I've *accidentally* missed the 9:30 and lied about it. Or at least, not been honest about it.

But how am I supposed to explain that I've been hanging out at Raleigh's after my shift to be alone with Cason? That Cason's been lying to his coach, saying his uncle's picking him up when, in reality, we're still there, hidden from view on the bleachers, sneaking out before the maintenance guy or Maya locks up for the night? That we've been getting closer, and before everything went wrong with Quinn, I'd invited him over on the night Kai was murdered. Alone. At midnight.

"It could have been you," Dad mutters.

My stomach knots at his words. "But it wasn't."

"Kai Harrison went to your school. He was your age."

"I know," I whisper. "He was my friend." Saying those words aloud makes me pause. Because I would have considered Kai a friend, once. He tagged along on our coffee trips and late-night snack runs to the gas station. But so much has happened over this past month, so much has changed.

Dad reaches across the counter and pats my hand. "I'm sorry. This is . . ." He trails off and shakes his head.

"I get it," I tell him. "Missing curfew, staying out late, it won't happen again."

"Maybe this job is too much for you. You're only seventeen—"

"But I'm saving for college. My tips are adding up to contribute toward housing, maybe even a car."

"There are other jobs," Dad points out. "Daytime jobs. Something closer to home."

I chew the inside of my lip.

"We can figure something out." Dad hesitates, and his hands twitch on the counter. "I'm here for you, okay?"

I muster a smile. "I know."

This is uncharted territory for us, tackling sensitive conversations. Usually it's just Dad and me, coexisting, watching movies and eating takeout. We both have to find our footing with this, and it's new.

"Detective Alanis said she might need to speak with you again," he adds. "How would you feel about that?"

My heart gives a slow thud. "Why? I already told them everything."

He flinches, trying too hard to keep his expression cool and collected. "It's just procedure. Now that they've identified the victim, they probably want to go over a few more details with you." He grimaces. "Victim," he mutters, echoing his own word. "I can't imagine how that boy's family must be feeling right now. You need to call your mom too. Call her before she sees this on the news."

"Okay," I murmur.

The coffeepot beeps, and Dad stands. "Don't worry about the police. It's just procedure," he says again. For me. For himself. I don't know anymore.

But it doesn't stop the dread from creeping into my throat, suffocating me. If the police start looking too closely, asking me questions about my relationship with Kai, it's only a matter of time before they find out that we've got history, and I've got motive.

POLICE DOCUMENTATION FOR CASE REF: 339KH

FILE_SEQUESTERED PHONE RECORDS

[RECOVERED JANUARY 31]

Hi, I found your note in my bag.

Good. I hoped you would.

Why did you give me your number?

Because I wanted you to text me. I guess it worked.

CASON:
You all free to meet?

MICHEL:
Yeah.

RUBEN:
?

FINLEY:
Why?

CASON:
Meet at the site.

FINLEY:
Is this about 19?

CASON:
Talk later.

Saturday, February 22

CASON

THERE'S THIS CONSTRUCTION SITE ALEC worked on a couple of years back. The project got shut down when they found something wrong with the soil, and the whole site got abandoned. It's like some forgotten junkyard now, with rusty nails, rotting planks of wood, and burned-out machinery. It's a graveyard for rusted poles and half-finished structures. No one's checking on this place anymore.

I climb the chain-link fence, gripping the wire rungs and jamming my sneakers into footholds. The fence shakes and creaks as I jump down to the other side. Wind rocks a skeletal support frame hanging on its hinges.

The sun is setting, stretching shadows over the cracked concrete. I take a seat on some blocks and listen for footsteps crunching over gravel.

Ruben's first; I see him, hood up, climbing the fence. He makes his way over to me.

"Hey." My voice sounds rough, cold air in my throat.

"Hey." He slaps my hand. "You good?" The muscles in his wide jaw tense with the question, but I nod.

Michel and Finley show up right after. They join us, finding a spot on the stacks of concrete blocks. For a minute, we just sit in silence, staring at the growing shadows.

"All right," I start. "I got to tell you what happened."

Their eyes are on me now, waiting. And I'm trying to find the words, because once I talk, we can't go back.

"You all know Nineteen is dead?" The wind steals my voice from me, it funnels through the site, rattling the fence.

Ruben drags a hand over his mouth. "Michel told us you saw him at the train station." He's looking at me when he says it. "You talked to him, right before."

Right before.

"Yeah, but . . ." My eyes move over the abandoned site. "I didn't kill him."

Michel's knee starts bouncing, and Finley keeps his eyes lowered while he messes with a rusted nail, scraping it in circles on the concrete. His shaggy hair is falling over one eye.

"Okay." I carry on, drumming my fist in my palm, "I'd just gotten off the train, I was hanging around, waiting for Sadie." A frown passes between them.

"Sadie?" Michel interrupts. "As in . . . ?"

"Yeah," I admit. "We've been meeting up." No one responds this time. I can guess what they're thinking. Since when am I involved with an Arcadia girl? But Sadie isn't one of them—she's one of us.

In their silence, I keep going. "I overhead Kai and Quinn

McKinley arguing on the street, right? Then it went quiet, and the next thing I know, he's up on the platform, coming at me, saying he knows one of our team has been hooking up with Quinn, and he wanted a name."

Ruben's thick eyebrows pull together. "What did you tell him?"

"Nothing! I didn't even know about it. He said he saw Quinn getting on the train with one of us, someone wearing our jacket. He said whoever it is better be ready because he's coming for them. Talking about how he's got nothing left to lose and all that."

"And what did you say?" Ruben presses.

I roll my eyes. "What do you think I said? I told him to pull up."

Ruben grimaces.

"Then I walked away. I only called Michel to see if he knew anything, to give the heads-up."

"Yeah, and that's why I called you." Michel nods in Ruben's direction. "Because I figured if anyone had something going with Quinn, it might have been you."

Ruben shakes his head. "I don't know anything about it."

"Ruben called me," Finley says, bringing his dark eyes up to us. "But I haven't heard anything about it either. No rumors going around or anything."

We all stare at each other.

"Okay." I press my hands together. "So Quinn was seeing someone from our team, but it wasn't any of us, and no one's heard anything about it? And then Kai—"

A shadow moves in my peripheral vision. Everyone's eyes dart across the site just as a rat streaks over the rubble.

I swallow. "Fin," I say, lowering my voice, "did the conversation go any further than you? Did you tell anyone else about what Kai said to me last night?"

His thin shoulders tense. "No."

"Just the four of us, then." I rub the nape of my neck. "Is this just a badly timed coincidence? Number Nineteen accuses one of us of making a play for his girlfriend, puts out a threat, says he's coming for whoever it is, it passes between the four of us, and he's dead an hour later?"

Michel glances between Ruben and me, and Finley starts scratching the nail along the concrete again.

Another beat of silence hangs between us.

Then Ruben speaks. "Does it matter?"

Something cold crawls down my spine. "What do you mean?"

Ruben hesitates, then says slowly, "What I mean is, maybe we don't need to dig too deep into this. I trust you all, I don't need to know anything more than you didn't do it. As far as I'm concerned, that conversation with Nineteen never happened."

Michel drags his hands over his face.

"It could have been anyone," I point out. "Just because Nineteen said some stuff last night doesn't mean his death has anything to do with us. He probably had a lot of enemies. Or he could have just tripped."

Michel exhales into the biting air. "Yeah. Of course. It's got nothing to do with us."

The scraping of the nail on the concrete stops. "What if the police want to look at our cell records?" Fin asks under his breath.

"Because of the fight last month. And they ask why we were calling each other right around the time Nineteen was killed."

Ruben brings a fist to his mouth, pausing before he speaks. "Okay. So if the cops check our call records, we just say we were talking about our game coming up, right? We had practice earlier that evening. We were just debriefing."

"Okay," Michel says, and Finley nods.

"Does that work with your story?" Ruben asks me.

My story.

"Yeah," I answer. Just a word, a breath, a signature in blood.

Ruben slaps his hand against mine. And it's done. We're all in.

No one's talking.

Saturday, February 22

SADIE

THE TRAIN SLOWS AS IT approaches Arcadia, and I brace myself, gripping the overhead handle and tensing in the press of bodies. The train cars are full this evening, and in the crush of people I can barely move. With services only just resuming, trains have been running sporadically, leaving commuters packed together like this, jostling for space and air.

I lied to Dad again. I told him I wouldn't leave the house, and that I'd lock up and get an early night. But five minutes after he left for his night shift, I was out the door.

The train reaches a standstill, and I tug anxiously at the hair tie on my wrist. The electric doors click open, and everyone moves. A guy carrying a bulky guitar case bumps into me, making me flinch.

"Sorry," he mutters, sidling past.

I shouldn't be on this train. Even as I was boarding, something felt profoundly wrong. Not only because it's late and I promised Dad I'd stay home. But standing at Hailing platform, with the crime scene area cordoned off to prevent contamination, and life just carrying on around it, it was all wrong.

But I can't just sit around my house going out of my mind wondering where Quinn is. I have to at least try to find her. There's still a chance I might.

I disembark at Arcadia as passengers flood the platform.

Weaving through the crowd, I head across the street toward Raleigh's, a blocky gray building looming at the back of a dimly lit parking lot. There are a couple of cars in the shadows, but it's quiet tonight, no big events or troops of people. Just darkness. Sometimes Maya closes early on slow nights like this. But the building lights are still on.

I draw in a deep breath and quicken my pace as I cross the quiet lot. At Raleigh's entrance, I push through the glass doors into the lobby. My shoes squeak as I half run along the polished corridor leading to the rink.

At once I'm hit by the icy air. The rink attendant has gone, and the stadium is empty, its metal bleachers creaking in the silence. Gone are the rowdy hockey fans, stomping their feet and waving their banners. The sound of skates carving through ice is replaced by the hum of the refrigeration system, and the chill of the arena seeps into my bones, penetrating my thick coat. Everything is frozen. Everything is cold.

I don't know why I thought Quinn would be here. It was a long shot, but I figured she might feel closer to Kai here. Or maybe it's me; *I* needed to be here. Some vague shred of normalcy.

This is where Cason and I meet. All those stolen evenings, waiting on the empty stands after my shift, and after his practice, strategically out of sight of the diner's interior window, where we can be *us*, with the thrill of our secret.

My footsteps clang on the bleachers, and I take a seat on the bench, gazing at the abandoned rink stretching out before me and the deserted stands surrounding me. I didn't expect to feel lonely here.

I slip out my phone and try Quinn's number again. The too-familiar sound of her voicemail echoes back at me.

"Hey," I murmur into the phone. "It's me . . . again. You probably won't listen to this, but if you do, call me back. I'm here for you."

As I end the call, a new notification pops up on my home screen.

TIKTOK: *@WildeOnCrime has posted a new video.*

I click the link, and my stomach flips.

TIKTOK

DARCY WILDE

@WILDEONCRIME

Season 19, Episode 2 #truecrime #forensic #fyp #HailingNY #JusticeforKai

Hi, guys. If you haven't already seen my last video, I suggest you go check it out. I talked about Kai Harrison, whose name was leaked earlier today as the victim of a fatal incident in Hailing. The story hit the news this morning, and Hailing is only a couple of towns over from me, so I've been doing some research. I can tell you, one of my former colleagues is working this case, and the facts are almost conclusively pointing toward homicide.

After my last video, someone who knew Kai reached out to me online. This person, who does not want to be named, shared some information regarding a school friend of Kai's who was also seen around Hailing train station late last night. Now, this could be a coincidence, but it does trigger some suspicion for me.

This correlation is interesting because, allegedly, this particular classmate—let's call them S.M.—was witnessed during school hours verbally attacking Kai Harrison, accusing him of taking a photo without consent.

My source has confirmed that although he personally wasn't present, the incident was witnessed by multiple people, and I understand it took place sometime last week. So really not that long ago in context. During the verbal dispute, things got extremely heated, and S.M. was overheard using threatening language toward Harrison. Something along the lines of "You're going to regret this. Don't think I won't see this through."

Very disturbing language, in my opinion. Part three to follow.

CASON

Sadie you good?

SADIE

No.

SADIE

[SHARED A LINK TO TIKTOK]

CASON

Where you at?

SADIE

Raleigh's. I don't know what to do. It's me, I'm S.M.

CASON

Wait right there I'm on my way.

Saturday, February 22

SADIE

THE RINK'S DOORS OPEN WITH a heavy thud. My eyes land on Cason as he jogs to the bleachers, and I stand to meet him, letting him fold me into a hug. It's only been about half an hour since I texted him, but that could have been an eternity—or maybe just a breath.

I practically fall into him, and for the first time all day, I feel like I can exhale. His skin carries the lingering cold of outside, but the closeness, the comfort, warms me.

"I'm sorry," he says, and just like that, I'm grounded again.

"Thanks for coming," I murmur as we sit together on the stands. "I hope I didn't interrupt anything."

He shakes his head. "It doesn't matter."

"I just needed to talk to someone." His gaze stays on me, even while mine wanders, roving over the rink below. "I didn't know who to call, but I had to . . ."

"You've got me," he says, reaching for my hand.

Under normal circumstances, those words from Cason would have made my heart skip a beat. But right now, my heart is racing for an entirely different reason.

"Kai," I manage, speaking quietly. Still, my voice seems to echo through the empty arena. "You've heard the news, right? You know that he's . . ."

He nods. "Yeah. I know."

I sit taller, prepare myself to face the moment I've been dreading. The inevitable. "Last night, after we left the train . . ." I can't bring myself to meet his eyes. Instead, I stare at the gleaming ice, the surface marked by the tracks of the Zamboni. "Did you and Kai . . ."

He tries to catch my gaze, but I'm too scared to look at him. I'm scared to see his face while I scramble for the question I'm afraid to ask. "Did you guys fight last night?"

There's a painful pause, and his hand slackens around mine. "No," he says, calmly, gently. "There was no fight. I promise you."

I let my eyes drift to him, and he tries to reassure me with a look, a nod.

"Do you hate me for asking?" I whisper.

This time, he laughs, just a quiet breath. "No."

I lean into him, listening to the steady beat of his heart.

He plays absently with the hair tie on my wrist, rolling the silver charm between his thumb and forefinger. In our silence, he pauses, studying the *Q* charm threaded through the elastic.

"Quinn," I explain. "She's got the *S*." I summon a smile. "Tacky, right? They were selling alphabet hair ties at the lake last summer. Quinn and I bought them, but we accidentally picked up the wrong bags, so we kept them on our wrists with the intention of switching back. But it never happened, and we ended up wearing them like friendship bracelets instead."

He touches the red-and-white striped hair tie bunched around my wrist. "How is Quinn?"

I exhale, and the cold air mists. "MIA, and her phone is off. I thought she might be here."

"I'm sorry," he murmurs. "She'll be okay."

"I don't know. It's so unlike Quinn to shut down and close off." A knot of guilt nags at me. Of the two of us, Quinn is the open one. The one who wears her heart on her sleeve and speaks with no filter. I've been lying to her about Cason for weeks, hiding the most exciting secret I have. How can I expect her to share her feelings with me when I don't do the same?

I heave a sigh.

"She'll get through this," Cason says. "It'll take some time, but she'll be okay." He pauses, lowers his gaze, then says it again, "She'll be okay."

Something in his voice has altered, as though he's lost in a memory. He's speaking as someone who knows. Someone who has lived through grief and loss.

We were in eighth grade when his mom died. It was on the local news, and everyone was talking about it at school. *That car crash,* they'd whisper. *It was Cason's mom.*

I remember the first day he came back to class after it happened. Everyone watched as he took his usual seat at the back of the room. He was different, though, like a part of him had died too. Cason was always the loud kid, the one who talked too much and challenged the teachers but was kind of charming with it. After his mom died, he shut down for a really long time, retreated into himself, and I never knew what to say to him. We drifted apart, and I let it happen because I didn't know what else to do. The pain poured from him.

I didn't have the tools to help him back then. I still don't. But I've always regretted letting him go.

Maybe that's why, when I was interviewed by the police, my first instinct was to protect him. Because I've witnessed his pain, and it's left a mark.

"I didn't tell the police I saw you last night."

He traps his lip between his teeth. "I didn't mention your name either. Our stories will track."

Our stories, like we have something to hide. My chest tightens at the thought. If the investigators decide to look closer at us, they'd only have to check our phone records to see the messages we've exchanged, the connection we have. Would they believe that we just didn't notice each other on the platform?

It makes my pulse quicken. I'm on the wrong side of this. I want to be the person investigating, scrutinizing the suspects, the crime scene, the impact. I'm not the person who lies to the police, or gets questioned, or gets called out by my initials in front of millions of viewers on a true crime TikTok account.

A few days ago, the idea that Darcy Wilde knew I existed would have felt like the greatest achievement of my life. I've been following her for years, daydreaming about working with her. The views on her latest video are already well into the thousands, and the comment section is blowing up, and she's talking about me. But not in a good way.

I take a deep breath. "Okay," I say to Cason, steeling myself. "So that video I sent you, calling out S.M. for yelling at Kai Harrison during school. Did you watch it?"

"Yeah," he says. "But don't worry. No one pays attention to that stuff."

I squint in his direction. "It already has tens of thousands of views."

His nose crinkles. "And you think S.M. is you?"

"I know it's me." My gaze wanders overs the empty stadium. "Because there was this thing that happened. At school." The words die in my throat. Across the arena, the deserted bleachers loom, casting long shadows over the ice. A faint mist rises from the surface, breath in our silence.

"Sadie, come on," Cason urges. "Whatever it is, you can tell me. Talk to me."

I keep my focus trained on the ice. "The only reason I didn't tell you sooner was because it would have escalated the tension between you and Kai. It would have made things so much worse."

He runs his thumb over mine, patiently waiting for me to explain.

"And I guess," I continue, "I was embarrassed." I slip my hand free from his and hug my arms around myself. "Okay. Last week, someone made an AI image of me and printed it out. They taped it to my locker at school."

Cason stays silent, but strain tightens his shoulders.

"It was my face," I elaborate. "On a different body. A naked body."

He shifts and his expression changes—brows pulling together, eyes narrowed. "You're kidding."

I shake my head. "There was no way of proving who did it. But," I draw out the word, "when I got to homeroom that morning, Kai made some comment about you. About *us*, and how I was trash, and a traitor. Because you *attacked* him." I make air quotes on the word.

"He knew about us meeting up?"

"He must have, right?" I comb my fingers through my hair, restlessly working through the cold strands. "I knew he was suspicious ever since that night I saw his car pull up in the lot. Clearly he made the picture to get back at me. Anyway, I accused him in front of our whole class."

"And he admitted it?"

"No. But he didn't deny it either. And the way he kept smirking . . ." I clench my teeth and shake the memory away. "I yelled at him in front of everyone. I told him he'd regret it, and I'd see it through. But I meant I'd take it up with the principal, not kill him."

Cason leans back on the bleachers, his chest lifting as he inhales. It's awhile before he speaks, and I find myself holding my breath. Countless thoughts run through my mind. Does he think I overreacted? Does he think I killed Kai?

Then he speaks. "I'm sorry Kai did that to you." I hear the meaning in his words, the sympathy.

All I can do is nod, because a lump has formed in my throat. When I found the picture taped to my locker, I went into fight-or-flight mode. It was hours before the humiliation hit me, the feeling of violation, like something had been stolen from me. I don't know how many people saw the image, how many people thought it was real, and those intrusive feelings are still running their course.

"I didn't do anything to Kai." I say it again, for Cason's benefit and my own. "I never would have." A frustrated breath escapes me. "Who is this source mentioned in the video, anyway? And how does Darcy Wilde even know that I was at the train station last night?"

He scuffs his sneaker on the dusty floor. "Someone must have told her."

"The thing that happened at school, sure. But the fact that I was at the train station last night? The police said I'd have anonymity, so how is this information out already? It's only been a day. And the only people who knew I was there would be you, Quinn, and Emma. Unless Emma told her brother, and it's spread around the hockey guys from my school."

"You've just got to ride this out," he says. "Don't let it get to you. Give it a day and they'll be jumping on something else."

I lean into his broad shoulder, taking comfort from his calm energy. Despite everything, every fear, every doubt, I know I'm safe with Cason.

I've always been safe with Cason.

Back in eighth grade, I was upset on my way to school. I was distracted and almost stepped out in front of a car. But it was Cason who pulled me back by my backpack. I still remember yanking out my earbuds and whirling around to see him behind me on the street, balanced on his bike with one foot on the ground, the other on the pedal.

He frowned at my glassy eyes, and I ended up telling him the whole story, that I'd had a huge fight with my mom, that I was scared my parents were getting divorced—I hadn't told anyone this, not even Quinn. Back then, Cason lived alone with his mom. I don't think he had contact with his dad. He probably didn't want to hear about my family drama. But he listened. He gave me a ride to school on the handlebars of his bike, and I poured my heart out to him as the wheels clicked and bumped us around over the uneven pavement.

There was always something about Cason, something reliable. I knew he wouldn't spread my secret around school or talk behind my back. My words were always safe with him. They still are.

Everything is safe with him.

Saturday, February 22

SADIE

CASON AND I SIT IN silence, the chill of the empty rink settling around us. There's so much I want to say but can't quite put into words. I steal a glance at him.

"Do you think it's possible," I start carefully, my voice low, "that one of the other Hailing boys, maybe . . ." I trail off, watching as he tenses, his eyes meeting mine. "I'm not accusing anyone," I add quickly. "It's just that Kai was in Hailing last night. You don't think maybe he ran into someone, and things just . . . got out of hand?"

He rubs the nape of his neck. The lack of response makes my skin prickle.

"Have you talked to any of the guys since this happened?" I press.

"I've talked to them, yeah."

I sit up straighter. "What did they say?"

"Nothing."

"And you don't think—"

"No."

The locker-room door swings open with a resonating thump.

We both turn as a group of girls glides onto the rink, their voices echoing in the cavernous space. They spot us on the bleachers, and one of them skates toward us, her blades carving the ice.

She leans against the barrier, sun-kissed highlights and bright blue eyes catching the light. There's something familiar about her. And for a second, it seems as though a flicker of recognition crosses her face too. "Hey," she says. "We have the rink between eight and nine tonight. It's up on the roster board. ACU women's hockey." She gestures toward the timetable attached to the door. The rest of her team has gathered at the edge, stretching and warming up.

"Sorry," I say, standing. "We'll go."

Her eyes land on Cason. "Wait. You play for Hailing, right?"

"Yeah," he says as he gets to his feet. "Do I know you?"

"Madison," she introduces herself. "I play center for the ACU Foxes. Listen, you guys are welcome to hang out and watch, if you want."

Cason glances at me before answering. "Thanks, but we should go."

"Okay," she says. "See you around." She turns quickly, and her glossy ponytail swishes behind her as she navigates the ice, skating back to her group.

The team begins its practice as Cason and I start down the bleachers. The clang of our footsteps reverberates.

"I'm sure I recognize her from somewhere," I whisper.

"She probably played in high school. Your school, maybe?"

I look back at the rink and the girls in their helmets. "Maybe."

Cason swings the door open just as my phone buzzes in my hand.

My eyes shoot to the screen, hoping to see Quinn's name. Willing it to be her. Because she still hasn't picked up my messages, and the day is rapidly slipping away.

But it isn't Quinn.

It's another app notification.

"I've been tagged in something on Instagram," I murmur. "Who's @AvaKava? What is this—" A breath catches in my throat, and I stop dead.

Cason stares at me, still propping the door ajar. "What's wrong?"

"I've been tagged in a photo." My voice suddenly feels scratchy. "In the comments. Quinn and Kai's handles have been tagged too."

Cason leans closer to see my phone and the picture displayed on the screen.

I swallow. "I guess this answers the question of how Darcy Wilde knew I was at the train station last night."

It's Quinn, Kai, and me. We're not deliberately in the frame—it's a selfie of the three college girls who'd been on the train last night. The photo was taken from the street, not long after they'd stumbled onto the platform throttling their beer bottles, the brunette giggling as she lost her footing. But behind their smiling faces, they've captured *us* in the background. I'm standing between Quinn and Kai with my hand lifted toward him, as though it's raised to hit him.

Cason has gone completely silent.

The same girls I casually chatted with on the platform, my

allies in the night, have shared a picture of me looking like I'm about to slap Kai Harrison, right before he was found dead a few feet from where we're standing.

"This isn't good," I say in a breath.

POLICE DOCUMENTATION FOR CASE REF: 339KH

FILE_SEQUESTERED PHONE RECORDS

[RECOVERED FEBRUARY 7]

I keep hearing that song you like. Do you think the universe is trying to tell me something?

What do you mean?

It's the Baader-Meinhof phenomenon. We studied it in philosophy class—when you notice something for the first time, then suddenly see it everywhere. It makes me think of you.

What, the theory or the song?

Both. You're always on my mind.

You have no idea how much that means to me. I feel so seen with you.

What are you doing later? I'm about to head into practice, but I need to see you.

I wish I could tonight. You're on my mind too.

Are you meeting him?

I was planning to go to his game. I just want to talk to him.

You're too good for him. He doesn't deserve you. Are you going to tell him about us?

No. I'm not telling anyone.

Neither am I. It's better this way. Then no one can get between us.

Saturday, February 22

CASON

I WALK SADIE TO HER door. We don't talk about the police tape snapping in the wind, even as we pass it. I stand on her stoop in the darkness, tell her good night, and watch her slip into the house. The lock clicks shut behind her.

It's heavy. All of it.

But I don't know how to make it better.

Alone, I cut through side streets where the walls are cracked and the streetlamps flicker, half broken. The roads are empty—no cars, no signs of life. It's late, and the quiet gets under my skin, pulling out the worst of my thoughts. I've been holding it together for Sadie, pretending this is no big deal. Getting called out on social media, tagged in a photo where she looks ready to take a swing at Kai—it's all going to be fine. The words leave my mouth while my heart smacks hard against my ribs.

I should have laid it all out from the jump, told her everything. I should have told her about what Kai said to me on the platform, how he knew Quinn was seeing someone from Hailing. But if I tell Sadie, then what? She'll think it was one of us. She'll think one of us killed him.

Ruben's house is just a few blocks away, so I make my way there. I text him as I walk. **You home?**

I wait a minute, stopping on the street corner outside his place, waiting for his reply. The lights are on in his house, and the beat of bass-y music is leaking from an open window upstairs.

Then his response comes. **Yeah. You coming over?**

Can you come out?

Ruben's got a big family, lots of people around. I like that. I like going over to his place, hanging out, getting lost in the noise. But I can't do that tonight. I can't have this conversation around anyone else.

I sit on the curb, staring into the shadows thrown by the streetlight, waiting for him. The front door creaks open, and I see him jog down the steps. He joins me on the curb, locking his hands in front of him.

"Sadie's been tagged in the comments on a picture," I tell him, keeping my eyes on the shadows. "It's bad, makes her look like she's involved in what happened to Nineteen."

He draws in a breath, saying nothing.

"I feel bad, man," I mutter, staring at my sneakers, the spatters of mud. "Because I didn't tell her about what happened between Kai and me. I didn't tell her about him threatening us."

He rubs the back of his neck. "What are you going to do?"

"I don't know." I glance at him, and he drops his gaze. "I don't want to lie to Sadie, because I like her. And even if what I'm doing isn't lying, I'm not telling her everything. So that's lying, right?"

Ruben lifts his hands, which doesn't help me.

"I'm leaving out facts," I keep going, more for myself than for him. "And now she's in trouble."

I want him to say something, tell me what to do. Tell me how I'm going to make this right without screwing him over, or Finley, or Michel, or myself. Because we're all involved in this; those phone calls will make us all look guilty if the police start looking our way.

Ruben's usually loud. He doesn't keep his opinions to himself, he's not that guy. I'm not that guy, either. But the one time I actually want his advice, he's giving me nothing.

"Say something, man."

"I don't know what to say."

"Sadie's in trouble," I mutter into the darkness, my voice rough. I swear, in every shadow I feel eyes on me.

"Yeah," he murmurs. "You are too."

Saturday, February 22

SADIE

MY BED FEELS RIGID, AND the comforter is scratching my skin. I can't seem to tear my gaze away from the shadows on the ceiling. My mind won't stop whirring, and it's taking all of my willpower not to check on @AvaKava's picture, and the comments that have been steadily building all evening. Going viral.

That girl definitely did it.

The two girls are in on it together, FOR SURE.

I bet they didn't plan for this photo to get released. They're done.

Somewhere in the distance, a siren wails and my stomach pits.

I concentrate on my breathing, slow and steady. But it doesn't quell the fears churning through my mind. I'm replaying everything. Every detail I gave to the police, every word that could have inadvertently landed me on their radar.

My phone buzzes, lighting up the dark room.

I almost ignore the incoming text, afraid of what I'll see. But when Quinn's name pops up, I sit bolt upright.

I'm outside.

I clamber out of bed and yank open the drapes. Only the lamplight glows on the empty street. My eyes frantically scan the pavement below and the shadows of the bare trees. But she isn't out there.

Where? I type back.

Her reply comes quickly. **Train station.**

I race downstairs and grab my coat.

Twisting the latch on the front door, I slip out into the moonlit night and pace across the quiet road.

"Quinn?" I call, searching for any sign of movement in the shadows of the streetlamp's light.

My heartbeat quickens, and it dawns on me that it isn't just Quinn I could find out here in the darkness. Kai's killer is still roaming free. I flip the flashlight on my phone and track it across the road, moving the beam over the storm drains and tire marks staining the asphalt. Police tape flutters in the wind, cordoning off the crime scene just beyond the platform. I sweep my flashlight over the stairwell, every sense on overdrive.

A chilling thought occurs to me. *What if it isn't her*? Why would she text me saying that she's outside, but not just come to my house? She's been missing all day; someone could have taken her phone.

But if someone does have her phone, if she's in trouble, I can't just leave her.

Shivering in the darkness, I try calling her, but it doesn't ring. It goes straight to voicemail, just like it's been doing all evening.

Alone on the quiet street, I glance back at my house, then grip my phone tighter, ready to dial 911 if I need to.

My breath turns shallow as I climb the steps to the platform. A strong gust of wind whips at the shelter, creaking the roof.

Edging forward, I move my light over the tracks and concrete. The graffiti on the brick wall arcs in florescent jagged letters and shapes, and a neon demonic-looking clown face leers at me with its sprayed-on evil sneer.

And then I notice the figure in the darkness, the shadowed silhouette standing perfectly still and staring silently back at me.

A breath catches in my throat.

Saturday, February 22

SADIE

I CLUTCH MY CHEST, RIGHT above my racing heart.

My light lands on her pale face, and the tear tracks staining her cheeks.

"Quinn," I whisper, rushing to her. "Are you okay?" I pull her into a hug, and she leans into my shoulder. "Where have you been?"

"Do you think he was right here?" Her voice trembles when she asks the question, and her gaze strays to the shadowed train tracks just beyond the platform. "Do you think it happened here?"

I can't bring myself to respond.

"I don't believe this is real, Sadie."

"I know," I murmur. "I'm so sorry, Quinn."

"No. I *don't* believe it." She steps back from me and takes a small breath. "Because what if they made a mistake? Someone's got this wrong."

The memory of the lifeless body on the stretcher flashes through my mind, making me shudder.

Quinn keeps going, overflowing with frenzied words, "At first the police made out like Kai just fell, right? Like it was an accident." She hesitates, and her voice wavers. "I told them we got into a fight, and that it was my fault he was in Hailing. He was probably waiting for the last train home, and he slipped and fell." Her thin shoulders start to shake. "And then," she whispers, "they said he suffered head trauma, and they started treating me like I did something to him. Like I killed him." She's wheezing, trying to get air into her lungs.

I reach for her trembling hand. "Don't do this to yourself. It's just procedure." I echo my dad's words—the tired stock response that we all need to hear. "The police have to ask questions. They were asking me questions too."

"No, but then everyone's been texting me, like they're trying to catch me out. Because they all know Kai would have only been in Hailing to see me. So everyone thinks he broke up with me, and I flipped out and killed him."

"But you didn't."

"What does it matter? Kai's gone." She presses her lips together, a fresh wave of tears threatening to spill. "He's gone, isn't he?"

"I'm so sorry." I sigh into the wind. "This is so horrible."

"It is horrible," she agrees, her eyes glistening in the low light. "And everyone is just making it worse, blaming me. Running this narrative that's so far from the truth. I never would have hurt Kai. Never."

"Don't do this to yourself, Quinn," I urge softly. "You can't assume people are suspecting you. Stop paying attention to what you read online. That picture is libel, and we should demand that it get taken down."

She stares blankly back at me, red, glassy eyes narrowing. "What do you mean? What picture?"

Her confused expression makes me wince. "You haven't checked Instagram lately?"

She slips her phone from her coat pocket and opens the app. Suddenly I'm faced with the image I've been trying so hard to avoid. Me, caught in the corner of the frame, with my hand raised toward Kai.

Quinn goes straight to the comments.

"Don't." I pry the phone from her grasp. But it's too late.

"Oh my god," she chokes. "They're saying it's us."

My heart sinks. "I'm sorry. I thought you knew. You said everyone's blaming you."

"I meant . . ." She exhales sharply. "I meant people from school. Not *everyone*. These people think it's us, Sadie!"

"It doesn't matter. *We* know it wasn't us." I muster confidence in my words, even though I'm quaking on the inside. "We were together, at my house. We're each other's alibi."

A shallow breath escapes her. "People are going to think we're covering for each other, though. The police were already asking me if anyone else can vouch for us."

I swallow the fear. "We just have to keep being honest with the investigators and trust that they'll believe us. Because we're telling the truth." My thoughts wander to Darcy Wilde's video. Thanks to this nameless source, everyone knows I've got motive. Or at least they know S.M. has motive.

But I've been so caught up with Darcy calling me out as a

suspect, I haven't had a chance to process her other content.

There was blunt force head trauma. . . . It's likely to have happened sometime between midnight and one a.m.

"What happened to Kai happened between midnight and one?" I say to Quinn. "We were together at that time, in my room. Remember? Because we . . ." I stop talking, and my breath hitches.

"What? What is it?"

"The car," I muddle on.

Quinn frowns back at me.

"We heard a car last night. Ten past midnight. Remember?"

She presses her fingers to her lips. "The tires screeching," she says quickly. "Do you think it was someone coming for Kai?"

"I don't know. But it's weird, right? Even at the time it was weird, before any of this came out." The screeching of rubber on the road, like someone was tearing down the empty street way too fast. It was swift, their arrival, the door slamming, and their getaway.

Quinn doubles over, clutching her stomach. "Oh my god," she half sobs. "It has to have been one of the Hailing boys."

I flinch at her words. "We can't jump to conclusions. The details around the cause of death haven't been confirmed. It could still have been an accident."

Quinn snatches her phone from me.

"What are you doing?" Panic rises in my throat. "Are you calling the police? Because if you are, people's names are going to get dragged into this over that fight, and I—" My voice falters in fear for Cason.

But Quinn doesn't answer. She opens the image again, the picture of us on the street, not far from the platform where we're standing right now. "This was posted at 11:51 on Friday night," she says. "We heard the car about twenty minutes later. What if someone saw this picture and came looking for Kai?"

She starts scrolling quickly through the likes and comments, probably trying to pick out names, but they're well into the thousands now, and increasing by the second.

Quinn tosses her phone onto the concrete, and the clatter echoes in the night. "I hate this," she whispers.

"I do too," I say, reaching for her hand. "But we don't know anything for sure. We can't do this to ourselves. And we can't start throwing peoples' names around either."

"Yeah," she says, shakily. "The Hailing boys wouldn't . . ." The sentence dies in her throat.

A bone-cold feeling comes over me. I glance at the tracks and the shadows curling around us, ghosts on the abandoned platform.

There are no certainties, no explanations yet, and we can't point the finger at anyone without proof. But there is one thing I feel sure of. I believe that whoever was driving that car murdered Kai. And I think Quinn knows it too.

POLICE DOCUMENTATION FOR CASE REF: 339KH

FILE_SEQUESTERED PHONE RECORDS

[RECOVERED FEBRUARY 14]

Happy Valentine's Day, babe.

Happy Valentine's Day to you too!! 

I wish I could be with you right now. I'd skip practice, but we've got a game coming up. You watching from the diner?

Yep, I see how hard you're working out there. He's really pushing your buttons tonight, huh? 🙄 But I love how you're handling it. You're amazing.

I feel the same about you. You mean everything to me, just want you to know that.

Thank you. You make me feel so safe.

Good. And don't worry about Kai anymore. If he wants to talk, I'll handle it.

AUDIO FILE_MP3

TITLE: CASE_339KH_SADIE MORELLI INTERVIEW

Hi, Sadie. Thank you for coming into the station today.

That's okay. Why did you need to see me again?

I'd like to get your thoughts on this. (PAUSE.) For the purpose of the tape, I'm showing Miss Morelli an image that was posted to a social media account @AvaKava. The image captures three people in the background who appear to be in the middle of what seems to be a heated confrontation. Sadie, can you confirm that one of these people is you?

Yes. Yes, that's me.

And the other two people?

Quinn and Kai.

Quinn McKinley and Kai Harrison?

Yes.

Thank you for confirming that, Sadie. Why don't you talk me through what was going on at this moment? Because it seems like you were raising your hand to hit Kai. Am I right in assuming that?

No. No, that's absolutely not what was happening. I was trying to mediate. They were fighting, and I was just calming the situation down.

They were fighting?

No, I didn't mean . . . They weren't physically fighting, but they were talking and . . . it's not how it looks. I was just trying to help. This isn't me. I'm not this person.

There was an incident at school too, wasn't there? You reported Kai for sharing a private picture of you.

It wasn't a real picture. It was an AI-generated image that Kai made.

And words got heated?

It was just a conversation. The school dealt with it.

Yes, I understand that. It's okay, Sadie. We're just trying to get a clear picture of what happened that night.

I know. But this picture isn't going to give you one.

Monday, February 24

SADIE

STANDING AT THE SCHOOL GATES on Monday morning makes my chest constrict. Over the weekend, the picture of Kai, Quinn, and me at the platform gained momentum, and the comment section is out of control. The possibility that the police think Quinn and I have anything to do with what happened to Kai makes me feel sick to my stomach. I can only imagine what theories my classmates are concocting.

The main building is fronted by a large stone archway, engraved with *Arcadia High School*, welcoming students into the halls. Even before I've reached the entrance, I hear the whispers. I feel everyone's eyes on me, watching me expectantly, like they're holding their breath, waiting for me to slip up and confess everything. That I did it. I killed Kai Harrison.

I force myself to walk forward, striding along the corridor. I need to show everyone that I'm not the person they're painting me to be. I'm not the intimidating S.M. on @WildeOnCrime, or the aggressive antagonist in @AvaKava's post. I would never have hurt Kai, no matter what our history was. And I'm going to prove my innocence, one painful step at a time.

While I wait for Emma to show up, I focus on my locker, busying myself arranging, then rearranging my books.

"Oh my god, Sadie." A voice makes me flinch, and someone grabs my arm. It isn't Emma.

I drop my dog-eared English lit book and spin around to face Hannah Sutton. She blinks back at me with wide eyes, her full lips parted in disbelief. "Kai," she whispers. "I can't believe it."

"I know," I manage. "I can't either."

"How's Quinn? Is she coming in today?"

"I doubt it. She needs some time, you know?" I didn't ask Quinn if she'd be at school today. Given everything that's happened, I'm sure showing up to class is the furthest thing from her mind right now.

Hannah frowns. "Yeah, but like, she and Kai weren't together, were they? I thought they broke up forever ago?"

"She loved him," I answer blankly. I return my attention to my locker, hoping to end the conversation there.

But Hannah doesn't pick up on my cues. "I saw that picture going around of you guys and Kai at the train station," she says. "So what actually went down that night? Did you all get into a fight or something?"

Heat flushes my face. "That picture is very deceptive."

There's a beat of silence before she fixes me with a too-sweet smile. "Of course. Because it looked pretty bad." She tilts her head in sympathy. "So deceptive, though."

I'm seconds away from crawling into my locker, hiding there

for the rest of the day amid the clutter where no one can find me. But then a memory creeps to the forefront of my mind, and I freeze. *Pictures can be very deceptive.*

"Hannah," I say quickly, "I just remembered something. You sent Quinn a text a little while ago, didn't you? About a month ago, you sent her a picture of Kai with another girl."

She nods knowingly, then I swear her big blue eyes light up. "Oh, shit. Was that what your fight was over?"

"No, no. It's just . . ." I hesitate, chewing over my words. I need to tread carefully with this. The last thing I want to do is provide more fodder for the Quinn-and-Sadie-killed-Kai narrative. But if Quinn's theory about someone seeing @AvaKava's post and showing up at the station is right, then there could be a connection here. From what I can remember, the girl Kai had his arm around, the lipstick-on-his-neck girl, looked like she might be about the same age as @AvaKava and the other girls who were on the train on Friday night. It wouldn't be impossible for them to know each other from college, or maybe even be friends. More than that, when the girls passed us on the street that night, I caught them whispering to each other. Now I'm wondering what exactly they were whispering about.

When I speak again, I try to keep my voice casual. "Can I see that picture?"

"I don't have it. I just saw it on my cousin's story and forwarded it to Quinn." Hannah leans closer, hushing her voice. "Why?"

There's no way to spin this without making Quinn look like the jealous ex, out for revenge. When Hannah sent her that picture,

Quinn had me analyze every detail until I finally convinced her to delete it the next day. It's been a month, so my memory is a little hazy, but it's still a lead worth considering—especially if it could exonerate Quinn, Cason, and me. "Just wondering who the girl was. Do you know her name?"

She shakes her head. "No. My cousin's a freshman at ACU, she remembered Kai from Arcadia. They were at some party, and he was wasted. Why do you want to know the girl's name?" She's already getting out her phone, finger poised like she's ready to text this information to everyone in her contacts list.

Fortunately, I catch sight of Emma heading our way before I have to figure out how to talk myself out of this conversation.

"Hey." I wave her over.

"Hi." She gives me a hug, then squeezes my hand. "How are you?"

I nod, mustering confidence as Hannah studies my every move. "How are you? How's your brother?"

She heaves a sigh, looking between Hannah and me. "I'm okay, but Brandon's not doing so great. The guys are all in shock, I think. They're planning a vigil for Kai. They're rallying, you know?"

Hannah pouts sadly. "For sure. Kai was literally their best friend." Her eyes skim over me again, checking for my reaction, probably.

The first warning bell drills through the corridor, and I hold my breath as people begin to flood past in a cacophony of voices. I pretend not to notice the side-eyes and awkward stares.

And then I see them. The hockey boys, heroes of our school. They're quiet and somber in their grief, all weaning Kai's number drawn in permanent marker on their shirts: *19*. People bow out of their way, letting them march in formation along the corridor.

I swallow as Jacob Ritter catches my gaze. The muscles in his jaw twitch, and he looks away.

When they pass, I turn to Emma, and the tremor in my voice betrays me as I whisper, "The boys don't think I had anything to do with—"

"Of course not," she answers quickly. Too quickly.

"Brandon hasn't said anything to you about me, has he?"

She squeezes my hand and forces a smile.

The lack of response is answer enough for me. Message received, loud and clear.

"They can't seriously think that I . . ."

"They don't." Emma fills in the blanks—the words that I couldn't bring myself to say. "They're just feeling it, you know? Everyone's in shock right now."

"Yeah," I murmur. "Yeah. Okay."

Emma and I are close, and I trust her completely, but deep down, I know her loyalty will always lie with Brandon and those guys. That's Emma's core group, and blood will always run thicker than water.

"We should go to homeroom," she says, and I let her lead me down the corridor, with Hannah in tow. Locker doors clang and voices start to peter off as everyone disappears into the classrooms. In the new quiet, my footsteps echo, and my breath rattles in my ears.

When Hannah waves and heads to her classroom, I grab Emma's arm and pull her to a stop in the corridor.

"Kai was partying with a college girl about a month back," I tell Emma, lowering my voice as I muddle through my thoughts. "Do you remember that Hannah sent Quinn a picture of Kai with another girl, and she was devastated over it?"

"Yeah, I remember."

"Did any of the guys ever mention it?"

Emma hesitates, glancing between me and our classroom farther down the hall. "I don't think so," she answers.

"Brandon never mentioned it to you? He never told you that Kai was seeing someone else while he and Quinn were on a break?"

"Nope."

My gaze wanders along the empty corridor, drawn by the faint echoes of footsteps. The bright ceiling lights bounce off the gray floor tiles, fragmented in their reflection, and the quiet is almost tangible.

"Maybe I should ask Jacob," I mutter. "Jacob would know, right?" Out of all Kai's friends, Jacob's the one I know best, thanks to our sort-of date over the summer break.

"Why, though?" Emma says. "What does it matter?"

"This could be nothing," I accept, "but what if it isn't?" A surge of hope rushes through me at the notion. "What if the mystery girl that Kai was seeing is a lead? What if she's connected to @AvaKava? Wait." I press my hand to my chest. "What if it's one of them? Ava, the girl who posted that photo—she and her friends *saw* Kai there that night. They walked right past us."

Emma makes a noncommittal noise. "But them seeing Kai at the platform doesn't necessarily mean anything."

I lift my index finger. "Unless one of those girls was the mystery person Kai was seeing while he and Quinn were broken up. Maybe she saw him with his ex and came back to confront him once Quinn was gone. I have to talk to the hockey boys. All I need is a name."

Emma traps her rosy lip between her teeth. "I don't think that's such a good idea, Sadie."

"Why not?"

"Well, I just—"

We pause our conversation as a group of freshmen troops past. I'm sure their steps slow as they weave around us, shooting each other looks.

I roll my eyes, and we wait until they're out of earshot before continuing.

"Okay, look," Emma says, pressing her palms together. "You know I love you, right?"

"Never a good intro, but okay."

She musters a smile. "The guys are mourning their friend. They're really feeling it. Just give it a minute, yeah? No one wants to be questioned about some random that Kai may or may not have hooked up with a month ago."

"And especially if *I'm* the one doing the questioning," I guess, reading between the lines.

She sighs. "Everyone's pretty convinced that the Hailing boys had something to do with what happened to Kai—"

"Baseless accusations."

"Kai was in Hailing when it happened, Sadie. They jumped him outside Raleigh's not that long ago."

"Or was it the other way around?" I venture. "Did *Kai* jump *them*?"

"Sadie!" She flings up her arms. "How can you say that?"

"We didn't see who started that fight," I remind her. "None of us did." My thoughts stray to my conversation with Cason. I believe his story. He had no reason to start that fight, and I trust him. But judging by the pursed-lipped look of disappointment on Emma's face, I don't think she's open to hearing Cason's side of the story right now.

"Kai is . . ." She rakes her hands through her curls, giving way to a frustrated breath. "Kai's dead."

I dip my gaze.

"And people are talking." Her voice softens a little. "Brandon and those guys know that you and Quinn have been hanging out with the Hailing boys."

"Quinn?" I frown back at her. "Quinn hasn't been hanging out with them."

"But you have," Emma says.

"Okay, but . . ." I stammer. "Is that really a big deal? We used to know them, way back."

"That's the point." She exhales slowly. "Full disclosure? People think that you and Quinn know something about what happened to Kai, or even had a part to play in it. All of you, together."

Her words hit me hard. For a second, I can't find my voice. "You actually believe that?"

"*I* don't," she says, touching her fingers to her heart, colorful rings catching the light. "But when that photo came out with you about to hit Kai—"

"I was trying to calm him. Like this," I say, raising my palm in a peace gesture, but she flinches a little.

My breath catches. "Emma, please," I murmur. "You know me. You have to believe that I had nothing to do with this."

Emma glances along the corridor. "I do," she says. "The guys will come around too."

"But they actually think that Quinn and I orchestrated some assault with the Hailing boys? Quinn loved Kai."

"And he broke up with her."

My lips part in disbelief. "She wouldn't kill him for breaking up with her, Emma. Come on."

"You don't think I've said that to Brandon and those guys? Sadie, I'm fighting in your corner hard."

"Are you?"

"Yes. And that's why I'm telling you this. Trust me, give it a minute."

A tightness pulls at my chest. A few weeks ago, I considered these boys to be my friends. Today, they consider me a murderer.

"It'll pass," Emma says gently. "Just hang in there." She reaches for my hand and leads me along the corridor.

Numb, I follow her to homeroom and slide into my seat. Quinn's desk is conspicuously empty, and her absence looms over me like a dark cloud. I don't know if I can get through today without her.

Mr. Jensen stands at the front of the classroom, his usual cheerful demeanor replaced by this strange solemn reflection. There's an uneasy silence in the room, broken only by the rustle of jackets and the soft sound of crying as our teacher commemorates Kai in a low and measured voice. He talks about how Kai would be remembered, how his legacy at the school would live on.

The weight of it aches.

But there are words he won't say—Kai was killed. And the person who did it still walks free. That realization scares me. I've listened to enough true crime podcasts and documentaries to know that sometimes there is no resolution. Sometimes the investigators get it wrong. And that scares me just as much.

When Mr. Jensen ends his speech, the room stays quiet in a collective show of respect. At the sound of the bell, everyone starts to stand, gathering their books.

I hold back, though. Slipping my phone beneath the desk, I search for @AvaKava's page and isolate her profile picture. Ava Kavanaugh. She must be a few years older than me, blond hair tumbling over one shoulder, eyes shielded by aviators.

Steeling myself, I open the comments on the picture from the platform. It's mostly RIP statements, or people throwing out speculations.

One person says, They must have been fighting over him. Look at the brunette, she's pissed, probably in love with the guy and he's over it.

My stomach lurches. *I'm* the brunette.

And the comments don't end there. There are arguments,

debates about who's prettier, comparing me and Quinn, our appearance, our flaws.

Grimacing, I exit the thread and start scrolling through Ava's grid, working my way through dozens of pictures. Ava on vacation or posing with her friends at theme parties in costumes. There's a shot of her in front of a white house, where bunting is strung from the porch and girls in oversized hoodies are lounging on lawn chairs beneath a Gamma Phi Beta banner.

"Sadie?" Mr. Jensen's voice makes my head snap up. "Is everything okay? It's time for class."

"Yes. Yes, sorry." I'm on my feet fast, almost knocking over my chair. I slip my phone into my bag before slinging the strap over my shoulder.

But I'm not going to class.

I'm going to find Ava Kavanaugh.

Monday, February 24

SADIE

THE GAMMA PHI BETA SORORITY house is a white-walled colonial with huge bay windows and a turreted roof. A brick path leads through the neat lawn to white columns and pastel bunting hanging from the portico, and a green-and-yellow ACU flag rippling in the breeze.

I climb the porch steps and press the bell. It chimes softly inside the house, just about reaching my ears.

A moment later, the door swings open and a petite red-haired girl wearing cutoffs and an ACU sweatshirt is standing in front of me.

There's a split-second pause, a moment where she studies my face.

I hold my breath.

She sweeps aside some stray strands of hair that have escaped her effortlessly messy bun. "Hey," she says, beaming at me with perfect teeth. "Freshman, right?"

"Oh. Yeah." The lie falls out too easily.

"Come on in," she says, swinging the door wider.

I step gingerly over the threshold. "I've come to see Ava Kavanaugh. She lives here, right?"

The girl glances into the wide hallway cluttered with discarded shoes and unopened mail. "Ava? Yeah, she's upstairs, I'll go get her for you. Make yourself at home."

Beyond the wood-floored hallway, she directs me to an airy living room with mismatched couches and colorful throw cushions, and a mantel with scented candles and candid photos in bright frames. The coffee table is littered with magazines and college textbooks, and an open family-sized bag of popcorn.

I sit tensely on one of the couches, waiting for the sound of footsteps. I'm pretty sure my entire house could fit into this living room.

"Hi."

I turn fast to see Ava standing in the arched doorway.

Her heart-shaped face falls, and she stops still. "Hi," she says again, slowly. "What are you doing here?" She glances over her shoulder, like she's about to call for backup.

I stand and lift my hands in peace. "Hi, Ava. I'm sorry to come over unannounced like this, but I had to talk to you. About the other night."

Her willowy shoulders tighten. "How do you know where I live?"

Heat flushes to my cheeks. "I figured it out." Admitting that makes me cringe—even I can hear how stalker-ish it sounds. "Your social media," I add. "This house is pretty distinctive. You probably should take a look at that."

Her chest rises. "I'm calling the police."

"No, wait," I say quickly. "I'm not here to cause trouble. I didn't even plan to come inside; I was invited in."

"Under false pretenses," she says, narrowing her eyes. "Naomi said you were one of the freshmen rushes. You're not."

"Please, Ava. I have to talk to you about Kai Harrison."

Her eyes move away from me at the mention of his name. "Why?"

"You were there on the night he died," I carry on. "Just like I was. You took that photo, with me in the background. You posted it."

"I didn't even notice you in the frame," she says. But her nose twitches. Together with the way she's playing with her hair, and the sharpened tone of her voice, it's Criminology 101. If there's one thing I've learned from Darcy Wilde, it's to watch out for the tells: grooming, fidgeting. Check. Vocal cues, a change in speech pattern. Check. And, most importantly, gut instinct.

Check, check, and check.

"You could have cropped us out," I forge on. "But you didn't. And now I'm dealing with the repercussions. Can you at least have the decency to have a conversation with me?"

She rakes her fingers through her glossy hair. "I told you I didn't notice you in the shot. What more do you want?"

"All I'm trying to do is figure out what happened to Kai. What *really* happened to Kai. Because contrary to the comments on your post, *I* didn't kill him. And neither did my friend Quinn."

She hesitates for a moment. "Okay," she says at last, reluctantly gesturing toward the couch. "But I've only got, like, ten minutes. Then you've got to leave."

"Thanks," I murmur. "Ten minutes is good."

She takes a seat on the opposite couch and crosses her lean legs.

"The photo you took when you were leaving the platform," I begin. "Kai, Quinn, and I were tagged in it—"

"That's not my fault," she interrupts. "I posted a picture of me and the girls, and some people started tagging you all in the comments."

"But you knew Kai," I hedge.

She shifts, uncrossing her legs. "I'd seen him around. I didn't *know* him."

My pulse races, and Hannah's picture flashes through my mind. Kai grinning sloppily at the camera, gripping a Miller bottle, with a lipstick mark on his throat and his arm slung around a girl's waist. A girl who, from what I can remember, kind of looked like Ava. Long blond hair, blue eyes, petite. "Did anything happen between you and Kai?" I ask.

"No. God, no." She exaggerates a shudder. "My friend had a thing going with him for a minute. But then he ghosted her."

"Do the police know about this?"

"What, that Kai Harrison ghosted my friend?" She tilts her head, a decidedly patronizing smirk playing on her lips. "It doesn't matter anyway, because she was waitressing that night, so she had nothing to do with what happened to him, if that's what you're getting at."

"What's her name?" I press.

Ava arches a perfectly sculpted eyebrow. “Look,” she says, “it’s cute that you want to play detective and all—”

“My best friend’s boyfriend is dead, and I’m being treated like a suspect. Nothing about this is *cute*.”

She stares at the woven rug beneath her fuzzy slippers. “Okay. I don’t think this conversation is going anywhere. I’m sorry you got identified from the picture, but . . .” She trails off and shrugs again.

The way she said *identified*, with a lilt, makes my stomach turn. “Your friend who had a thing with Kai, do you think she’d talk to me?”

“Probably not,” Ava says, and she stands.

I force myself to follow her lead. “Okay.” After a moment, I add, “But I don’t deserve any of this. I haven’t done anything wrong, and I think you know that. You know I didn’t hit Kai, because you were there, beyond the split-second frame of that picture.”

She purses her lips, and something close to sympathy crosses her face. “If you want me to take the photo down . . .”

I summon a smile. “It doesn’t matter now. It’s already been shared. People have already drawn whatever conclusions they want from it. The police included.”

“For the record,” she says quietly, “I posted it before I knew about what happened to Kai. Probably before anything *had* happened to him. To be real, when I took the photo I just thought you all were having some typical high school drama.”

A shiver moves over me.

“I saw you leaving that night,” she adds. “I know my picture made you look way more involved than you were, and I told the police that when they interviewed me."

"Thanks for that," I say as she leads me to the door.

"Yeah. I told them it didn't seem like you were acting aggressive."

We stop for a minute in the open doorway, cold air stirring our hair. She rests her hand on the frame.

"Good luck with everything," she says. "I hope this blows over for you, all the hype."

I nod.

Ava closes the door behind me with a soft click, leaving me on the porch. Mind racing, I make my way along the brick path and onto the sidewalk. Alone on the leafy suburban street, I turn my conversation with Ava over in my mind. She said she'd probably posted the photo *before anything had happened to him* . . . 11:51.

I heard car tires screech outside at ten past midnight. That's a nineteen-minute time gap between Ava's post and the sound of tires. According to the coroner's estimate, Kai died somewhere between midnight and one a.m.

There's a ton of college housing in this neighborhood—it's known for it, because the places are huge and cheaper than renting in Arcadia, closer to campus.

I open up the route planner on my phone and set a course to the Hailing train station. If someone had seen Ava's picture at the time it was posted, it would have taken them thirty-one minutes to walk to the platform from here. Less if they ran.

And even less if they drove.

AUDIO FILE_MP3

TITLE: CASE_339KH_AVA KAVANAUGH INTERVIEW

Good morning, and thank you for speaking with us today. My name is Detective Alanis, and this is my colleague, Detective Sampson. For the purpose of the tape, please state your full name.

Ava Rose Kavanaugh.

Thank you, Ava. I'd like to talk to you about Friday, February 21, and a photo you posted online that evening.

Sure. Have I done something wrong?

No. But we're investigating an incident that took place near Hailing train station during the early hours of Saturday morning, and I understand you were in the area shortly before.

Yes. I caught the last train from Arcadia that night. What's going on?

For the purpose of the tape, I'm showing Miss Kavanaugh a printout of an image she posted to a social media account, @AvaKava. The image shows Kavanaugh and two other females at close range, with three people captured in the background, seemingly embroiled in a dispute. Ava, can you identify the people pictured in the background?

I . . . No. I don't know them. The guy, maybe. He was at an ACU hockey party I went to about a month back, but I don't know him.

You met him at the party?

No. Actually, no. I didn't know him, one of my friends did, and she tagged him in the comments as a joke. I think his name's Kai. Why? What's going on?

What about the two girls seen with him right here?

I don't know them. This one, with the ginger hair, she was arguing with Kai, and the other girl just passed them on her way out of the station. She stopped to talk to them for a minute.

Did you hear any words exchanged between these three people?

Um, a little. The one girl was trying to reason with him, but he kept shutting her down. She was pleading with him, like "Please don't do this." And he said something like, "You did this to us, not me. I don't owe you anything anymore." When the other girl joined, she was trying to mediate.

Okay. Thank you, Ava.

And . . . (PAUSE.)

Ava? Is there something else?

Well, maybe. It's just that when my friend met this guy Kai at the party, she said he was wasted. Like, really drunk. She was into him at first, but he was obsessing over his ex, almost crying, you know? She asked him to come back to our house in Hailing, just to hang out, and he flipped. I guess because his ex lives in Hailing. He was really cut up about it, like losing it.

I see. And did your friend see him again after that night?

No. Not as far as I know, anyway.

Ava, I'd like to take your friend's name, please? Along with the names of the other girls featured in this picture alongside you.

Okay, sure. My friends in the picture are Chloe Bridges and Shona Stone. My friend who'd been talking to Kai is Madison Dane.

Thank you.

So what's this about? Has something happened?

Unfortunately, we're investigating the death of the young man in this picture, Kai Harrison. He was found this morning. If you have any more information, it's important that you share it.

No. No, I don't. I . . . I'm sorry, I'm in complete shock.

Of course. We have trauma counselors on hand to help support anyone struggling with this.

Yes. Yes, okay. I . . . I need support.

SADIE

I think someone saw the photo Ava Kavanaugh posted on Friday night and drove to the station looking for Kai.

CASON

Who?

SADIE

I haven't figured that part out yet. Someone who wanted Kai dead. Or at least, someone who saw something in that picture that they didn't like.

Monday, February 24

CASON

THE LIBRARY AT SCHOOL IS a long, windowless room with a couple of computers at the back. Wooden shelves are packed with books that look like they've been around longer than I have. Larsen sends us here to watch our game footage whenever it's uploaded. We all group in the back corner, ducking out of lunch to study the video and strategize for our next game.

But hockey is the least of my problems right now.

It's already started, just like I knew it would. The cops looking our way. They were at school this morning, questioning the guys and some of the teachers about the fight with Arcadia last month. We all said the same thing, kept it consistent. We've just got to hope they don't pull our cell records and connect the phone calls that went from me to Michel, to Ruben, to Finley. It's going to look like we were all in on it together. I'd buy that.

"Hey, Mrs. Edwards," Michel calls to the librarian. She's at her desk, surrounded by stacks of books, turning one over and flattening out some damage on the cover. But she stops and looks up.

"Hi there, boys," she says. "How can I help you?"

We head for the desk, and Michel hands her his student card. "Can we get the code for last week's hockey game, please?"

"Sure," she says, setting the book on top of a pile. "Just hold on one moment." Her eyes move fast over the computer screen. "Did you win?" she asks, half glancing at us.

"Yeah," Michel tells her. "Five to three. Their offense was pretty good, but we blocked most of their shots. . . ."

He reels off a play-by-play, and I'm trying to focus, trying to remember the game, but I can't concentrate.

I hate that I haven't been completely honest with Sadie, and it's been getting to me, like poison under my skin. I should have been straight up with her from the start. I should have trusted her to keep it between us. But I made the call in the moment, and now the truth seems a whole lot worse.

Mrs. Edwards hands Michel a piece of paper with the system code scrawled on it. Then she says, "I knew you'd kill them."

My eyes shoot to Michel, but he's smiling his wide chipped-tooth smile.

"Yeah," he says. "Thanks."

The game. She's talking about the game. I drag my hands over my face.

I thought I could do this, pretend like I don't know anything. I thought I could do it, but the guilt is tearing me up inside.

Michel starts toward the back of the library, and I hitch my backpack on my shoulder and follow him. He takes a seat at one of the ancient computers and logs on to the network.

I pull a chair next to him. "I'm thinking I should talk to Sadie."

"Talk to Sadie about what?"

I give him a look.

His heavy eyebrows pull together. "Are you serious?" he says, lowering his voice. "You're going to tell Sadie what Nineteen said to you?" He checks over his shoulder, scanning the quiet library. "I thought we agreed it never happened?"

"Yeah, but . . ." I squeeze my eyes shut for a second.

"Why would you tell Sadie, of all people?"

"Because she'd know who Quinn had been seeing, right?"

"Why do you want to know that? I don't want to know," he says, pressing his hand to his chest. "I don't want to know any of this."

I rub the back of my neck. "But I can't lie to Sadie."

He squints at me, probably wondering why I'm so messed up over this. A month ago, Sadie was no one to me. Just a memory. "You like her that much?" he asks.

"Yeah," I admit. To him. To myself. "I do."

The computer hums as the game footage loads on the screen. And there we are, all of us on the ice, caught in jerky angles as the camera moves fast from one player to the next.

Any minute now, the others are going to start showing up. They'll crowd around the screen, commenting on the game, filling my head with noise.

"Just forget you ever spoke to Kai," Michel says. "Like we agreed. Because once you start telling more people . . ." He drops the sentence. "Just be careful who you talk to about this stuff. Trust me, I'm looking out for you."

I work my lip between my teeth. I get it. I don't want to see him get pulled into this either.

"Sadie thinks someone saw a photo that was posted that night," I tell him, "and that they came to the station looking for Nineteen. Not us, someone else."

Michel's eyes dart to me, and I see the pause, the moment where he stops and considers that. A shadow of relief flashes over his face.

Then he claps my shoulder. "Exactly. It could have been anyone. It wasn't you, that's all that matters."

His attention moves back to the game. "Did you see that turnover? When we play Bridgewater, we're going to need to tighten up our positioning in the neutral zone. Write that down."

I reach across the desk and take control of the mouse.

He frowns at me. "What are you doing?"

"Hang on." I close the footage and scroll through the upload history, all the way back to January. The Arcadia game. The file loads on the screen, and my hands twitch on the desk.

Michel leans back in his seat and presses his knuckles to his mouth.

He's there on the screen, Number 19. I watch him, watch everyone around him. Quinn cheering for him from the stands, her hands burrowed into the sleeves of a big coat. Our team, playing hard, clocking him, marking him as one of their stronger players. *His* team, challenging him on decisions, going for the puck when he has it.

I glance at Michel, and he quirks an eyebrow. Because he's

seeing it too. The rivalry in that game wasn't just us and them. It was them and 19 too.

I skip ahead to the moment in the footage where 19 takes me out, then he raises his hands like it was nothing, an accident.

Even the kid filming cusses under his breath.

I glance over my shoulder as Finley comes up behind us. He tenses when he notices what's on the screen.

"What are you doing?" he rasps under his breath. Before we can answer, he grabs the mouse and exits the video.

I frown at him as he drags his hands through his shaggy hair, pushing it back. He looks pale, sick.

"The others are on their way over here," he says through his teeth. "Be a little more discreet." He sinks onto the chair next to me.

"Relax," I tell him as he slouches forward. "We're just watching the game."

But Fin looks like he's about to chuck.

"No, he's right," Michel mutters. "We got to stop." He jiggles the mouse and opens up the Rochester footage just as a couple of the guys head our way through the rows of bookcases, their barks of laughter announcing their arrival.

Every muscle in my back tenses as last week's Rochester game restarts.

Ruben comes up behind us and grips my shoulder. "What's going on? You started without us?" He bares his teeth into a tight smile. His eyes move over the three of us, Fin, Michel, and me.

Paranoia's creeping in, spreading like a virus. I know, no matter how hard we try to ignore this, it's coming for us. The cops are looking at us. *We're* looking at us, even if we're not saying it. We might not be the only suspects, but we're the ones that make the most sense.

And what happens if the cops come down on me because I was at the station that night, because of my history with 19? Is everyone still staying quiet? Or is someone going to come forward to admit they were the person seeing Quinn? If one of my friends did it, are they going to let me go down for it?

Every time I glance at Ruben, all I can see is the tension in his neck. And Fin, he won't look at me. His eyes go everywhere, landing on everything but me. It makes me doubt him. Makes me think he's hiding something. Or maybe he thinks *I'm* hiding something, and that's why he won't look my way. And Michel, my best friend since we were kids, I can trust him, I know I can trust him.

Right up until I can't.

Because how come this isn't getting to him like it's getting to me?

I can't squash the feeling that it could have been one of them. It could have been any of them.

Just like they might think it could have been me.

AUDIO FILE_MP3

TITLE: CASE_339KH_MICHEL KONAN INTERVIEW

Good morning, Michel. Thank you for taking the time out of class to speak with us today. Do you know why you're here?

Should my parents be present for this?

This is just an informal chat, Michel. Are you happy to proceed?

(PAUSE.)

Michel, we can rearrange this conversation if you'd feel more comfortable in a formal setting?

No. This is fine.

Then let's begin. We have a few questions regarding an altercation that took place on Friday, January 24, outside Raleigh's Recreation Center in Arcadia. Do you know the incident I'm referring to?

Yes.

I understand you witnessed an altercation involving your teammate Cason Tano?

Yes.

Can you explain what you saw, please?

It was after the game. I was looking for Cason in Raleigh's lobby, and then I saw him through the glass doors. He was walking across the parking lot, heading toward the Arcadia train station, and Kai Harrison came up behind him. I saw Kai hit him with a hockey stick, twice to the back of the head, and then when Cason was down, Kai started going for his legs. So I got out there fast, I restrained Kai and pulled him off, I'm admitting to that. Then other people started coming outside,

and we couldn't get a handle on it.

I understand. What do you think would motivate an assault like this?

We think Kai was fired up because he fouled Cason, which got him pulled from the game—and scouts were there.

I see. How did Cason respond to this incident in the parking lot, after the fact?

What do you mean?

Did he ever indicate to you any signs of seeking retaliation?

No.

You play on the school hockey team together, is that correct?

Yes.

Have you ever felt concerned about Cason's behavior? Any signs of excessive aggression during your games?

No.

We've received some information that suggests otherwise.

What? What information? It's not true.

Okay. Thank you for your help, Michel.

Cason isn't aggressive or violent. It wasn't his fault.

Okay.

Please listen. The fight wasn't his fault.

TIKTOK

DARCY WILDE

@WILDEONCRIME

Season 19, Episode 3 #truecrime #forensic #fyp #HailingNY #JusticeforKai

So I have a little update for you guys on the Kai Harrison case. If you haven't heard the news, this has now been confirmed as a homicide investigation, meaning they are looking for a murderer.

I'm building up my own file on this, and I managed to obtain a police document relating to rioting that happened some weeks ago involving Kai Harrison and several others. Now, this was all reported in the media too, but at the time it wasn't considered particularly newsworthy. My understanding is that some kind of dispute took place after a high school hockey event between Arcadia and Hailing. The coaches issued a statement shortly after, and the players faced some minor consequences. Not a big deal, right?

Not a big deal until one of the people involved is found dead in Hailing, several miles from his own home in Arcadia. Yes, you've guessed it . . . Kai Harrison.

I've been given some information on another individual who was heavily involved in this incident, but since he's a minor, I'll just refer to him as C.T. What I can say is that this young man, C.T., was seen assaulting Harrison, and allegedly suffered injuries of his own when Harrison fought back in self-defense.

I'm assuming C.T. will be investigated as standard procedure. But I have every reason to believe he'll be high on the suspects list, and it's just a matter of tying this up. As I said, I've been looking into it myself, and my source mentioned in my previous video just so happens to have a close personal relationship with C.T. and has confirmed that he is widely known to be aggressive, dishonest, and dangerously impulsive.

Monday, February 24

CASON

I CATCH UP WITH RUBEN at the vending machine outside the canteen.

"Hey."

"Hey, man," he says, but his eyes stay focused on the rows of snacks. He punches in the code on the keypad to release a packet of M&Ms, and they fall into the dispenser drawer with a thump.

"Got a minute?"

"Yeah." He grabs the M&Ms and pops them open, then tosses a couple my way.

"So, tell me straight." I glance over my shoulder to make sure no one's close enough to overhear. "Are we good? Feels like things have been off today."

"We're good," he says, giving my shoulder a quick clap.

"All right, but seriously," I say, lowering my voice. "Are you sure? Because I've been thinking it over. I'm going to tell Sadie about Friday night. About me talking to Nineteen and all that stuff he said about coming for whoever has been with Quinn."

"Yeah, I know."

"What? How do you know?"

"Michel told me."

I check over my shoulder again. There are people passing through, coming in and out of the canteen, but no one's close enough to hear us. "And you're okay with it? You're okay with me bringing Sadie in on this?"

"Yeah," he says, crunching on a mouthful of M&Ms. "Are you okay with it, though?"

I frown. "Yeah. Why wouldn't I be? It's my idea."

"Why wouldn't *I* be?" He keeps crunching.

"Well, if I tell Sadie, she might know who Quinn was seeing. So then if one of us isn't owning up to being *him*, it's going to look shady on them."

"Okay," he says. "As long as you're prepared for that." His stare sharpens on me.

"Why are you looking at me like that?"

"Like what?"

I copy his expression, narrowing my eyes the same way he did.

He doesn't respond right away, and I tense, waiting. "Look," he mutters, "all I'm saying is it might not be in your best interest to let this get out. There are some parts of your story that sound kind of sus when you think about it."

It takes a second. Then it hits me, knocking the air out of me. "Hold up. You don't think . . ." I lower my voice, "You don't think *I* killed Nineteen, do you?"

"No. Of course not." But he won't look at me.

My lungs tighten. "Come on, Ruben," I say under my breath.

"Don't start doubting me now."

"I'm not." His voice sounds different, too hoarse, too hesitant. "I won't."

I stare back at him, numb.

"Cason, you know I always shoot straight with you." He glances over his shoulder to make sure we're still alone. "And I told you, man, I'm not talking. None of us are."

"It wasn't me."

He lets out a deep sigh. "I know that. All I'm saying is, don't go telling Sadie any more than she needs to know. Just in case." He slaps his hand to his chest. "You wanted my advice, and there it is. If you're not going to listen, that's on you. You're on your own."

Those words hit me harder than anything.

There's nothing more to say. He claps my shoulder again, then he turns and walks away, leaving me standing there. Alone.

It's been a long time since I've been *on my own*.

I was pretty messed up for a while after my mom died. Back then, I did things without thinking, things that scared me later. I remember one day in eighth grade, after a rough morning, I was walking in from the baseball field. Someone had left a bat on the edge of the turf, and before I even knew what I was doing, I had it in my hands, swinging it with all the pent-up anger I had inside, smashing it into the bleachers, doing some damage. Ruben ran over, knocked the bat out of my hands, just staring at me while I stood there, sweating and breathing fast.

The wild thing is, I didn't even remember picking up the bat.

If it weren't for the ache in my arm, I probably wouldn't have believed it was me.

Ruben took the fall for me that day. A couple of months later, when he got called out for skipping study hall, I lied through my teeth that I saw him there. I swore I sat right next to him. Borrowed his pen. Shared his drink. I would have died on that hill.

That's just how it is with Ruben and me. We've got each other's backs, no matter what. We're never on our own.

Until we are.

AUDIO FILE_MP3

TITLE: CASE_339KH_RUBEN HERNANDEZ INTERVIEW

Good morning, Ruben. Thank you for speaking with us today. Do you know why you're here?

Because of the kid that died, right?

Yes. We'd like to talk to you about Kai Harrison.

Why me?

We're talking to a lot of people, not just you. But there was some history between yourself, Kai Harrison, and a few others, wasn't there? A fight that happened after a hockey game? We have the police records from Arcadia right here.

Yeah, there was a fight. But it wasn't as bad as it sounds. All I was doing was trying to calm it down, then someone called the cops.

You were trying to calm everyone down?

Yeah. Ask anyone. I was trying to break it up. What does this have to do with anything, anyway? Because if you're jumping from a scrap to a murder, then I know my rights, and I'm going need a lawyer present for this.

No one's accusing you of anything, Ruben. This is just a conversation so that we have a clear picture of Kai Harrison's movements before his death.

Okay, well, I don't know anything about that. All I know is that a month ago his movements were to smack my buddy over the head with a hockey stick.

Your friend's name, please?

(PAUSE.) Cason Tano.

Are you aware that some of Kai's friends are claiming that they witnessed Cason Tano attacking Kai Harrison, unprovoked, in Raleigh's Rec Center parking lot that night?

They would say that, though, wouldn't they?

You're suggesting it was the other way around? And you were trying to intervene?

Exactly.

What about Cason? What was he doing at this point?

Trying not to die, probably.

By that you mean . . . ?

He was defending himself.

By retaliating?

These questions are leading. I'm not answering anything else without a lawyer here.

Tuesday, February 25

SADIE

KAI REACHES OUT TO ME, *clawing through empty space as he grasps for my hand. His strong fingers seal around mine, squeezing tight. Tighter. My bones begin to crack, but he won't let go. His face hollows and grays, skin turning to bone before crumbling away, disintegrating in the wind. I push him as hard as I can, and I watch him fall onto the tracks. . . .*

My breath catches in my throat as I wake with a jolt. Damp with sweat, I untangle myself from the nightmare. My fingernails have left tiny half-moon imprints on my palms.

"I'm not there," I murmur, because I have to hear it. I have to say it out loud. I'm not standing on the edge of the platform, watching Kai fall onto the train tracks. I'm in my room, safe. It was just a dream. A horrible, twisted dream.

But it lingers all too vividly.

The distant sound of clattering dishes comes from the kitchen, followed by the whirring of the coffeepot.

I crawl out of bed and pad downstairs.

Dad is at the breakfast bar, pouring himself a bowl of granola.

"Morning," he says. His gray hair looks rumpled, and his eyes are still heavy with sleep. "Do you want one of these?" He lifts his coffee mug, and I nod.

Things have been stilted between us over the past few days. Understandable. The fact that I was on the last train home that night has knocked Dad's trust in me, I know it has. And if I'm honest with myself, I don't blame him.

"How did you sleep?" he asks.

"Okay," I lie.

He pours a coffee and passes me the steaming mug.

I wrap my hands around it, savoring the warmth. "How about you?"

"I've got a lot on my mind," he says, swerving the question. "I'm sure we both have."

I take a small sip of coffee. The bitter taste catches me.

"Sadie," Dad says, placing his cup on the counter and folding his arms, "why did I wake up to a voicemail from your school informing me that you weren't in any of your classes yesterday?"

I scramble for a response. "I wasn't feeling great."

Dad musters a closed-lipped smile, not condemning, but not exactly forgiving. "Let's talk," he says, pulling out a seat at the breakfast bar.

Reluctantly, I follow his lead. "Sorry I didn't tell you right away. I just couldn't face class. Everyone was staring at me, talking about me, treating me like a suspect." My throat tightens, making the words sound strangled.

He reaches across the counter and pats my hand. "Honey. Why

don't I talk to your principal—"

"No." I cut him off. "God, no. It wouldn't help, anyway. People are going to gossip, no matter what. I've just got to ride it out."

"You shouldn't have to," he says, grimacing. "If you're being bullied, the principal needs to know. This can't continue."

"It'll pass. Honestly, it's not a big deal."

I stare at my coffee and the tendrils of steam lifting from the mug. It's only been a week since I had to tell Dad about the picture taped to my locker. I didn't tell him that I suspected Kai. It was painful enough having to explain about the picture, let alone that I suspected someone I considered to be a friend of having made it. I hated having to relive it out loud to Dad, and to Principal Marcus. A part of me just didn't want to admit that it had happened.

"On a different note," Dad moves on, clearing his throat, "I talked to your mom last night."

My grip tightens around the mug. "Okay," I say slowly.

"She's been trying to get ahold of you. She's going out of her mind with worry, Sadie. Why haven't you been picking up her calls?"

"I don't know," I stumble over my response. "I've just been so busy."

He arches an eyebrow, unconvinced. And I get it. There's been plenty of opportunity to call my mom. I've texted her, standard responses like "I'm fine" and "Everything's okay." But the truth is, calls with Mom have been strained since she moved away. Neither of us wants to admit it, but our conversations always seem to be overshadowed by her guilt around leaving Hailing. Leaving Dad.

And me. I was mad at her for a long time, because she chose to leave. She moved on, and we didn't. But I'm not in that space anymore. I'm fine here. At least, I was until a couple of days ago.

I draw in a small breath. "I haven't been deliberately avoiding Mom's calls, just with everything that's been going on, what happened to Kai, and Quinn going AWOL, it's been a lot."

"You need to check in with her," he says.

"I know, and I will."

"You need to check in more with me too," he adds. "Skipping school is not okay, no matter what the circumstances. I need to know where you are. I need that peace of mind."

"It was just once. You know I never ditch."

He can't argue with that. Dad knows I care way too much about proving myself in Arcadia, living up to the standard of excellence in the graduating classes that came before. I work hard, and my GPA is high. I'm going to get into the University of Buffalo and then go on to law school, achieve my dreams, and uphold the standards that I've set for myself.

As long as I don't get wrongly accused of murder.

"Okay," Dad says, knotting his rough hands on the counter. "But what troubles me is that you wouldn't have told me you skipped school. You wouldn't have told me you were on the 11:20 train if it hadn't come out during the police investigation."

"I thought you wanted me to take the train."

"*The* train," he says, lifting an index finger. "Not the *last* train."

A few weeks back, Dad gave this whole speech about the benefits of public transportation versus the dangers of poorly lit roads at night—especially after the hit-and-run on the byway. That night clearly shook him up pretty bad.

"And you weren't supposed to be catching the train alone," he carries on. "You promised me that you'd buddy with Quinn. Out close to midnight, by yourself? Sadie." He blinks in a show of total disbelief. "Come on. I was never going to be okay with that."

"I'm sorry," I manage. "It won't happen again."

I see it then, the flash of something in his eyes. Something close to remorse. I brace myself.

"Your safety isn't a joke. Living in Hailing, after everything that's—"

"I'll take this seriously." I jump in because I can sense where this is heading. "I won't go out at night. You can trust me."

He heaves a sigh. "Look," he says, pressing his palms flat to the counter, "let's just start by having some stricter rules around here. Your mom thinks the same."

"What happened to Kai won't happen to me," I say, for my own sake as much as Dad's. Because the truth is, I'm scared too. Whoever did this is still out there, a monster in disguise.

The concern is still etched on Dad's face, deep frown lines denting his brow. "I only care about your safety, and there are some risks that I'm not willing to take." The alarm on his phone buzzes, and he checks the time. "I've got to leave for work. We'll pick this up later and come up with a plan."

"Okay," I murmur. "Sounds good." But my heart sinks as he heads for the door.

SADIE
How are you? I miss you.

QUINN
I miss you too.

SADIE
Are you coming to school today?

QUINN
I'm not ready. My mom already called the school for me. I can't be there without Kai. It's never going to get better.

SADIE
I'm here for you, Quinn. You don't have to go through this alone.

QUINN
I want to know who did this to him. They deserve to be suffering like how I'm suffering.

SADIE
Maybe they are.

Thursday, February 27

SADIE

I ARRIVE AT THE SCHOOL gates a little before the first bell. Wide stone steps lead to the building, surrounded by red maples that will soon bloom scarlet beneath the spring sunshine. But for now their branches are bare, and the sky above is an endless expanse of steel gray.

Despite the pit in my stomach, I hold my head high and stride along the corridor. There are people loitering at their lockers or hanging out in classrooms, but it's quieter than usual. It isn't by chance that I'm here early. Jacob Ritter is on the dance committee with Emma, and I happen to know they meet in the media block on Thursdays before homeroom.

Whatever the narrative is about me right now, there's a chance that Jacob won't be buying into it. He and I had something for a minute. Okay, so our almost-thing didn't go anywhere, but it counts for something.

At the media room, I crack the door ajar. The voices stop, and everyone turns to look at me. Emma and Jacob are among the half-dozen faces staring at me from the center table.

"Hey, Sadie," Emma says, her brow creasing. "What are you doing here?"

I wave awkwardly back at her. "Actually, I was hoping I could talk to Jacob for a second. Is that okay?"

He frowns and glances at the others before standing. "I'll be right back," I hear him mutter to them, and I swear he rolls his eyes.

He follows me into the corridor as the rest of the committee resumes their conversation. Emma's trying to rally, pulling everyone's attention back with buzzwords like *layout* and *theme.* But judging by their wide-eyed stares, I'm pretty sure their thoughts are with me, wondering what I need to talk to Jacob about that can't be said in front of them. They probably think I'm about to confess. Vultures.

Jacob lets the door fall shut behind him, and just like that we're alone in the hall. His angular face pulls into an expression that I can't quite make sense of—mouth pressed into a tight line and one eyebrow lifted. "Hey," he says flatly.

I inhale. Okay. I wasn't expecting such a frosty response from him. Clearly I underestimated the influence of these rumors. "How are you?" I ask gently.

He tilts his head. "My best friend's dead. How do you think I am?"

It takes everything I have to hold my gaze on his. "I'm sorry," I murmur.

"Yeah, we're planning a vigil for him." He locks his hands behind his head. "But it's not going to bring him back."

"That's a lovely idea."

He laughs, a short, sharp sound. "Yeah. Are we done?"

"Well, actually . . ." I stumble to regain my composure. "Actually, Jacob, I wanted to talk to you. About Kai."

His jaw tics.

Suddenly I can't find my voice. Emma was right; none of the guys are going to be receptive to this. To me.

But if there's even the slightest chance that Ava's friend is connected to Kai's death, then I can't just let this pass. I'm a suspect in a murder investigation. Cason and Quinn are too. No matter what alibi Ava claims her friend has, I can still bring this to the police—I just need a name. And Jacob might have that information.

"I spoke to a girl from ACU," I press on. "Her name's Ava Kavanaugh. She posted that picture with Kai, Quinn, and me in the background."

Jacob's expression gives nothing away, no recognition or reaction. He keeps his stony stare fixed on me.

"Ava told me that one of her friends knew Kai and—"

"Everyone knew Kai," he says, cutting me off mid-sentence. "Everyone liked him. Apart from you," he adds under his breath.

"That's not fair. Of course I liked Kai."

He scoffs at that. "You think we don't remember what you did?"

My pulse starts to quicken, thundering in my ears.

And he mimics me. "'You're going to regret this. Don't think I won't see this through.'"

"But . . ." My stomach dips. "Was it you who contacted Darcy Wilde about what happened in class? You told her all that stuff about me? Made it sound like I was threatening Kai?"

"No, but I saw the TikTok about it. And they got you down pat, because you *were* threatening him. I was there."

I narrow my eyes. "Yes, I said those things, but you know full well I was talking about reporting Kai to Principal Marcus. I know Kai was the person who edited that image of me. And I'm starting to think you guys all knew it too. Besides, I know that between the two of us, I wasn't the only one who had issues with Kai."

Jacob shakes his head and runs his tongue over his teeth, like he can't believe I'd have the audacity to remind him that for the two weeks we almost-dated, all he did was talk shit about Kai, complaining about Kai being made captain and about how he threw his weight around to control the team and played dirty, reflecting poorly on the rest of them.

"Maybe you should be questioned," I say before I can stop myself.

His lip curls, but he keeps going as though he hasn't heard me. "Nice. You're just trying to stir shit up to distract the attention from yourself." Towering over me, he aims a trembling index finger at me, but I refuse to shrink back. I notice the cues—the tremor in his hand, the sweat on his brow, the fear he's trying to hide. "You might have some people fooled, but not me. I see through you, Sadie."

My throat tightens at his words.

"You act all innocent, but I see the real you. And I know where your loyalties lie." The way he says it makes me feel cold all over. "You and that guy Cason, you deserve each other. We all know you've been creeping around together at Raleigh's. And you're both going to get what's coming to you."

AUDIO FILE_MP3

TITLE: CASE_339KH_JACOB RITTER INTERVIEW

Good morning, Jacob. Thank you for coming in today. You were close friends with Kai Harrison, I understand?

Yeah. We've been best friends since the start of high school. I loved him like a brother.

I'm so sorry for your loss, Jacob.

Yeah. Me too.

Can you share with us any thoughts on Kai, any fears you might have had for him? Perhaps there's information he might have shared with you that could be relevant to our investigation?

For sure. That's why I'm here, and I'm going to keep it one hundred. Some kid jumped Kai after our hockey game last month. Cason Tano, he's from Hailing. And there's a girl from my school too, Sadie Morelli. Both of them are from Hailing. Sadie lives right by where Kai was found.

You're saying these two might know something about what happened to Kai?

No, I'm saying they did it. They killed him. Both of them, together.

What's made you reach that conclusion, Jacob?

Sadie went off at Kai during class last week, in front of everyone. She was basically threatening to kill him.

Why was that?

Something about a picture. But she makes up lies.

How so?

Trust me, this girl lies about everything. She's delusional. She told people we were dating, but I swear it never happened. I've never talked to the girl in my life.

Right. I see.

Straight-up liar. And everyone knows it.

Thursday, February 27

CASON

THE STREETLAMP CASTS A GLOW into the living room, reflecting off the TV and the NHL game playing on the sports channel. But my thoughts keep drifting back to my conversation with Ruben. Does he think I'm lying? Do all my friends think I'm lying? Worse, do they think I'm a murderer? The idea makes my stomach turn. And then another thought creeps in, leaving me cold—have they lost trust in me . . . or have I lost trust in them?

I crane my neck at the sound of the front door opening, followed by laughter floating through the hallway. Thalia's laughter, light and high. I drop my feet from the coffee table as they walk in.

Alec stops short when he sees me. He's carrying a bottle of wine in a brown paper bag—the bag creased around the neck where he's gripping it.

"Oh." Thalia's hand goes to her chest, red-painted nails shining in the light from the TV. "Cason. Hi, honey." She smiles, but it looks strained. Disappointed.

"Hey."

"Hey, buddy," Alec says. He glances at Thalia and gives her

an apologetic look, the mouth-pressed head slant. Like he thinks I won't notice. His eyes come back to me, and he frowns. "Don't you have practice tonight?"

I clear my throat. The commentator's voice is still hollering in the background. "And it's Burrows. Burrows is going for the puck. It's a two-goal lead, with everything to play for . . ."

"Yeah, I did. But Coach Larsen rescheduled because something's up with the rink. But also one of the guys overheard him on a call with his girlfriend, talking about meeting up tonight. So we think he just bailed for a better offer."

Thalia touches her heart. "Oh, cute."

"It's not cute, Thalia," Alec says, frowning. "It's unprofessional, is what it is."

She nuzzles into his shoulder. "Well, I think it's cute. It's romantic."

"Maybe Larsen's going to propose or something," I add, just for the hell of it. "Maybe that's what he's doing tonight."

Alec takes the bait, balking. "Propose? He's just a kid." Seeing my uncle squirm at the marriage talk never fails to get a smile out of me. The guy's a commitment-phobe. Or he was, up until a couple of months ago.

"He's twenty-three," I tell Alec.

"That's my point. Too young."

Thalia swats Alec's arm. "Not everyone stays a bachelor into their forties, Al. Maybe you're the anomaly. Ever considered that?"

His neck turns red, and he rubs his jaw. "Yeah, well. Maybe I was holding out for the right person. How about that?"

She touches his chest, playing with the top button on his shirt, and I try not to hurl.

"We're ordering takeout tonight," Alec tells me, "if you want to join us?" That last part sounded forced as hell. Almost as forced as his easy smile.

I grit my teeth into an *easy* smile back. "Thanks, but I'm about to head out."

I see the relief on both their faces, the way their shoulders sink with the exhale. But man, it takes effort to switch off the game and stand, act like I have somewhere to go.

Alec's already punching numbers into his cell, dialing for takeout.

Thalia practically skips to the kitchen. She selects a couple of wineglasses from the cabinet. I swear, we never had wineglasses before she came into our lives.

"Babe," Alec calls to her from the living room. "Are you getting the usual?"

"Yeah, babe," she calls back. "But with a side of the feta salad."

"Gotcha."

I shrug into my coat. "Bye, babe," I mouth to Alec as I sidle past him.

He cuffs my shoulder. "Get out of here."

"Bye, Cason," Thalia sings. "Have a good night, honey."

"Thanks. See you later."

I half expected Alec to ask where I'm going or toss out a cursory "Don't stay out too late." But he's already talking into his cell. ". . . I'll get a number eleven, and a number four with extra sauce and a side of the feta salad." Then he laughs. "Right. But with some extras tonight."

I pull the front door shut behind me, and it's done. I'm out, breathing cold air into my lungs, wondering if Burrows made the shot. Streetlamps light the dark road in pools and stripe the pavement with shadows.

I stuff my hands into my pockets and walk along the street. Farther down the block, Michel's place is lost in darkness. The curtains are drawn, the lights are out, and their family SUV isn't in the driveway.

I slide my phone from my pocket and text him. **Where you at?**

It's a minute before the reply comes. **Family dinner at the steakhouse. Why?**

Nothing. Have a good one.

I drop onto the curb. Usually I'd head to Ruben's place if Michel is busy, but after our conversation at school? Yeah, that's the last place I want to be—if he'd even want me there. Finley's house, maybe. But his foster family is weird about him having people over. With nowhere else to go, I grab a twig and start digging at the mush of leaves clogging the storm drain.

Kai Harrison crosses my mind. And I let myself go there. I let myself think about him, and how it happened. Blunt trauma, that's what they're calling it. Something, *someone*, hit him hard enough to wipe him out.

On reflex, I touch the back of my head, the spot where he took a swing at me with his hockey stick in Raleigh's parking lot. The impact left me spinning, seeing stars. And it makes me wonder . . . did he want to kill me that night? If Michel, Ruben, and Finley hadn't stepped in, would he have done it? All because we won the game? I love hockey, it's my ticket out of Hailing. In so many ways, it's my life. But I wouldn't kill for it.

My phone buzzes, and I expect to see a message from Michel at the top of the screen, offering to bring me back some leftovers or something.

I'm good with that.

But it isn't Michel, and my heart picks up at the sight of her name. Sadie.

Today sucks.

I don't even pause to write back. I hit call instead, and she answers.

"Hi," she says, and her voice stirs something in me. Smooth, calming, affecting in more ways than I can explain. I'm floating when I'm talking to her, tripping on a wild high.

"So today sucked, huh? How bad?"

She sighs softly down the line. "Kai's friends think I have some disturbed vendetta against him and . . . well, you know. Between this, Darcy Wilde's video, and Ava Kavanaugh's photo, I'm unequivocally guilty."

The weight of my own guilt drags me down to earth. I'm not floating anymore, I'm on the cold, hard pavement. "I'm sorry, Sadie."

"I thought I was okay," she carries on. "I thought I was above it all, the gossip and rumors. But I'm not."

"Yeah." I jam the twig into the storm drain, impaling the wet leaves. "I get that."

We fall silent, but it isn't awkward. It's company in the darkness.

"Where are you?" she asks after a moment. "It sounds like you're outside."

"I am. I'm unblocking a storm drain."

"Really? Why?"

I scrape the twig along the metal grate. "The short version is that my uncle and his girlfriend seemed like they wanted alone time. So I'm having alone time too."

"Oh. Sounds lonely."

A smile tugs at my lips. "It's not so bad."

"You can hang out at my house if you want. My dad's at work so I'm alone too. We can be alone together."

It makes me stop when she says it, because not only is this new territory for us, it's proof. Proof that she trusts me. She's not afraid of me, or suspicious.

"Cason?" she prompts. "Are you still there?"

"Yeah, I'm here."

"You don't have to come over," she says quickly. "If you don't want to. It was just a suggestion, but—"

"No," I jump. "It's not . . . I mean, yeah. I want to come over." I stare at the full moon above, too bright in the void of black sky. "Sadie," I add, chewing over my words, "I really like you. I want you to know that."

"I like you too." She says it so softly, so sweetly, that I feel like the worst person in the world.

"I'll come over," I tell her. "I'll be there soon."

My heart sinks as I stand, because I know what I've got to do.

I look up at the sky again, finding the stars. It makes me wonder if my mom is up there somewhere, watching over me, telling me to do the right thing.

Because I feel it.

The truth needs to come out, and I'll take the consequences, whatever they are.

Thursday, February 27

SADIE

I WAIT ON THE PORCH for Cason, shivering in the night air. Across the street, the wind howls though the platform, making the shelter groan and creak. Police barricades still cordon off the crime scene area, and the echoes of Kai linger. His ghost haunts everything.

From the other direction, a silhouette moves in the lamplight, walking toward my house. I stiffen, a moment of unease tightening in my chest, but then he steps into the pool of light. He walks casually, hands in his jacket pockets, short hair tousling in the breeze.

My heartbeat quickens at the sight of him. It gives me butterflies.

Cason jogs the rest of the way to reach me. "Hey." He folds his arms around me, and I rest my chin on his shoulder, breathing in the familiarity.

"Hey," I echo.

He follows me into the house, and I lock the door behind him. But I already feel safer just having him here. Safer than when I was home alone, anyway, with only the creaking pipes and the wild gale tapping at the windows.

I lead him to my room, and he sits on the edge of the bed, an apparition in my space. He's never been inside this house before, and it feels surreal. It's as though he and I have only ever existed in Raleigh's, or beneath the cover of moon shadows. Suddenly everything is illuminated.

I like this. I want more.

"I'm glad you're here," I say, sitting beside him.

He locks his hands and his broad shoulders hunch forward. His smile looks different, faint. Even sitting right beside him, there's distance between us, I feel it.

It takes me back to eighth grade, after his mom died. There was a hollowness behind his eyes back then, like he wasn't even in there. I see it now too.

"Is everything okay?" I ask.

He doesn't respond. His gaze stays on his sneakers.

"You can talk to me, Cason," I urge, touching his hand. "Whatever's on your mind, whatever you're going through, you can talk to me. I'm here."

He draws in a slow breath. "Life is so fragile."

I lower my gaze. "Yeah."

"The things that matter, they *matter.* You matter to me. You always have."

"I know," I whisper. "You matter to me too."

I thread my fingers through his. He brings our joined hands to his lips and plants the smallest of kisses on my wrist. The simple act makes my pulse quicken.

But when he speaks again, his voice sounds hoarse. "I have to tell you something, Sadie."

My heart starts beating a little faster, with a different kind of nervousness. "Okay." Every instinct I have is telling me that I don't want to hear this. That I want to pause this moment, stop him from going any further.

He won't meet my gaze—he's looking down at our joined hands, and then his fingers slip away from mine.

Somewhere in the distance, I hear the train on the tracks, the mechanical squeaking and screeching. It's a sound I hear from my room often. A sound that's been creeping into my nightmares lately.

"I didn't leave the station right away on Friday night."

My breath stalls. "Okay."

"I was waiting on the platform, waiting for you to text me back. I knew you were talking to Quinn, and after I got your message about something coming up, I was going to leave, but then Kai showed up."

Suddenly I can't breathe. I can't do anything but stare at him.

"He came to wait for the train and looked surprised to see me there, but he was all worked up, and he started grilling me about Quinn."

"What?" My brow knits. "What about Quinn?"

"He told me he saw Quinn with one of the boys from my team. He didn't get a close enough look to see who it was—"

I hold up my hands, stopping him. "Wait. *Kai* said this?"

"Yeah."

I stare back at him, confused. My mind is a jumble of thoughts, none of which I can make sense of. "Quinn? With one of the Hailing boys?" Instinctively, my gaze wanders to the pictures of Quinn and me tacked to the wall. The snapshots of us over the years, the smiles, and the closeness. "Like, *together*?"

"Yeah. I didn't know anything about it," Cason says. "And no one's admitting to it." His eyes search mine, like he's waiting for me to piece the puzzle together.

"Quinn never mentioned this to me." I pause, frowning. "I mean, I knew she'd been texting other guys, but she was always super casual about it." I think back to the times I pressed her, and she'd just brush it off, like it wasn't worth talking about. I figured it was because she felt weird about talking to other people while still holding out for Kai, like she didn't want to make it a thing. But maybe . . . maybe there was more to it.

Cason drags a hand over his face. "Do you think Quinn would tell you who it was, if you asked her?"

"Yes."

There's a flash of fear in his eyes, as though he was hoping my answer would have been *no*.

"What, you think that this person has something to do with Kai's murder?"

He twitches, shifts. "The thing is, that night at the station, Kai told me he was coming after him—whoever *he* is. So yeah, it's possible someone got to Kai before he got to them."

I press my hand to my mouth. "Oh my god. Who?"

He shakes his head in response.

Something else occurs to me then, and I tense. "You told me you didn't speak to Kai that night."

"Actually," he says, working his lip between his teeth, "I told you there was no fight. And there wasn't."

I choke out a sound. "Semantics, Cason. You *intentionally* didn't mention that you spoke to Kai, about something pretty colossal." Up until now, we've been sitting close, his arm touching mine. But I move away, forcing space between us.

"I know, and I'm sorry," he says. "But my head was all over the place. Imagine if this was Quinn, and you knew you were about to drop her name into the fire."

I rake my hands through my hair, trying to catch up with his thoughts. Trying to catch up with my own thoughts. "But none of the boys are admitting to anything?"

"No one knows anything."

"Do *you* think it was one of them, though? Do you think one of the Hailing boys came to confront Kai?"

"No."

My heart twists because I see the lying signs. His too-fast response. The fidgeting, rubbing his thumb and forefinger together.

And my gut instinct.

"You're lying," I murmur. "Who do you think killed Kai?"

He closes his eyes for a second. "I don't know."

He flinches as I seize my phone and unlock the screen with trembling hands. I dial Quinn's number, then hold my cell close to my ear and wait. A sense of dread slithers down my spine as it rings, and rings, and rings, before connecting to voicemail.

I end the call and toss my phone onto the bed. "This just doesn't make any sense. Quinn's my best friend. Surely she would have told me if she'd been seeing someone from Hailing, someone we both knew. That's a big deal."

"Did you tell her about me?"

I can't respond. Because he's right. I didn't tell Quinn about Cason, so why should I expect anything different from her?

"Quinn loved Kai," I say instead. "If she'd been involved with someone from Hailing, then she'll have recognized that this person would have motive to hurt Kai after that fight, regardless of any threats made to you. She wouldn't let someone get away with that."

I remember Quinn sitting on my bed that night, hugging a pillow to her chest right after Kai broke up with her. She said Kai was angry because she'd been talking to other people during their time apart. Was *this* what had caused their eventual break-up? Quinn seeing one of the Hailing boys?

After Kai distanced himself from Quinn, she stopped hanging out at his house in Arcadia and started taking the train home after work. The Hailing hockey team caught the train on Fridays too. And that night we saw the boys in Raleigh's diner, Quinn joined their table. While I was busy talking to Cason, was Quinn forming a connection with someone too?

Cason's voice jolts me back. "I'm sorry I didn't tell you about this right away. For what it's worth, it tore me up inside."

"Yeah," I say thinly.

"I had to give them a chance, right?" he says. "Those guys are my best friends, they've been there for me and I have for them. Look at that fight in the parking lot, they saved me. Michel, Ruben, Finley. They didn't have to step in. They could have left me out there, but those three, they stayed. If they hadn't . . ." He trails off, and I swallow.

We fall silent for a minute.

"Do you want me to leave?" he asks.

He lied to me. I understand his reasons, I understand it all. But I put my absolute trust in him, and he lied.

I breathe slowly before I can bring myself to say the words, "Yes. I think you should."

POLICE DOCUMENTATION FOR CASE REF: 339KH

FILE_SEQUESTERED PHONE RECORDS

[RECOVERED FEBRUARY 18]

I can't stop thinking about you. I know it's wrong, but I'm falling for you.

You mean that?

I love that you trust me. And yes, I mean it, I'm falling for you.

I feel the same way.

Forget about everything else. Forget about Kai. You have me.

Friday, February 28

SADIE

THE SOUND OF FOOTSTEPS ON the staircase wakes me at dawn. I lay still, listening to the heavy tread on the floorboards. *It's Dad*, I have to remind myself. *It's just Dad.*

I must have fallen asleep on top of the bed covers, fully clothed, because the last thing I remember is staring into the darkness, hyperaware of every sound. The distant cars, the creak of branches in the gale, birds of prey keening as they hunt in the moonlight. I stayed wide awake for hours, just listening to the night, wishing I hadn't told Cason to leave.

But I did. And he did.

Dad's bedroom door clicks shut as he turns in for the night. But the sun is starting to rise outside, and I'm already too alert to fall back to sleep.

Questions still whir around Quinn, and Kai, and the possible third person in their relationship. Their argument on the street that night keeps replaying in my head, the fragments of conversation.

I'm done, Quinn.

You can't do this to me. To us.

I don't owe you anything. Not anymore.

I reach for my phone. My last message to Quinn is still unread.

We need to talk. Please call me.

With low sunlight streaming through my window, I force myself to get up and dress for school. Because life has to go on. I have to keep going to class, pretending like the side-eyes and whispers aren't getting to me.

Outside, the street is quiet, bathed in the golden light of dawn, a stolen moment before the day has fully begun. I stand at the platform and pull my coat tightly around myself. The early mist has settled on the tracks, making the station feel slick and damp. The memory of Kai clings to the breath of cold air. I don't think his ghost will ever leave.

Footsteps clang on the stairwell behind me, and when I turn, my heart leaps into my throat.

"Quinn," I whisper.

She buries her hands in the sleeves of her puffy coat. Her usual flawless makeup is replaced by real, bare-faced rawness. For the first time in a long while, I feel like I'm seeing *her*. The person she was back when we were kids, before the contouring and concealers. I see the freckles on her cheeks and pale lashes framing glassy eyes.

"How are you?" I murmur.

She sucks in her top lip and shakes her head.

"Why are you here?"

She tries to smile. "School. I knew I'd have to face it eventually." She runs her fingers through her ponytail. "I have to go back to classes without Kai sooner or later, right?"

I manage to nod.

"Anyway," she says, "I could use the distraction. Being at home all day with my mom analyzing my every move . . ." She exhales, and her breath fogs the morning air.

She's broken. And worse, she has no idea what's awaiting her at school.

We both turn as the train rumbles into the station. Together we board and find two seats next to each other. It's pretty quiet today, with a few commuters working on laptops and people with earbuds in. I gaze out the cloudy window as we slowly leave the station behind.

"I'm sorry I've been so distant," Quinn says, tracing her thumb over a snag in the plastic seat. "It's not you. It's just . . ." She heaves a sigh. "I just don't know what I'm supposed to say, you know?"

"Have you talked to anyone from school?" I broach carefully.

"Not really. Everyone's been texting, but I'm not even thinking about that right now. It's too much."

My eyes drift to the window as the train shudders along the tracks, rolling through the urban landscape, wheels screeching on the bends.

"Okay," I say, drawing in a deep breath, "so there's something you should probably know."

She sits rigid. "Oh, no. What?"

"A few things, actually. People at school, some of the guys," I stumble over my words. "They're kind of mad. Well, they're grieving. . . ." I adjust with Emma's kinder phrasing. "They have this theory that you and I have been hanging out with the Hailing boys, and we're somehow involved in what happened to Kai. Like we're all in on it together."

Her mouth falls open. "You're kidding."

I shake my head. "I wish I was."

Her eyebrows pull together. "They actually believe we'd team up and conspire to kill Kai? Who thinks this?"

"Just some of the guys. Jacob and the hockey boys."

She presses her fingertips to her temples. "I can't believe this shit," she hisses. "How dare they? Kai was the love of my life, you think I'd—" She abandons the sentence, ending with a tearful breath.

I wrap my arm around her. She seems thin and fragile, as if she has no strength to hold herself upright anymore.

It makes me wince, and I brace myself to drop the next bombshell. "The night that Kai died," I begin gently, "you told me that he was mad at you for talking to other people while you were on your break."

"Sadie," she mutters. "I don't want to talk about this. It's not the memory of Kai I want to focus on."

"I know, but I have to ask. Were you seeing one of the Hailing boys?"

She stares at me for a second. "Who told you that?" My pulse quickens when she doesn't deny it. She doesn't look surprised, either.

"It's true? Who is it?"

Her eyelashes sweep downward. "We were just texting, it's not a big deal. It was never going to be anything serious."

"Who?" I press.

And then my entire world comes crashing down around me when she says the name. "Cason."

Friday, February 28

SADIE

MY HEART FEELS LIKE IT'S dropped through my body. I feel sick. I can barely breathe.

"Cason?"

"Okay, I know it sounds bad," Quinn says. "Especially after that fight he started." She grasps my hand, her cold fingers sealing around mine. "Please don't tell anyone, Sadie. I should never have gone there, but I was so hurt when I saw that picture of Kai with another girl—"

"Cason?" I manage to get the word out. "You and Cason?"

Quinn's eyes fill. "You think I'm the worst person ever. Like, literally, of all people, I chose the guy who started a fight with my boyfriend. There must be some screwed-up psychology behind this. Some Freudian crap that I'm going to need therapy for."

All I can do is stare at her, speechless. This can't be real. "When?" I ask her, weakly.

"Since the night we bumped into them at the diner. It was after I saw that picture of Kai, when Hannah sent me that text. I wasn't thinking clearly, I was just so hurt." She pauses, her cheeks flushing. "I hope you're okay with this, Sadie. I know you used to have a thing for him years back, but—"

"I've been talking to Cason too." The words sting my throat.

She falls silent and frowns at me. Then, after a really long pause, "What, as in, *talking*?"

"We've been meeting up in secret. Since that same night at Raleigh's."

"No way," she says, blinking back at me. "Are you serious?"

The train pulls into Arcadia, but as everyone else starts moving around us, I can't bring myself to stand. We're two statues, frozen in our seats.

The automated announcement grinds out, "Please make sure you take all your personal belongings."

Quinn pulls me to my feet, and we blindly follow the commuters onto the platform. The brightly lit tunnel blurs around me.

Cason and Quinn?

I clench my teeth, holding back the swell of emotion building inside my chest. Cason has been texting my best friend.

"I can't . . . ," I murmur, grabbing Quinn's sleeve. "I can't go to school today." My voice sounds scratchy, and the words waver. We stop in the throughfare of the busy platform, and Quinn's eyes roam across the street as people shove past us.

"Raleigh's?" she says.

I nod, and I let her lead me across the road, even though my heart twists and burns at the thought of going to Raleigh's. Our place. Mine and Cason's. The place where he and I have been growing closer, more intimate. And now I find out he's been doing the exact same thing with my best friend. My skin crawls.

"How could he do this to us?"

She grimaces "He's a dog, and he played us, Sadie."

We slip into the building, and Quinn tosses her bag onto a bench in the lobby. She taps fast on her phone before angling the screen toward me. And there it is, the truth. The weeks of messages they've exchanged, rolling before my eyes as Quinn scrolls through their thread.

She stops at the most recent messages, the last ones in their conversation. I want to look away. I wish I could.

CASON

I can't stop thinking about you. I know it's wrong, but I'm falling for you.

Friday, February 28

CASON

I STOP AT THE FENCE surrounding school. The wire links are rusted and broken in places, and people have jammed trash into some of the gaps. Ahead of me, the school is dull gray, a grim prison, shadowed beneath heavy cloud. And I know I've got to make myself walk toward it. Because I know what I've got to do. I've got to admit to everything.

It'll get into their heads; I know it will. Ruben, Finley, even Michel. They won't be able to trust me after this. Because I did it; I told Sadie about that night. Now she's going to talk to Quinn, and Quinn is going to call someone out. Whether they killed 19 or not, if it was one of them, they'll be exposed. And because of those phone calls, we'll all look guilty.

I drag my hands over my face.

Across the parking lot, Larsen pulls up in his busted Ford. He climbs out of the driver's side and double-checks the lock. I swear, he doesn't trust any of us around here. I can't blame him for that.

His eyes slide over me and he frowns. "You okay, Tano? You look sick."

I rub the nape of my neck. "No, yeah. I'm okay, Coach."

He winces. "You sure about that? You haven't got the same thing Ty's got, have you?"

"What's Ty got?"

"Some stomach virus." His mouth quirks. "Better believe I'm not asking for details."

I muster a smile. "I'm okay. Just tired, you know?"

"Well, wake up. We've got a game tonight." He aims his car keys at me. "Don't be tapping out sick on me. I need you at your best, yes?"

"Yes."

He hesitates before walking away. Then he says, "If you're *not* okay, Cason . . . I mean, if you need to talk about anything, you know where to find me."

"Yeah." It catches me off guard, the gesture. And I can tell from his steady expression, the sincerity in his voice, that these aren't empty words. He means it. "Thanks," I tell him, and I mean it too.

"Remember, I was where you are once," he adds. "You're on the right track. Just keep that focus and you'll be set."

I swallow. "Yeah. Thank you."

"You remind me of a guy who played center on my team in high school. Rollins. He got drafted for the NHL right out of college. You think you can stay on that trajectory?"

"I hope so."

He slaps my shoulder, then he's gone, heading toward school with his bag slung over his shoulder.

I watch him walk away, lanky and loping across the lot. He's thin, all limbs, doesn't look much like a hockey player. But he's good. He probably could have had a shot at playing in the NHL himself if he hadn't busted his knee in a college game.

But I let his words sink in, and something lands.

Now is not the time to fall apart.

My phone buzzes as a new message from Sadie lights up the screen.

Quinn told me. I frown at the words. Then my heart slams. **She told me it's you.**

Friday, February 28

CASON

I'M SPUN OUT, STANDING IN the school parking lot, staring at my phone while people move around me.

"What?" I murmur.

Everyone's heading inside, leaving me alone with the silent cars parked skewed in the faded lines. The wind picks up, sending a soda can rolling along the asphalt.

I write back to Sadie, **What do you mean? What's me?**

Her reply comes back quickly.

I've seen the messages you sent to Quinn. You've been lying to both of us this whole time.

I have to read her text a couple of times over, because the words don't make sense to me. There were no messages to Quinn. There never have been.

I hit dial on Sadie's number, half expecting her to send the call to voicemail. But she doesn't. She picks up on the third ring.

"It's a lie," I say before she has chance to tear into me. Then I wait for her to hang up. But I can still hear breathing on the other end of the line.

So I keep going. "Whatever you've heard, it's wrong. The only person I'm talking to is you. The only person I'm interested in is you. You've got to know that."

"I . . ." She falters. "I've seen the messages on Quinn's phone."

I scrub my hand through my hair. "What messages? I don't even have her number!"

There's a voice in the background now. Quinn's voice.

"Where are you, Sadie?" I press. "Can I meet you?"

"I don't know about that," she says.

"Please. You've got this wrong. Trust me, this is wrong."

There's a stillness, quiet breaths down the line. And Quinn's fast chatter in the background. "What's he saying? Let me listen."

Sadie speaks again, "We're at Raleigh's."

I glance at the gray-walled building where I'm supposed to be. Rain has started to spatter, stabbing at my jacket. And before I can change my mind, I'm out of there, sprinting toward the train stop, my sneakers smacking the pavement and breath coming fast.

In a daze, I'm on the train, tearing through the town. Buildings and fields bleed together outside, and I grip my seat, reeling.

From Arcadia station, I jog the rest of the way to Raleigh's.

I bust into the rink and the icy air hits me. The bleachers are empty apart from two girls at the top. They turn my way, and I climb the stands to reach them.

Quinn's arms are folded, and she's glaring at me. Sadie's eyes are fixed on the rink below. She stays silent. They both do.

"Why are you doing this, Quinn?"

She splutters out a sound. "Me? You're actually mad at *me* about this? Don't try to gaslight us, Cason. You're the snake here, not me."

My pulse is hammering in my ears. "But you know that you're lying. There's nothing going on between us. There never was."

She scoffs and turns her head away from me, muttering under her breath.

"I don't even have your number!"

"I gave it to you!" she yells back. "I slipped it into your bag, and *you* texted *me*."

Sadie heaves a sigh, and my attention goes to her.

"You've been texting her, Cason," she says, and I hear the hurt in her voice. I hate that I can hear that. "I've read the messages."

"Okay, well, can I see these messages, since apparently I'm the only one who *hasn't* read them?"

Reluctantly, Quinn passes her phone to me, and I skim through the conversations.

CASON
I keep hearing that song you like. Do you think the universe is trying to tell me something?

QUINN
What do you mean?

CASON
It's the Baader-Meinhof phenomenon. We studied it in philosophy class—when you notice something for the first time, then suddenly see it everywhere. It makes me think of you.

QUINN
You make me feel so safe.

CASON
Good. And don't worry about Kai anymore. If he wants to talk, I'll handle it.

CASON
I love that you trust me. And yes, I mean it, I'm falling for you.

QUINN
I feel the same way.

I squint at the screen. "What is this? I didn't write any of this." I tap on the contact and open the number connected to my name. "This isn't my number."

A flicker of relief crosses Sadie's face. And I feel it too, tenfold.

"You're such a liar," Quinn scoffs. "You can't just snake your way out because you got caught, Cason."

"I'm telling you I didn't write this stuff. For one thing, I've never taken a philosophy class. I didn't even know my school did that."

Sadie looks nervously between us. "These messages don't *seem* like Cason's writing," she ventures, shooting a quick glance at Quinn. "I mean, these sentences have commas."

My eyebrows pull together.

"You don't use commas," she adds.

I frown. "I didn't realize this was counting toward my final grade, but okay."

Sadie picks up her own phone and starts tapping on the screen. She jumps to her feet and huddles close to me to compare her phone with Quinn's, her eyes flitting between the two contacts.

"These are different numbers," she says.

Quinn's face flushes red. She's on her feet now too, and she yanks her phone out of my hands and cross-checks it with Sadie's.

"Whoever you've been texting, it wasn't me."

Quinn takes a shallow breath.

Sadie turns to her. "You haven't met this guy in person?"

She juts her chin. "Well, no. But we've been texting, and . . ." She presses her fingers to her mouth. "Oh my god. I think I'm going to puke."

"You've been catfished," I tell her.

Her eyes snap to me. "Yes, thank you, Cason," she says sharply. "I think we've established that already."

Sadie and I swap a look.

"Why would someone pretend to be you?" Quinn cries. "Who would even do that?"

"You said you dropped your number into my bag?" I toss my backpack onto the floor. "This one?"

"Yes." She huffs and pinches the bridge of her nose. "I don't know. It was dark, we were on the train. I was trying to be subtle, and whatever." She mutters the last few words, red creeping down her neck.

“Call the number,” Sadie says, gesturing to the phone.

Quinn presses dial, and the preset words leak out.

“This number has been disconnected.”

“Maybe it’s a burner,” Quinn says, and I see the shifty look she gives me, like she still doubts me. A part of her is still second-guessing.

“I swear,” I tell them again, lifting my hands. “This isn’t me. You think I can afford a burner? I can’t even afford the phone I have.”

“Let me take another look.” Sadie pries the cell from Quinn and opens the number. “See if it matches with any of the guys from the Hailing team.”

I go to my contacts list and start trying to pair the number, checking them one by one. Every nerve is on edge as I work through each name, scared to find a match.

But none of the numbers align.

Quinn combs her fingers through the ends of her ponytail. “This just doesn’t make sense, though.”

“When did this person last text you?” Sadie asks.

She hugs her arms around herself. “Not since before Kai died. I mean, I haven’t been messaging him, either. Because of Kai,” she adds, gnawing on her lip. “I felt sick at the thought of texting Cason after everything.” Her eyes come to me, then she half-heartedly corrects herself. “When I thought it was you.”

Sadie’s gaze moves carefully over me. The glimmer of trust is still there, somewhere.

“I should never have started this,” Quinn says with a terse breath. “But I was hurt, I was angry. I would have ended everything, though, if Kai had taken me back."

"Okay," Sadie says, clasping her hands. "This is going to sound really out there. But what if Kai was the person behind these messages?" Her focus lands on Quinn as she says the words. "What if he was trying to test you, to catch you out or something?"

Quinn rubs her eyes with the heels of her hands. "I don't know. You really think he would do that? On a burner?"

Sadie shrugs. "Maybe."

"I don't know." Quinn's face scrunches. "If he wanted to test me, why close things off between us? Why hook up with other girls on our break?"

"Or it could still be someone from the Hailing team." Sadie's attention comes back to me. "Someone who found Quinn's number in the wrong bag. If that's the case, this person could easily be connected to Kai's death. They clearly weren't afraid to confront him. One of the texts even said if Kai wanted to talk, he'd handle it. Maybe they wanted Kai out of the picture for good. I mean, these messages are pretty intense."

A visible shudder moves over Quinn, and she shakes out her shoulders.

"You should show these messages to the police," Sadie says. "They might be able to trace the number."

"Okay. Can they track disconnected numbers?"

"I don't know. But you should tell them that you were catfished." Sadie presses her palms together and brings her fingers to her lips. "Cason," she says. "Gut feeling, who do you think could be behind this?"

I look out over the ice, its sleek, scarred surface reflecting the light. "Out of everyone from my team?"

"Yeah. If you had to call it, who would write messages like this, pretending to be you?"

I just shake my head.

While Sadie and Quinn keep talking about who it might be, my thoughts are on Finley.

He had a knife—a box cutter. I caught him using it to carve *RIP* into a bench in Raleigh's locker room a couple of months back. When I took the knife from him, he looked up at me like I'd pulled him out of a trance. I've been in that state myself, a couple of times. I recognized it. Larsen came over and started popping off, so I jumped in. "Sorry, Coach. I did that. Sorry."

Larsen short-circuited, gave me the whole lecture. Bringing a knife to practice? Damaging Raleigh's property when you're representing our school?

Finley tried to step in, but I booted his sneaker. I took the hit that day.

Later, we went to the construction site, just me and him, tossing scraps of wood and old nails into the empty void, listening to them clink and clatter in the darkness. He opened up about losing him mom when he was a kid, because I've been there. I am there. He asked how I act like nothing bothers me, like nothing gets to me. I shrugged it off, told him I'm just good at pretending. Then he said he wanted to be me for a while, see where it takes him. And he launched another brick into the blackness. My flashlight caught the shards as they shattered.

AUDIO FILE_MP3

TITLE: CASE_339KH_FINLEY DUNCAN INTERVIEW

Hello, Finley. My name is Detective Alanis. Thank you for speaking with us today.

Okay.

We're following up on an altercation that you were involved in recently. January 24, outside Raleigh's Rec Center. Are you aware of the incident I'm referring to?

Yes. My friend was attacked that night.

Your friend's name, please?

Cason Tano.

Who attacked him, Finley?

Kai Harrison.

Okay. I can see that you're finding this distressing. Do you need a minute?

I didn't want it. I didn't want any of this. Cason is my friend. He's a good person, I couldn't leave him out there. They were coming for him too hard, those Arcadia guys.

You mean Kai Harrison? Is he your friend too?

No. He's no one's friend.

What do you mean by that, Finley?

I noticed it. People didn't like him, and he didn't like them. He thought he was better than everyone, and anyone who didn't treat him like the best, he'd be gunning for them.

Who are you referring to when you say people*?*

Everyone who knew him.

EMMA
Why aren't you in class today?
Are you okay?

SADIE
Yeah, I just couldn't face it. I'm with Quinn.

EMMA
I'm sorry. I know Jacob went off on you yesterday. I've talked to Brandon, and he's going to tell Jacob and the other guys to back off.

SADIE
Thanks.

EMMA
Please come back to school. No one really thinks you did it.

SADIE
Jacob does.

EMMA
Jacob knows it wasn't you. He's just grieving. Kai was his best friend, and he's super emotional right now. But that's no excuse for yelling at you, and I told him so.

SADIE
Thank you.

EMMA

Okay 🩶 There's something I want to talk to you about too. Nothing big, I'll explain when I see you.

Friday, February 28

SADIE

THE RINK'S DOOR SWINGS OPEN with a heavy thud, and the sudden interruption catches us by surprise.

Quinn, Cason, and I turn toward the entrance as Maya marches in. She strides to the bleachers, arms folded tightly, her skirt whipping around her lean legs, shoes clicking fast on the concrete.

"What are you three doing in here? I know for a fact that you should *all* be at school right now." She comes to a stop at the bottom of the bleachers. Her hardened gaze skims over Quinn and Cason before settling on me. And she's singling me out, giving me this look, like of all of us, *I* should know better.

My face flushes. I glance up at the glass wall overlooking the stands, where the diner's lights are on and there's a bottle of detergent spray on the inside ledge.

Busted.

When none of us responds, Maya tries again, "What's going on? One of you needs to start talking."

Cason clears his throat, and Quinn draws in a deep breath. "Well," she says, "my boyfriend is dead."

Maya heaves a sigh. "Okay." She presses her palms together and gathers herself. "Okay, I'm sorry. But that doesn't answer my question. What are you all doing in here at nine in the morning on a school day?"

I stare down at my shoes while Quinn adds, "Also, turns out some creep has been catfishing me. So I'm basically traumatized right now."

Maya's brow knits. "Excuse me? I'm confused."

"We all are," Cason mutters, and her attention lands on him.

"*You* definitely shouldn't be here," she says, frowning as she gestures to him. "Don't think I've forgotten you started a fight on this premises."

Wearily, he gets to his feet. "Sorry. I'll leave."

I shoot him a helpless look. "Cason didn't start that fight," I say to Maya.

She purses her lips, clearly skeptical.

"It's okay," Cason says—to me, mostly. "I got to go, anyway. I've got to get back to school and figure out how to explain where I've been."

My eyes follow him as he vaults the barrier and heads for the door. He lifts his hand in a wave, and my heart gives a little tug at the sight of him walking away.

Even with everything that's happened, I still believe I can trust him. He's always shown up for me, and deep down, I know that those messages weren't his words. The way he speaks with sincerity, his eyes on mine—those are the signs I can trust.

When the door thumps shut behind him, Maya relaxes a little.

Her arms fall to her sides. "Girls," she says, "talk to me. Come on."

But my thoughts are still with Cason. "Aren't there security cameras at the front of the building?" I ask Maya. "Can't we prove who actually started that fight?"

"Cameras only cover the back of the lobby," Maya says, "not the parking lot. Management already checked, and the security system only picked up people coming and going through the foyer, and a bunch of muffled conversations."

I sigh as she climbs the stands and takes a seat next to Quinn. "I'm sorry, sweetie," she says, rubbing Quinn's arm. "I know how much you liked Kai. I can only imagine how devastated you must be feeling."

Quinn's lashes sweep downward. "It's cruel. Like some sick joke where Kai's gone and I'm the punchline." When Maya frowns, she adds, "People think I'm involved. As if I would ever . . ." She sucks in a sharp breath.

"Is that why you're not at school?"

"Pretty much," I answer for both of us. "There are so many rumors going around about Quinn and me. People have drawn their own conclusions."

"Because of that picture at the platform?" Maya asks.

"You've seen it?" I don't know why I'm surprised. @AvaKava's post certainly made an impact.

"Social media garbage," Maya scoffs. "You two are minors, you should never have been exploited like that. Ava Kavanaugh is a twenty-something-year-old woman, she should have known better."

I sit straighter. "Do you know Ava from ACU?"

"I don't know her, but I've seen her around. We have some mutual friends."

"It's not just social media, though, is it?" Quinn says. "It's school, our friends, the police."

"The police have to question everyone," I remind her. "It's their job. They don't really think we had anything to do with it." The words sound stilted as they leave my lips. Because I know I'm forcing them out, not entirely sure if they're true or not. From what I can gather, Quinn is a suspect. *I'm* a suspect.

"But that doesn't make it better," she says, grimacing. "I'm still scared the investigators might get this wrong. Aren't you?"

A knot forms in my stomach. "No."

"And it's textbook," Quinn adds. "The perpetrator is always someone close to the victim, right? Like the spouse. That's *me.*" She presses her hands to her chest. "I'm the girlfriend."

"Ex-girlfriend," I point out.

"Sadie, that's worse!" she exclaims. "I'm the rejected ex-girlfriend."

"It's just a statistic, it's not the rule."

"We don't even know who's been texting me," Quinn carries on. "If it isn't Cason, I mean. But it has to have been one of the Hailing boys. It was one of their bags, and after the fight they had with Kai last month . . ." She trails off, and the icy chill in the arena slithers over my skin.

Maya reaches for Quinn's hand. "Don't worry. The police will be watching those boys, no doubt about it."

I inhale slowly, trying not to think about what that means for them.

Quinn rubs her eyes with her sleeves. "It just sucks because . . ." She hiccups in a breath. "I don't know what I'm supposed to do. It's like I keep forgetting, just for a second, that Kai is dead. And then I have to remember all over again."

Maya seals an arm around her. "You're bound to feel like that now, it's still so fresh. It'll take time."

Quinn swipes at a tear as it rolls down her cheek. "How am I supposed to move on from Kai? He's the only person I want. He was the love of my life."

"You're grieving," I murmur.

"Can I be honest with you?" Maya says, and Quinn gazes at her through watery eyes. "You *will* be okay. You *will* get through this. Quinn, you've spent weeks heartbroken over this boy. Every shift at the diner, all you've been doing is questioning your own worth because of him. I heard you, constantly wondering why he hasn't texted or called. What's he doing? Why doesn't he want me? He hurt you badly."

Quinn bristles and sits bolt upright, slipping free from Maya's arm. "How can you say that to me? Kai and I fought a couple of times, sure. But we would have fixed things."

"Quinn," Maya says softly. "I know you don't want to hear this, and hate me if you have to. But . . ." She pauses and shakes her head. "One day you'll find someone who loves you deeply."

Quinn scowls at her. "You don't know what you're talking about. You didn't even know Kai."

“I’m sorry,” Maya says gently. “I just hate seeing you go through this.”

“Well, I *am* going through it,” Quinn retorts, her voice sharp. “And you’re not helping. You don’t know the first thing about my relationship, so keep your opinions to yourself. Kai was the best person I knew; he would never have hurt anyone.”

I want to comfort Quinn, to tell her that she’s right, and Maya has got this wrong. But I can’t stop thinking about the image Kai made of me. Quinn *must* have suspected him, just like I did. But she never wanted to admit that he did it. She kept trying to convince me that it couldn’t have been him. That Kai would never have done that to me. And I didn’t challenge her on it because it was easier for all of us. But I knew. I *know*.

Quinn stands abruptly and starts making her way down the bleachers.

I shoot Maya a helpless look as I jump to follow her.

“Oh, and Maya,” Quinn yells over her shoulder. “Consider this my resignation from the diner. Because I quit.”

I’ve barely made it down the bleachers when the door slams shut behind Quinn. The rink roster sheet flutters in the gust, and as I reach for the handle, something on the paper catches my attention.

ACU women’s hockey practice. Saturday 10 a.m. – 12 p.m.

INSTAGRAM

ACU WOMEN'S ICE HOCKEY

@ARCCITUWOMENSHOCKEYCLUB

1,891 FOLLOWERS | 302 POSTS

You don't follow each other on Instagram.

View profile

Friday, February 28 at 16:43

Hi, my name's Sadie Morelli, and I'm trying to contact your team captain, Madison. If she could call me, that would be great. I'll leave my number below.

AUDIO FILE_MP3

TITLE: CASE_339KH_CASON TANO INTERVIEW

Hi again, Cason. Thanks for coming down to the precinct today. Are you sure you're happy to waive your right to have a legal guardian present for this interview?

Yeah, it's fine. What's this about?

We spoke with you a while back about the events at Hailing Train Station on February 22, the night Kai Harrison was found dead.

Yeah, I remember.

We also went over a prior altercation with Kai on January 24. It's recently come to our attention that there were text messages exchanged between you and Quinn McKinley, Kai's former girlfriend, in the weeks leading up to his death.

I've already talked to Quinn about this. She thought she put her number in my bag, but it was someone else's, and whoever had her number is the one who's been texting her, not me. It wasn't my phone. You can check—I've got nothing to hide.

We've analyzed the messages. Some of the language used could be considered threatening toward Kai. Are you sure you don't recognize these? For the purpose of the tape, I'm showing the interviewee a printout of text messages exchanged between Cason Tano and Quinn McKinley.

I didn't write those messages.

Do you have any idea who might have?

No.

Look, Cason, it's in your best interest to be honest with us. (PAUSE.)

I'll ask again. Did you send those messages to Quinn?

No. It wasn't me.

Okay. We'll need to investigate this further and may need to speak with you again. Cason, I advise you to consider obtaining legal representation. If you're unable to arrange that, we'll ensure that a lawyer is provided for you.

I don't need it. I haven't done anything wrong.

Friday, February 28

CASON

THE FINAL SECONDS OF THE game tick down on the scoreboard, and the crowd stomps in the stands. Ruben's moving fast toward the goal, going low after the puck, blades carving the slick ice. Bridgewater's goalie braces, getting ready, and Ruben takes the shot. The puck hurtles toward the net, and I hold my breath. It ricochets off the post and Ruben slams his stick on the ice, cussing under his breath.

The final whistle blows, and the arena erupts in cheers.

5–1 lights up the scoreboard. There's a clear winner, and it isn't us.

Bridgewater rushes the ice, jumping on each other, and their fans shake the stands.

At the edge, Larsen has his fist pressed to his mouth.

Yeah. He's pissed.

Michel pats my shoulder as he passes. No words.

We messed up. All of us—but mostly four of us. Ruben missing clear shots; Michel, fumbling, hitting the ice instead of the puck; Finley tapping out early with an injury. And me, mentally somewhere else. My head still in the police station. I didn't tell

Alec about how serious things got when they pulled me in today. I didn't tell anyone.

But it's over. For now.

The locker room is humid and reeks of aerosol spray. I'm on the bench when Larsen comes in.

"Okay," he hollers, slapping his hands together. The tendons in his neck are showing. I swear, half the reason he gets so worked up is because he's stuck wrangling us instead of playing in the NHL. I'd be mad about that too. "Gather up."

A couple of the guys stop what they're doing. Ruben takes a seat beside me on the bench, the short spikes of his hair still wet from the shower.

Larsen looks at us all. "Is this everyone?" His eyes move over us, doing a quick head count.

There are a few murmured responses, and I glance around. Hudson and Ty are standing in front of their lockers with towels draped over their shoulders. Michel and Finley are on the back bench, heads dipped and muttering under their breath.

A stab of paranoia hits me. What are they talking about? Why are they sitting so far away from me?

Larsen slaps his hands again. "So, let's debrief. What was that?" he says, addressing all of us. "What were you *doing* out there? Is this a joke to you, boys?" His voice rebounds through the room, and I drop my gaze to the wet floor tiles.

"You let me down," he adds. "You let yourselves down. You've got every opportunity at your fingertips, and I'm watching you piss it away."

We all stay silent, some of us looking at Larsen, the rest of us looking at anything but him. Because he's right. The season's coming to an end. We're supposed to be showcasing ourselves, proving that we're worthy of moving up to the college leagues. We had an opportunity tonight, and we blew it. There were scouts watching this game.

"I've backed you guys all year," he carries on. "I've gone to bat for you. Plenty of boys at school would kill for your spots, and they're good enough. But I keep giving you chances, time and time again. After the fight last month, I busted my ass doing damage control for you."

"It wasn't our fault," Ruben jumps in.

And for a beat, I wonder what he means. The lost game? The fight? Number 19's death?

Larsen's hard stare lands on Ruben. "You think it matters who started it? Them? You? You should have walked away."

"And what about Cason?" Ruben says. "We were just supposed to leave him to get beat down?"

"Cason shouldn't have been out there with those boys in the first place," Larsen fires back. "He should've stayed inside with the rest of us until I gave the okay for him to leave."

I grit my teeth, because it doesn't matter what I say, or what Ruben says. Larsen has already made up his mind. But that night in Raleigh's, I *was* walking away. I felt the tension in the diner, and I was walking away *because* of it. Kai had followed me outside.

"It makes the school look bad," Larsen says. "It makes *me* look bad." He presses his hand to his chest. "You get that? I gave you too much rope, too much trust. Letting you boys roam free, starting fights over a damn hockey match? A boy *died.*"

And there it is.

This isn't about the fight anymore. It's about a murder. A murder that, judging by the way Larsen's eyes dart to me, he thinks I committed.

Ruben mutters under his breath.

"Got something to say, Hernandez?"

Ruben takes a shallow breath. "No, sir."

"No?" Larsen folds his arms. "Are you sure about that?"

Ruben's jaw tightens, and I nudge him, telling him to stop. But he doesn't. "Number Nineteen was a dick. He had it coming."

I freeze up, and the room falls dead silent.

Larsen just stares at him, stunned, mouth gaping. "I know you didn't just say that, Hernandez."

Ruben's throat bobs.

"Whatever problem you had with the Arcadia boys," Larsen says, his gaze jumping between Ruben, Michel, Finley, and me as the other guys edge back, "a life lost is still a tragedy, and you're lucky it wasn't you. If I catch you talking like that again, Hernandez, you're off the team. That goes for all of you." He sweeps his finger across the locker room. "I'll be waiting in the lobby. Move."

When the door thumps shut behind him, the voices start up again, metal doors clang, and words bounce.

Ruben scrubs his hands through his wet hair. "Like he'd kick *us* off the team." He clicks his tongue against his teeth. "This is bullshit."

Michel and Finley head over to our bench. Michel takes a seat beside me, and Finley stays standing. When my eyes land on Fin, he flinches and looks down.

Tension tightens my back. "What's up with you?" I ask, my voice coming out sharper than I mean it to.

He glances over his shoulder, then at Ruben. "Nothing," he says, looking shifty as hell. "I'm good."

I want to ask him outright if he did it. If he's the one who's been texting Quinn. But I can't. The words won't come out.

Ruben's head is still with Larsen. "Kicking *me* off the team? *Me?* Tripping."

Michel's sneaker starts tapping on the damp floor tiles. "It's empty threats, he's not going to follow through with it this late in the season. But you shouldn't have said what you said."

Ruben blinks back at him.

"Number Nineteen had it coming," Michel mimics him.

"Well, he did," Ruben says. "I'm just saying what we're all thinking. If Cason took a shot at him—"

"*I* didn't."

Michel's eyes fix on Ruben. "You're drawing attention to us with shit like that," he says under his breath. "We're *all* still suspects because of that fight."

I watch Ruben's reaction. He sucks in his cheeks, and his mouth twitches. I watch him, everyone, everything.

The other guys start leaving the locker room, and I grab my

bag, but we're the last to move. It's quiet in here now, apart from a steady drip of water leaking from one of the showers.

Too many questions hang over us. Too many unspoken words.

Our silence echoes.

Friday, February 28

SADIE

SOME OF THE HAILING PLAYERS are already out in the foyer, and their coach looks mad. After my shift, I stayed to watch the end of the game. They lost pretty badly tonight.

Cason comes out with Michel, Ruben, and Finley, their sports bags slung over their shoulders.

They look stressed, but Cason smiles when he sees me, and my heart skips a little. No matter how many times he's smiled at me like that, it never fails to give me butterflies, in spite of everything.

I cross the lobby toward him, and he hangs back, allowing the other boys to walk ahead.

He pulls me into a hug. For the first time, we're acknowledging each other publicly. And it's kind of a relief. Secrets aren't fun anymore.

I tighten my arms around him. "I'm sorry," I murmur into his shoulder. "About tonight's game."

He shrugs heavily. "It sucked. We sucked. And there were scouts watching."

"Sorry, Cason. I know how important this is to you." I glance across the lobby to where the Hailing team has gathered. Everyone looks forlorn, glum expressions and slumped postures.

"We messed up," he says. "I hope we'll get another chance."

"Of course."

Cason keeps his arm around me as we follow the group into the parking lot, heading for the station across the street.

As the distance between us and them grows, I tug at his sleeve, signaling for him to slow our pace. "I messaged the ACU women's hockey team tonight," I tell him.

He drops his gaze down to meet mine. "How come?"

"Do you remember that girl Madison we met at the rink last Saturday, right after the news broke about Kai? She and her team came onto the ice, and she introduced herself. I think I've figured out where I recognized her from."

He frowns. "Okay."

"About a month ago, someone sent Quinn a picture of Kai looking cozy with another girl, and he had lipstick on his neck. At first I thought the girl might have been Ava Kavanaugh or one of the girls from the platform, but now I think it's Madison, the captain of the ACU women's team. I'm almost sure that's where I recognized her from, the picture."

His brow knits as we stroll through the lamplit lot. "She was hooking up with Kai?"

"I think so. What if my first theory was right? Madison saw Ava Kavanaugh's post from the platform, drove to the station to confront Kai, the guy who'd ghosted her, because she saw him . . ." I throw up my hands. "I don't know, talking to his ex or something.

They got into a huge fight, and it got out of hand."

Cason chews on his lip, considering my logic. "And you messaged her about this?"

"Not in so much detail. I just asked her to get in touch. I'm hoping she'll talk to me, so I can at least try to get some clarity on her situation with Kai."

We follow the rest of his team onto the platform, where our voices turn hollow in the tunneled station with its too-bright lights and chipped tiles lining the walls. Cason drops his bag, scraping the concrete floor.

"Do you really think she'll talk to you?" he asks under his breath.

"Maybe. I'm almost positive she's the person who'd been seeing Kai while he and Quinn were on a break. If I can just confirm that, I can give her name to the police, and they can take it from there. The timing of Ava's photo being posted and someone showing up at the station feels too suspicious to ignore. We need to at least explore that possibility."

"She could be the person messaging Quinn too," he says. "If she was that into Kai, maybe she got Quinn's number somehow and was trying to catch her out or set her up or something?"

"And in that case, Madison could have been the person who told Kai that Quinn was seeing someone else," I finish. "But it was all a setup to mess with their relationship."

A muffled announcement crackles on the platform, and I glance up at the display board, where neon letters indicate a delay to the next Hailing service. We've already missed the 9:30 because the game ran over, but at least I'm not alone tonight. Cason and I take a seat on a metal bench while the others stand around checking their phones, sometimes glancing our way with curious expressions.

But Cason doesn't seem aware of them. He stares at the tracks stretching before us. "Quinn said she slipped her number into my bag, though. Madison wouldn't have known that."

"Could be a coincidence."

"Kai told me he *saw* Quinn with someone."

"He was probably bluffing. Quinn didn't even know who she'd been texting—they'd never met in person. And even if Madison has nothing to do with the messages, I still don't think we can rule her out."

"You believe Quinn's story?"

I think on it for a moment, then nod. "Honestly, I do. I know when Quinn is lying, and I really don't think she is in this case. She wouldn't have told me she'd been texting you if she didn't wholly believe it herself. It must have been awkward for her to admit, especially because she knew I had a crush on you in middle school."

A grin lights up his entire face. "Oh, you did?"

The teasing tone of his voice flusters me, and I trip over my response. "Well, maybe, but—"

He jumps in. "I had a thing for you too. Ever since I saw you in that Sabres cap." He blows out a breath and tugs at his collar, pretending to overheat.

I laugh and swat his arm. The first time Cason and I met in

middle school, he walked by my desk and tapped the peak of my NHL cap down over my eyes. I pushed it back up, frowning, only to find him standing there with a grin. He asked if I was a Buffalo Sabres fan because of the cap. I told him I wasn't—I just liked the color blue. And that was it. From then on, we were friends.

"That was the moment I knew you were the girl for me," he adds, nudging his shoulder against mine.

"But it was just the hat," I remind him. "I wasn't a *real* Sabres fan."

"Doesn't matter. You were still the girl for me. Anyway, I know you're a Sabres fan deep down. Everyone is."

I smile back at him.

"And you believe me about the Quinn thing too?" he asks, searching my gaze. "You know it wasn't me messaging from a burner?"

"Yes, I believe you."

"Because of the commas?"

I shake my head. "I just know you, Cason." The words come out quietly, with meaning.

He draws me closer and plants a kiss on my forehead.

I believe him. I just hope the police do too. Quinn took the messages to the investigators, but as we'd feared, she said they didn't seem hopeful about tracking a disconnected number.

"I keep coming back to something, though," I say to Cason, shuffling on the bench to face him. "If it wasn't you texting Quinn, and it wasn't one of your friends, or Madison, is there someone we've overlooked? Maybe we need to widen our perspective and see who connects everyone. You and your friends, me and mine, and Madison and the college girls."

We fall quiet, contemplating our own thoughts.

The train finally pulls into the station, and we join the crowd boarding. As I pass, Michel gives me a small smile, and once we find our seats, I lean into Cason's shoulder. After a minute, the train lurches forward, screeching on the tracks. The darkness outside intensifies, pitch black against the windows. No one's high off the game energy like they'd usually be. Everyone is tense and on edge. I feel it in Cason's touch, the way his fingers tap restlessly on my hand.

A wave of fear ripples over me. Because whatever theories we toss around, we do know one thing for sure: someone murdered Kai. It's possible that someone aboard this train, someone sitting close to me, is a cold-blooded killer.

And they're lying their ass off to get away with it.

TIKTOK

DARCY WILDE

@WILDEONCRIME

Season 19, Episode 4 #truecrime #forensic #fyp #HailingNY #JusticeforKai

A lot of you commented on my last video following the Kai Harrison case, and you guys have some pretty wild thoughts on this. One popular theory going around is that there could be more than one person involved. Someone actually responded to my video saying, "Imagine if they're all in on it." It's an interesting idea, and I can't lie, I've wondered the same thing myself. Particularly regarding C.T. and S.M.

At the moment, these two are standing out as my red flags. C.T. because of the altercation that happened the month prior, and what I've been told about his character. *Dangerously impulsive* was the term used to describe him. And S.M. because of the direct threat she made to Kai during school. I also have reason to believe that these two individuals are connected.

Their online profiles are both set to private, but my source has confirmed that the pair know each other. Allegedly.

Synchronicities mean everything, guys. This shouldn't be overlooked.

I do have a contact working this case for the Hailing police department, and I know that C.T. and S.M. are both on the radar. Also, when C.T. and S.M. were interviewed, neither of them admitted to seeing each other on the night of Kai's murder. Strange, right?

Because, purportedly, they were both on the 11:20 train from Arcadia to Hailing. To my knowledge, there were only a handful of people around Hailing Station that night. Doesn't it seem a little off that two people who knew each other just didn't notice each other?

Doubtful, if you ask me.

Now, just to be clear, the fact that they didn't disclose seeing each other that night doesn't necessarily mean they planned it together. One of them could be under the other's influence, for instance. Let's see how this unfolds.

Friday, February 28

SADIE

WE DISEMBARK THE TRAIN AT Hailing, and Cason walks me to my door. Beneath the moonlight, my eyes land on Dad's car parked in the driveway. I thought he was working tonight.

"I would invite you in," I whisper, "but . . ." I nod toward the car.

His mouth lifts at the corner. "Do you think you'll ever introduce me to your family?"

I laugh quietly. "I hope so. Do you think you'll ever introduce me to yours?"

He nods, smiling, then leans in to plant a small kiss on my lips. "Anyway," he adds, "I've seen your dad around. Back in middle school."

"We weren't together then, though." As soon as the words are out, I realize what I've said. Rewind. *Rewind.*

He raises his eyebrows, playing. "Are we *together*? Officially?"

"No. I mean, no. That came out wrong." We've never defined what we are. Up until recently, no one even knew we were anything.

Cason laughs, just a quick breath. "I like *together*," he says. "Do you?"

I manage to nod. "Okay." A rush of something stirs in me,

something like falling, in a haze of whispered words in the darkness.

"See you tomorrow?" he asks, threading his fingers through mine.

"Yes. Tomorrow." With one last kiss, I slip into the house and close the door softly behind me. I lean against the wall, smiling so hard my cheeks ache.

"Sadie?" Dad's voice jolts me from my euphoria. Fast footsteps thud down the staircase, and he appears, looking stressed.

"Hey, Dad. I thought you were working tonight?"

"Where have you been?" he says in a ragged breath. "I've been going out of my mind. You weren't picking up my calls, it's late, I called the diner and your boss told me you'd left already."

I slide my phone from my pocket, noticing, for the first time, the many missed calls from Dad. "I'm so sorry," I say quickly. "There was a hockey game. I just went to watch the last couple of minutes, and I missed my usual train—"

"You're supposed to check in. I've been waiting for your message. When I couldn't get hold of you, I abandoned my shift because I was so worried," he exclaims. "Then I got home, and you weren't here. I was seconds away from calling the police, Sadie."

"I'm sorry," I say again. "My phone was on silent. I had no idea you'd been trying to reach me. I was planning on texting as soon as I got home."

He gives way to a short breath. "Why is your phone on silent mode? What's the point of having a cell if you don't answer anyone's calls?"

I glance at the time displayed above the missed call notifications.

"I'm only an hour late, and I would have been here sooner if the train hadn't been delayed. Is it really that big of a deal?"

He chokes out a sound. "Yes. Yes, it's a huge deal. A boy your age, from your school, a friend of yours—he *died*, just a stone's throw from this house." He flings his arm toward the window, toward the train station just beyond.

"I know that," I murmur. "And I've said I'm sorry. I didn't realize you'd been calling."

"I work nights, Sadie," he says. "What am I supposed to do? What, do I need to quit my job to keep an eye on you?"

"No. Of course not. Look, it won't happen again." I reset my phone, cranking the volume to the max. "There, see?" I twist the screen to face him. "Sound on."

Dad runs his hands over his face. "This isn't working."

"Okay, well, I won't forget to text you updates in the future. Honestly, I would have, but I assumed you'd be at work. There would've been no point."

"Your mom and I talked," he mutters, and I feel the shift in the air. This strange energetic shift that makes my pulse quicken. "We have to rethink the arrangement we have."

His words knock the air from my lungs. "Okay," I say slowly. "What does that mean?"

"You mom thinks . . ." He pauses and presses his knuckles to his mouth. "We both think that our current situation isn't working."

I'm frozen to the spot. The world seems to still around me, as though time has stopped.

Dad's voice sounds weak when he speaks again. "Your mom and I think you'd be better off living with her, where she and Bryce can give you more supervision."

I can't find my voice.

When I finally muster a response, it's just a breath. "But this is my home."

Dad closes his eyes for a second. "I know, and I don't want this, either. But I'm scared, Sadie. I'm scared for you, your safety. If living with your mom will give you a better life, a safer life—"

"It won't." My throat tightens. I love Mom and my visits with her, even if things have been strained between us lately. But *this* is my home. It's where I grew up, where everything I know is. Even with the situation at school, and with the police, I can't leave Hailing. Dad, Quinn, Emma . . .

Cason.

Dad rubs his temples, furrowing his lined skin. "We don't have to formalize anything tonight. It's late, emotions are running high, and I'm going to have to get back to my shift now that I know you're home safe. We can think on this, and then we'll call your mom and come up with a plan that works for everyone."

"Okay," I whisper.

"Okay," he echoes, and his eyes turn glassy.

There's an unspoken time-out, where he heads to his corner, and I retreat to mine. I hear him clattering around in the kitchen as I go upstairs.

In my bedroom, I close the door and try to steady my trembling hands. My fingers are locked too tightly around my phone, and it's all there: the missed calls and unread messages from Dad, even some from Mom.

Check in. Where are you?

Call me.

If you don't call me back, I'm coming looking for you.

I lean against the window ledge, staring at a sliver of moonlight reflecting in a puddle, savoring the smell of the iron tracks and damp leaves as though it might be the last time. As though it could all be taken away. A car drives beneath the lamplight, its tires splashing through the puddle, shattering the iridescent reflection of moonlight.

I close the drapes and crawl onto my bed. I can still feel Cason's touch on my skin, on my lips, and a lump forms in my throat.

My phone pings loudly in my hand, jolting me.

There's a new text message on the screen, sent from an unknown number. I open it and frown. It's just a picture. The image is dark and blurry, and I can hardly make anything out. Then I realize what I'm looking at, and my stomach flips.

It's a picture of my house, taken from the lamplit street outside. But the shot is zoomed in, focused on a window—my bedroom window, with me leaning against the ledge in the clothes that I'm wearing right now.

My heart smacks in my chest.

The message alert pings again, but this time, it's just words.

I see you.

Friday, February 28

CASON

ALEC IS IN HIS RECLINER, and there's some DIY show playing on TV.

I toss my bag down and sink onto the couch. "We lost."

He pauses the TV. "Against who?"

"Bridgewater."

"Aw, bud," he says. "Next time, huh? Pull out the win."

I scuff the edge of the coffee table with my sneaker. "There were scouts watching."

"Next time," he says, outstretching his fist to mine. "You'll get your shot. Don't worry about that, kid."

We fall quiet, and he starts the TV up again.

I wait a couple of minutes before I speak. "We're playing Newport next." I try to make it sound casual, like hey, I just remembered. Just a casual mention. But the words came out too loud.

"Oh yeah?"

I thought about telling him weeks ago, as soon as the game was confirmed. But I talked myself out of it. Then I talked myself in.

Then out. I tap the arm of the couch, and Alec cranes his neck to look at me.

"Newport's a big game for you guys, right?"

"Yeah." I scratch at a tear in the leather.

"You beat them last year, didn't you?"

"No, we lost."

His lips twitch. "Well, this year you'd better win, eh?"

"Yeah. So it's Saturday after next if you want to come? Seven o'clock at Raleigh's."

"Sure, I'll—" He stops short. "Oh, buddy. I'm going to dinner with Thalia's sister and brother-in-law that night." He winces, the lines on his forehead denting.

I keep my expression even, like it doesn't matter. "No worries, man. It's not that big a game."

It's our biggest game. Newport is really good. East Coast scouts will be there, like they have been on and off all season, watching out for us. I catch their eyes in the stands sometimes and start sweating.

Alec drags a rough hand over his mouth. "I could try to rearrange," he says, still looking pained. "Let me call Thalia right now." He reaches for his cell.

"No." I stop him. "Come on, man. Don't do that. It's just a hockey game. Whatever."

He's fumbling, tripping over words, trying to explain himself. "Thalia's sister's only in town for the weekend. I've never met her. Apparently her husband's some big-shot banker in the city. Stocks and shares and all that."

"Man, you think he'll foot the bill?" I drum the heel of my hand on the frayed leather arm of the couch.

But Alec doesn't smile. "I'm sorry, buddy."

I wave my hand. "No worries. You better bring me back some leftovers, though."

He presses his lips together, looking all sorry for me. I hate that shit.

"So, what's this?" I ask, nodding toward the TV and the old guy in a hard hat examining a plywood shed.

"Next time," Alec says, not taking the hint, "count me in."

"Yeah."

"You know I'm in your corner, right?" he adds. "There's nothing I wouldn't do to make sure you get where you need to be. You know that?"

"I know."

"Next game, I'm going to be there." He salutes me, and I mirror it.

I don't bother telling him that Newport is the last game of the season.

My eyes stray to one of the framed photos of my mom on the mantel. It's funny, but my memories of her exist more in pictures than they do in my head. It makes me wonder if I've blocked her out, to protect myself or something. I wish I could apologize to her for that, because I swear, I'm not doing it on purpose. I want those memories back.

One thing I do remember is that she showed up to every junior league game I played. Sometimes she was the only person in the stands, cheering, clapping her hands, freezing her ass off.

When I play now, I pretend I can see her there. I pick some random person out of the crowd and squint my eyes just enough until they kind of look like her. I always play better when I pretend she's there.

"You okay, kid?" Alec asks, jolting me from my trance.

"Yeah, I'm good." I crack a smile. "So, meeting the family, eh? Never thought I'd see the day."

He looks uncomfortable, jerks his shoulders up and down a couple of times.

"Things are getting serious between you and Thalia?"

He thinks on it for a moment. "I'd say so."

"Are you going to marry her?"

"Maybe," he says, running a hand over his stubbled chin. "Maybe."

The question hangs over me. The elephant in the room. When Thalia moves in, do I move out? Does she want me here? Does *he* want me here?

I don't ask because I don't want to know the answer.

So I just keep my mouth shut and focus on the DIY show, watching the presenter get hyped over a drill bit.

My phone starts buzzing in my pocket, and I jump at the chance to get out of this room. Sadie's name lights up my screen.

"I'll be right back," I tell Alec.

He waves a hand as I head for the kitchen.

"Hey," I say into the phone.

"Hi."

I hear it in her voice right away, the tremor.

"What's up?"

When she responds, her words sound choked. "A couple of things. My parents want me to go live with my mom in the city. Staten Island."

"Oh." I sink into a seat at the table. "That's . . ." My heart slams in the worst way. Those words were like a sucker punch. I already lost her once; I don't want to do it again.

Her voice reaches me. "Something else happened too. I'm pretty shaken up, and I don't know what to do about it."

My breath stops. "What happened?"

"I don't know if I should tell my dad," she says slowly. "He's left for work already, but I could call him. But it'll just prove his point about sending me to live with my mom—"

"What happened?" I grip the phone tighter.

"I got a message from a number I don't recognize. It was a picture of me in my room, tonight, taken from the street outside my house."

And just like that, I'm on my feet. "You're kidding."

"No. There was a second text, as well. All it says is 'I see you.'"

I'm up, pacing around the small kitchen. The DIY show is still playing in the background, but I can hardly hear it because my blood is rushing in my ears. "You've got to take that to the police."

She goes quiet for a second.

"Sadie?"

"It's just someone trying to intimidate me, right? But it's not going to work. I'm not going to let them scare me away from my home, my friends. You," she whispers the final word.

I scrub my hand through my hair. "Sadie, this is serious. Someone's been outside your house. They know where you live."

"I'm not scared." I hear the kink of fear in her voice.

"You should be," I tell her, and my tone, the cut of my words, it makes her breathe differently. Faster.

Hell, I'm breathing faster too.

"If I take this to the police, they'll tell my dad for sure," she says. Then she sucks in a breath. "I bet it's Madison from the ACU women's hockey team. She knows I'm looking for her. In my DM, I gave my name and number. It has to be her, right?"

A dozen other possibilities run through my mind. The guys, Michel, Ruben, Finley. Any one of them could have taken a look through my phone and found her number. I always leave my cell in a locker during practice, and they all know my passcode.

Finley tapped out of the game before the final whistle tonight. He went to the locker room.

But Fin wouldn't do something like this. None of my friends would.

"Take the messages to the cops," I tell her. "Let them deal with it—"

"Cason, do you realize what this means?" she says, a breathiness to her voice. "We're on to something. If someone considers *me* to be enough of a problem to send me these messages, to find out where I live, surely it means they think I know something. I'm close to something."

"Yeah, that's not a good thing."

"But it is," she shoots back. "I need to talk to Madison. If she won't respond to my DM, I'll just have to show up at their practice tomorrow."

I press my palm on the cold counter, staring at the darkness beyond the kitchen window. The deceptive shadows of the night.

"Kai was murdered." My voice sounds scratchy. "Someone killed him."

She exhales in frustration. "Yes. And I'm a suspect. You are too."

Tension locks up my whole body. "I don't want what happened to him to happen to you."

She goes quiet.

"Sadie? Are you still there?"

While I wait for her response, my shoulders tighten. The window reflects my face back at me, distorting my features, shadows bruising me.

"I just need a minute to think this through," she says at last. "I'll talk to you later."

It's not the outcome I was hoping for. But it's better than nothing. The tension doesn't leave me, though.

"Are you okay?" I ask her.

"Yeah. Yeah, I'm fine." Nothing about her tone convinces me. "Bye, Cason."

"Bye, Sadie."

Friday, February 28

SADIE

AFTER MY CALL WITH CASON, all I can do is sit numbly on my bed with my phone still in my hand. *I see you. I see you. I see you.*

My heart is racing. Whatever lies I try to tell myself, I *am* scared.

I should be calling the police right now. I should be calling my dad, asking him to come home.

A pipe creaks somewhere within the walls, making me flinch.

"Stay calm," I tell myself, out loud. Because I need to hear the words.

All I have to do is think about this logically. There'd be no point in dragging Dad out of work *again*, worrying him, adding fuel to the already blazing fire. These texts were only meant to frighten me. If this person wanted to do something more, they would have done it already. Hiding behind an anonymous cell phone shows how cowardly they are.

This is going to be okay. Because it has to be.

A knock at the front door stops me cold. It's way too late for visitors.

I hold my breath as it comes again, louder this time.

Sliding off my bed, I head downstairs slowly, my cell gripped in my hand. Behind the frosted glass panel, a broad silhouette waits. A familiar figure.

"Cason?" I call, my fingers resting on the handle. "Is that you?"

"Yeah." His voice reaches me from the other side.

I flip the latch and swing the door open to the night. Beyond him, the lamplit road is quiet and striped with shadows.

"What are you doing here?"

"I took a look around," he says, and my stomach knots. "There's no one out here."

On the road, an arc of lamplight catches the tread pattern of tire marks. Just like the marks on the asphalt I noticed in the aftermath of Kai's death. And I wonder, was the car that screeched down the road just after midnight that night the same car that passed by my window tonight?

Cason follows me into the house, and I bolt the door behind him.

"You didn't have to come over," I tell him as we stand in the hallway. "I'm fine."

"I know." He presses his lips together, dimpling his cheeks. "But I wanted to check, to make sure."

"You could have put yourself in danger."

He half smiles. "I wasn't thinking that far ahead."

"Thank you for coming," I say quietly. Just him being here steadies me; even if I don't spell it out, I think he knows. Darcy Wilde's words about him come to mind—*dangerously impulsive*, she'd called him. Maybe there's nuance to that. "Did you tell your uncle you were coming here?"

"No. He doesn't even know I left the house." As we head upstairs to my room, Cason adds, "But you need to be honest with your dad about these messages. He needs to know what's going on."

We slip into my room, and I heave a sigh as I sink onto my bed. "I don't know. I don't want to overreact."

He frowns. "I think you're *under*reacting."

"I'm not. Trust me, I'm taking this seriously."

"Then why aren't you calling the cops?"

I press my palms together. "Okay, look. We know the ACU women's team trains on Saturday mornings at ten, that's what it said on the roster sheet. We could show up tomorrow and confront Madison about this. We don't even need to get the police involved. It's too coincidental that I left my number for Madison and then was sent anonymous texts that same night."

"But you're not going to achieve anything by ambushing her."

I purse my lips.

"If you really think Madison is behind this, then tell that to the police," he adds.

"I know I should, but . . ."

He sits beside me on the bed. "I get why you don't want your dad finding out about this. But someone's been outside your house." The muscles in his jaw twitch and he shakes his head. "You can't keep this to yourself."

My gaze wanders to the window and the darkness beyond the pane. Everything he's saying makes sense.

"What do you think?" he nudges.

"Okay," I answer at last.

"Okay? You'll report it?"

"Tomorrow."

His shoulders relax as I huddle closer to him. When I kiss him, though, it catches him off guard, and he hesitates.

But I just want to forget about tonight. In this moment, I can pretend, just for a little while, that everything is fine. Everything is going to be okay.

So I lean into him, letting the warmth of his body draw me in. When our lips meet again, I lose myself in it. The world around us fades, leaving only the heat between us, and I disappear into a reality that isn't this.

AUDIO FILE_MP3

TITLE: CASE_339KH_SADIE MORELLI INTERVIEW

Good morning, Sadie. You requested to speak with me today?

Yes. Hi. Good morning, Detective Alanis.

I understand you have some concerns? Why don't you talk me through what's going on?

Okay, so maybe this is nothing, but last night I got a text message from an anonymous number. Two messages, actually. Here.

(PAUSE.) For the purpose of the tape, Miss Morelli is showing me two messages displayed on a cell phone. Your cell phone, I presume?

Yes.

The text reads, "I see you." And there's a picture of . . .

Me. In my room. Taken from the street outside. I know it was taken last night, because those are the clothes I was wearing.

Right. And you have no idea who sent these?

No. Well, there's this girl, Madison. She plays for the Arcadia City University women's hockey team. It might not be her, of course. It might have nothing to do with her. But I gave her my number, hoping she'd call me about Kai.

Why did you want to talk to her about Kai Harrison?

Because I think she might have dated him. Or almost dated him, I'm not sure.

(PAUSE.) Sadie, I noticed you came into the precinct today with Cason Tano.

(PAUSE.) Yes.

You previously mentioned that you have a close friendship with Kai Harrison's former girlfriend, Quinn McKinley. Is that correct?

Yes, she's my best friend.

Sadie, are you aware that someone has been texting Quinn from an unregistered number for some weeks? Someone presumed to be Cason Tano?

Yes, but it wasn't Cason. Quinn was catfished by someone* pretending *to be Cason.

Right.

Cason wasn't the person who messaged me last night, if that's what you're thinking.

Sadie, how well do you really know Cason Tano?

I know him very well. And I know that these threatening messages aren't from him. He wasn't the person texting Quinn either.

I see. When we first interviewed you on February 22, you neglected to mention that Cason was on the 11:20 Hailing train on the night of Kai's murder. If you claim to know him, how did you not notice him among the few people disembarking that evening?

No, but . . . well, maybe he was on the train. I just wasn't . . . I was in shock, confused.

I see. Did Cason influence your decision to not mention him?

No. It's not . . . I mean, Cason didn't do anything. It's Madison. It has to be Madison. She goes to ACU, she's friends with Ava Kavanaugh, and she met Kai at a party about a month back.

Okay. Thank you for this information, we'll look into it.

But . . .

If you think of anything else—anything you might want to share with us about Cason, perhaps—please come back as soon as possible.

Saturday, March 1

SADIE

MY THICK COAT IS PULLED around me, shielding me from the fierce wind. The weather is buck wild today, and Arcadia is busy with Saturday crowds and traffic. But I hardly notice any of it.

Cason and I leave the train station and begin down the busy street.

"I just fell apart in that interview room," I mutter, gnawing on my thumbnail. "Detective Alanis was asking me questions, and I just fell apart. I'm scared I've made everything so much worse. For you," I add quietly.

"It's okay," he reassures me. "You did the right thing reporting those messages."

"But they weren't even taking it seriously. They think it's . . ." I swallow before I can say, "They think it's you."

His jaw tics. "You did the right thing."

We head away from the bustling train station, and my eyes land on Raleigh's gray building across the street, with its weather-worn sign on the front facade, illustrated with the logo of a silver-accented pair of ice skates.

"Are you sure you want to do this?" Cason asks, noticing my hesitation.

I breathe steadily. "We have to take this chance. Madison and her team will still be on the ice." I don't wait for his response. I pace quickly across the street toward Raleigh's.

Cason lopes alongside me.

The drop in air temperature hits me as soon as we step into the arena, and a shiver crawls down my spine. It was cold outside, but in here it's bitter. The sound of skates slashing across the ice and teammates yelling back and forth echoes through the empty stands. The ACU team is at the far end of the rink, gliding over the ice as they battle for control of the puck.

Cason and I swap a glance before taking a seat on the bleachers. I study the team, trying to pinpoint Madison in her helmet and kit.

When their practice draws to an end, the players gather at the edge of the rink, flushed and out of breath.

I stand, my hands knotted in front of me, and Cason follows my lead.

"Excuse me, Madison," I call as the girls glide past, taking off their helmets as they head for the changing rooms.

One of them turns, blond bangs clinging to her damp brow. She frowns for a second before a look of recognition crosses her face. Reluctantly, she skates toward the barrier.

"Can I help you with something?" She looks like she's forcing a smile, her bright blue eyes sparkling beneath the arena lights.

Adrenaline spikes through me. It *is* her—I'm certain of it. The girl from Hannah's photo, the lipstick stain on Kai's throat. Quinn had me analyze that picture so many times, and now I'm mad at myself for not recognizing her sooner. The birthmark on her temple, the tiny gap between her front teeth, it's all there. "I've been trying to contact you," I forge on. "I was hoping we could talk."

She keeps her expression amiable. "I'm sorry, do I know you?"

"No, but you dated my friend Kai Harrison."

Her pleasant smile falters.

"My name's Sadie," I add. "You might have seen my DM on the ACU women's hockey account. I left my number for you to call."

She glances over her shoulder as the rest of her team disappears into the locker room. "Okay, I don't know what you've been told, but I didn't date . . ." She lowers her voice when she says his name. "Kai. We hung out once."

Next to me, Cason shifts and the bench creaks. She admitted it.

"I heard about what happened to him," she adds.

"Were you and Kai still in contact when he died?"

She double-takes. "No. God, no. It's so sad about what happened, though."

"He liked you."

Her eyebrows shoot up in surprise. "He did?"

"What, you didn't think so?"

"Honestly, no. He seemed way too obsessed with his ex. All my friends were like, Maddie, don't even go there. But I gave him a shot, and then he ghosted me."

I stare back at her, thrown by her words. "Wait. Kai was obsessing over his ex? Quinn?"

"Yeah." She leans against the ledge, swiping loose strands of hair from her face. "He was pretty drunk when I met him, and he got a little intense. He was talking about this girl Quinn, saying, 'I can't get over it. I'm never going to get over this, I don't know how she can.' You know, all that still-in-love-with-the-ex kind of talk."

My brow knits. "Kai said those things about Quinn? That *she* was over it? Because Quinn was definitely *not* over it."

Madison just shrugs.

"When was this?"

"A few weeks ago, I guess." She checks over her shoulder again. The rink is abandoned. All her teammates are gone; the locker room door is long closed behind them. "Anyway," she says, "I'd better go. Sorry again about what happened to Kai."

She moves to skate away, but I stop her.

"Did you tell the police this?"

She halts and stares at me for a moment. Her eyes sweep over Cason too. "Did I tell the police about what?"

"That you dated Kai. Because friends and family have been asked to come forward, so I'm just wondering if you told the police that you were dating him right before he died."

She lifts her chin. "I don't see how that's any of your business."

"If you've got nothing to hide . . ."

"I don't have anything to hide." Her eyes narrow, and what remains of her smile vanishes completely. "I don't appreciate the insinuation, either."

"You texted me last night, didn't you? You took a picture of my house."

A look of confusion crinkles her forehead. "I think you're mistaking me for someone else."

I glance at Cason, and he shakes his head. But I can't give up now. "Why keep this from the police if you've got nothing to hide?"

"Not that it's any of your business," she interrupts, "but I have spoken to the police."

"Did they ask you where you were on the night of Kai's murder?"

She splutters out an angry laugh. "This is ridiculous."

"Did you see the picture that your friend Ava Kavanaugh posted?" I carry on, keeping my cool. "Did you see Kai at the station with Quinn and drive to Hailing to confront him? Because he chose her over you?"

Madison's jaw drops. "Oh my god. You are out of your mind."

"Sadie," Cason says under his breath. He touches my arm, urging me to stop.

But I can't. I've shown all my cards now, and I won't get this chance again. "Where were you that night, Madison?"

She folds her arms. "I was working at Sierra's Restaurant on the night that it happened," she says through her teeth. "I have plenty of witnesses to back that up. Now leave me the hell alone before I call the police on you. Stalking is a federal offense."

And with that, she's gone.

Saturday, March 1

SADIE

CASON AND I SIT ON the sidewalk opposite Raleigh's. Rain has started to fall, spattering the pavement.

"She might be lying," I murmur.

"She has an alibi," Cason says, running his hand over his mouth. "The police would have checked that out."

I purse my lips. "Unless . . ."

"I don't think it's her, Sadie. I really don't."

My shoulders sag. I didn't realize how disappointed I'd be to rule out Madison's involvement. But it's knocked me. I thought I had a solid lead, something that I could tie up. And for a moment, it had almost felt reassuring, less scary, to believe I'd unmasked the culprit. Turns out, my judgment was wrong. If I'm this far off the mark, how can I trust myself to build a future in this field?

I take a deep breath. "Okay," I say to Cason, "so if it isn't Madison, that leaves who?"

He glances across the street to where Raleigh's stands behind a mist of rain. When he turns back to me, I see the conflict in his eyes. I can feel the words he doesn't want to say.

"One of the Hailing boys," I hedge. "We're back to that? One of them came to the station to confront Kai?"

He doesn't answer. He doesn't have to.

I sigh into the damp breeze. "It's weird. After everything that's happened here, I should want to get as far away from this place as possible."

He locks his broad hands in front of him.

"But I don't. I don't want to leave."

"I don't want you to leave either." The clouds darken above us, and I lean into him.

"This past month has been a lot, hasn't it?" I say as I watch the raindrops form a pool on the ground. "The fight, Kai's death, everything that's happened at school. The way people are treating us like suspects. I hate it."

He falls quiet for a moment. "We trust each other," he says at last. "That's all that matters."

"Yeah," I whisper.

"There's no proof, anyway." When I frown, he adds, "Because we didn't do it. There's no proof."

"Right."

"The cops haven't even found the murder weapon."

I hesitate before responding. "If the murderer left a weapon to find."

From what I've read, the type of weapon used in an assault is often a focal point in criminological study. Accessibly, environmental context, demography. A hunting knife would likely point to a hunter, just like, say, a hockey stick, would point to a hockey player.

"Are you okay?" Cason's voice pulls me back, grounding me.

"Yeah. Sorry, I was just thinking."

"Do you want to go home?" he asks.

"Yeah."

The rain is getting heavier, dampening our hair and clothes. As we head into the shelter of the train station, a thought strikes me: Maybe I've been searching for leads in all the wrong places. Instead of chasing motives, I should have been focused on uncovering the evidence.

Because most of the time, the perpetrator leaves a trail.

TIKTOK

DARCY WILDE

@WILDEONCRIME

Season 19, Episode 5 #truecrime #forensic #fyp #HailingNY #JusticeforKai

There's one element of the Kai Harrison case that's been nagging at me. Something that the police ruled out early on, but I'm not so sure it should have been dismissed so quickly.

We know Kai Harrison played in a Hailing-Arcadia hockey game on Friday, January 24. That game ended in an altercation where police were called to the scene. That same night, there was a hit-and-run on the byway between Hailing and Arcadia, reported shortly after the fight broke up. A local construction worker named Jon Reese died, and the driver was never identified. And it makes me wonder . . . there could be a connection here, right? The timings are just too close to overlook, especially when you add in riled-up teenagers with brand-new driver's licenses.

Listen, guys, working in this business for as long as I have, these synchronicities often connect the dots. A murder needs a motive. Kai Harrison wasn't robbed, he still had his cell, his keys, everything. So why was he murdered? What's the motive, you guys? That's what I'm stuck on. The girls in the photo, I don't know if that's enough for me. C.T. and S.M. together, maybe. But throw in a hit-and-run, and bam, you've got yourselves a motive.

Friday, March 7

CASON

RIP. IT'S STILL CARVED ON the bench in Raleigh's locker room.

"Let's go, let's go," Larsen shouts, slapping his hands together. "Hustle. Get out on the ice. Only one week until we face Newport." He gestures for the others to leave, but when I move to pass him, he stops me.

"You okay?" he asks under his breath.

I nod.

He lifts his finger, signaling for me to stay, waiting until everyone else has left the locker room before he says, "I don't buy it. All week, I've noticed you walking around school on your own, looking like a lost dog. What is it, fallen out with the boys? Girlfriend troubles? All of the above?"

My focus drops to the damp floor tiles. "No. I'm good. Just tired." *Tired of all of it.* The words are trying to edge out. I want to say that I'm tired of being doubted. Tired of not being able to protect the people I care about. Tired of *losing* the people I care about. To death. To Staten Island. To a jail cell, maybe.

It almost makes me laugh, because I must be pretty close to rock-bottom if I'm legit considering pouring my heart out to Larsen.

"I know you're lying," he says, and I stiffen. Then he adds, "I know you're not okay. You've been different these past couple of weeks. You're not the same kid who gave me hell all season." He attempts a smile. Then he glances around the empty changing room, where the steady drip of a leaking shower echoes. "If there's something . . ." He pauses and drags a hand over his sharp jaw. "Cason, if there's anything you want to talk about, disclose—"

"No," I say it too fast. "No, there's nothing."

"Okay." He lifts his hands. "Okay. You don't have to tell me," he says, clapping my shoulder. "Maybe I don't need to know. But whatever it is, whatever's messing with your head right now, leave it in here. Okay?" He grips my shoulder over the padding. "Game face. Yes?"

"Yeah," I mutter.

"You've got this."

I work my lip between my teeth.

"Focus on what is within your control. Stoic principle," he says, and when I frown, he adds with a quick grin, "Sorry. Former philosophy major."

"You studied philosophy at ACU?"

"All four years. Believe it or not, I have a life outside of hockey." He slaps my shoulder again. "But not tonight. Now let's get out there." He tosses his gym bag into the nearest locker, and I notice something on his wrist. A flash of something striped red-and-white. A silver *S* charm hanging from it.

He turns his back to me for a moment, but I see when he tosses the hair tie into his locker with his bag and punches in the combination code. I watch as the metal door clicks shut. And I repeat the code over in my mind.

"Get out there," he says, nodding toward the exit. "Game face, remember?"

"Yeah. Just a second." I jog to my own locker, acting like I forgot something. While Larsen waits at the door, holding it ajar for me, I reach into my locker and fumble out a quick text.

I hit send, and the metal door clangs shut. Then I put my game face on and pretend like nothing happened.

AUDIO FILE_MP3

TITLE: CASE_339KH_ZACH LARSEN INTERVIEW

Good morning, Mr. Larsen. Thank you for speaking with us today. My name is Detective Alanis, and this is my colleague Detective Sampson.

Hi. How can I be of help?

We're investigating an incident that happened in Hailing over the weekend, resulting in the death of a young male from Arcadia. Kai Harrison. Is this name familiar to you?

Yes. Yes, I'm so sorry to hear this. He played center for the Arcadia High School team. I know them well.

Right. In line with our investigation, we're following up on an altercation that happened on January 24 outside Raleigh's Rec Center. I understand you were supervising the Hailing High School hockey students that evening, and you witnessed the incident I'm referring to?

Yes. Myself and the Arcadia coach, Richard Johnson.

Could you help us understand the motivation behind this fight, how it happened, from your perspective?

Our two teams had just come from the game, and there'd been some problems on the ice, questions around players' conduct, that sort of thing. One of my boys, Cason Tano, flagged Kai Harrison for a foul that wasn't caught by the ref.

Are you suggesting this was the instigating moment that led to the fight that evening?

I believe so, yes.

You mentioned your student Cason Tano. Did you witness him assaulting Kai Harrison that night?

(PAUSE.) Yes. Yes, unfortunately I did. He followed Kai Harrison outside.

I see. Can you tell us a little about your own experience with Tano? As his teacher, how would you describe his character?

Wow, okay. Okay. He is one of my more challenging students. He can be great, he has a lot of potential, but he can also be quick-tempered, and I have known him to be destructive and aggressive at times. On and off the ice.

Could you give some specifics here, please?

(PAUSE.) A few months ago, I did have to confiscate a knife that I found in his possession. He'd been using it to deface a bench in Raleigh's locker room. I believe he could have used the knife on a fellow teammate had I not intervened when I did.

Right. I see. Was this reported?

No. I made the call not to escalate it on this occasion. He's a good kid, most of the time. But I think he needs intervention that stretches beyond my capabilities as his coach. As much as I've tried to reach him, he's not receptive.

Are you saying you have concerns for Cason Tano's behavior and stability?

Yes. I believe that he's a risk to himself and others. Yes. From what I've observed, he's dangerous.

CASON

Locker 3 combination 9965 hair tie looks like one you and Quinn have. My coach wearing it on wrist. He studied philosophy. We are on ice until 9.

Friday, March 7

SADIE

IT'S 8:45.

My eyes move fast over Cason's message, making sense of the words. I drop the cleaning rag onto the booth table in the diner. Beyond the glass wall, the Hailing team is still on the ice, soundtracked by muffled shouts and clashing sticks. But I've only just checked my phone.

"Maya!" I call. "Do you mind if I leave early tonight?"

Over at the counter, she glances up. "What?" She checks the time on the red wall clock behind her. "You mean right now?"

"I don't feel so good." I hurry to the counter with the cleaning rag, already untangling myself from my apron. The diner is empty, and since Raleigh's is quiet tonight, Maya was planning on closing soon, anyway.

"Honey." Her brow creases, and she reaches out to touch my arm. "Are you okay?"

"Yeah. I'll be fine." I grab my jacket from behind the counter. "Is it okay if I leave?"

"Sure. I mean, I'll probably call it a night around now too. Do you need a ride home?"

"No, thanks," I call over my shoulder, practically tripping over myself to get out the door. "I'll catch the train, and I'll work the time back."

I don't hear Maya's response. The door closes behind me, and I race through the squeaky corridor toward the stairwell. My breath escapes in quick rasps as I hurry down the stairs, my hand skimming the rail.

I sprint to the boys' locker room with my heart racing. In the silence of the empty corridor, I push the door and take stock of the damp shower room.

I hurry through the numbers marked on the rows of metal doors, and I find locker number three. Shaking, I grapple with the combination Cason sent me. The latch clicks open, and I start rummaging around the shelves. A bag, a padded jacket, a cell phone . . . and a small red-and-white striped hair tie with a tiny silver *S* charm hanging from the band. Identical to the hair tie that I wear on my wrist. Only mine has a tiny silver *Q*, for Quinn. *Quinn* has the *S* for Sadie.

I slip the *S* band onto my wrist alongside my own before leaving the room.

Out in the hallway, the boys are coming in from the ice, with their coach leading the way. When his eyes land on me, he gives me a strange look, and my heart stops.

"Excuse me," I say, sidling past him. Heat flushes my cheeks as his gaze wanders to the boys' locker room door behind me. "Just looking for a bathroom." The stammer in my voice betrays me, and I sense his stare on my back as I pace toward the stairwell.

I duck out of sight and hurry upstairs.

The *Sorry, We're Closed!* sign is hanging from the diner's door and the lights are off. Looks like Maya already locked up, and there's no sign of her or Joey.

I grip my phone tightly as I pace back to the stairwell. Taking a seat on the top step, I type a response to Cason's last message.

Got it and I'm out. He saw me leaving the locker room, though.

As soon as Cason gives me the all-clear, I'll sneak downstairs. The last thing I want is for their coach to see me again, especially if he notices that the hair tie is missing from his locker.

But the Hailing boys always take the 9:30 train after practice, so all I have to do is wait right here until they're gone.

Drawing in a shaky breath, I call Quinn.

"Hey," she answers.

"Quinn, why does the Hailing hockey coach have your friendship bracelet?"

There's a beat of silence, and I hold my phone a little tighter.

I hear her move, the background noise around her becoming quieter. Her voice is lower now. *"What?"*

"Cason caught him wearing it on his wrist."

"Are you sure it's mine?"

I twist my wrist, rolling the tiny *S* charm between my thumb and forefinger. "Yes, this is too weird to be a coincidence. Did you give it to him?"

"No!" she cries. "Ew, of course not. It went missing a couple of weeks ago, I thought I lost it."

"Maybe you lost it at Raleigh's?"

"And he picked it up? But why?"

"That's not all—he studied philosophy, like the guy in the texts. If he's the person who's been texting you, pretending to be Cason, maybe he's stalking you. We met him that night in the diner, when you joined the Hailing boys' table. He sat down next to you and Ruben, remember?"

While Cason and I hashed out our differences that night, Quinn had joined the others at their table. Their coach kept looking at Quinn from the edge of the booth. I had seen it. But I hadn't thought anything of it at the time.

"Oh my god," Quinn whispers.

It makes me think of the car that drove past my house, and the anonymous text messages that followed. *I see you.* Cason leaves his phone in the locker room during practice. Their coach could have taken it while the boys were on the ice and found my number, just like I took the hair tie. He could have told them he had to step out for a moment. As simple as that.

Right before I got those anonymous messages, I'd been with Cason, with his team at the train station. I'd been throwing out theories that Larsen could have easily overheard.

"The car tires outside my house," I say to Quinn, "on the night that Kai was murdered . . ."

"*Shit*," she hisses. "You think it was him?"

"Hold on." Keeping Quinn on the line, I open Ava Kavanaugh's Instagram account. I click on her followers list and start scrolling.

I spent so much time looking for Kai's mystery ACU girl,

I never thought to look for other people who might've known him. "Larsen graduated last year, in Maya's class," I remind Quinn. "Maya knew him—she chatted with him at the bar after the Arcadia game. Maya knew Ava Kavanaugh too; she said they had mutual friends. So, what if Larsen and Ava know each other? Larsen saw Ava's picture, with Kai and us in a standoff or whatever, so he came down to the station to protect you or something."

I hear Quinn's fast breaths down the line, but I'm working fast through @AvaKava's followers list, until I see it. @ZLarsy_beastmode. Zach Larsen. I remember his name from the press statement he gave with Coach Johnson, after the fight that broke out between the two schools.

I select his profile, and my breath falters. "It's him. He follows Ava Kavanaugh."

Quinn's voice comes out quickly, almost frantic. "Sadie, where are you?"

All of a sudden, the stairwell lights cut out, and my stomach flips as I'm plunged into blackness.

It's okay, I tell myself in the darkness. *It's okay, it's just the building shutting down for the night.* Sometimes Maya or the maintenance guy will lock up early once the diner closes and the rink is empty. But panic still spikes through me.

I check the time on my cell . . . 9:31.

"Quinn, I've got to go." I don't wait for her response; I end the call and race down the stairs. The last thing I need is to get locked inside Raleigh's after hours. I'll go to the platform and wait for the next train. As long as the Hailing team got onto the 9:30, I'll be safe at the station.

I burst through the stairwell door and into the corridor. Everything's quiet and the lights are all out, but there's a soft glow coming from the safety trip hazards lining a path to the exit. Farther along the hallway, the rink is closed, and I can just about hear the hum of the cooling system beyond its heavy doors.

At the other end of the corridor, the lobby is empty, and glass doors lead out to the dim parking lot. Someone is outside, locking up for the night.

"Wait!" I call, breaking into a run. Whatever happens, I can't get stuck in here overnight. To my relief, the person outside stops, and the door opens.

But my heart smacks in my chest when I realize who's on the other side.

Zach Larsen steps into the lobby and closes the door behind him.

Frozen in fear, all I can do is stare as he twists the lock and the latch snaps shut.

Friday, March 7

CASON

THE TRAIN DOORS SHUT WITH the heavy click of the mechanism. Up and down the aisle, the guys are taking their seats, but I stay standing, checking the faces as the train moves forward, clacking over the tracks beneath us.

I can't see her.

Voices buzz around me, and I head for the next car. The windows are fogged against the black night. It's started to rain, drops streaking down the glass and leaving trails. I jog through the aisles, searching for a sign of her. Row after row of people in plastic seats, staring out the window or down at their phones.

I check Sadie's last message. Got it and I'm out. He saw me leaving the locker room, though.

I type out a reply. I'm on the train. I can't find you.

She said she was out, so she's got to be on this train. Unless she caught a ride home.

I head back to the car where the guys are sitting. Ducking through the dividing door, I drop into the empty spot next to Michel.

"Have you seen Sadie?"

He sits higher, looking over my head, peering into the chaos of the train car where everyone's talking about practice and strategizing for the Newport game. "Nope," he says. "Why?"

I lower my voice. "Okay, I gotta tell you what I saw earlier." I glance over my shoulder. Larsen can't hear me talking about this. My eyes move over everyone. Ruben, Finley, Ty, Hudson . . .

I turn back to Michel. "Where's Larsen at?"

"I don't know, he wasn't on the platform."

My breath stalls. "What do you mean, he wasn't on the platform? He didn't catch the train with us?"

"I don't know," Michel says with a half laugh. "I'm not checking for Larsen, bro."

"No," I murmur. "No, no, no. She said, 'I'm out.' Out of the *locker room*, not out of Raleigh's."

"What's up?" Michel's thick eyebrows pull together. "What's going on?"

I'm not listening. My phone is in my hand, and I'm trying to call Sadie, but we're in a dead zone and my cell won't connect.

I jump to my feet as the city shoots by outside and we head farther and farther out of Arcadia. The wind and rain drown out the screech of the train on the tracks.

There's nothing I can do but leave her behind.

Friday, March 7

SADIE

"HI THERE. IT'S SADIE, RIGHT?"

Zach Larsen's voice sounds too loud in the eerie calm of Raleigh's locked building. His face is warped in the shadows cast by the soft trip lights.

"Yes," I manage. "Where's Maya?"

"Oh, she's gone." He glances over his shoulder. "I told her I'd lock up for her tonight."

"Okay. Would you mind opening the door, please? My friends are waiting for me." He's blocking the exit. Through the glass doors behind him, the dimly lit parking lot stretches beyond, and the single streetlamp exposes the emptiness. No more parked cars. No more people. We're alone.

"Sure." Larsen slips the keys into his pocket, and I swallow as he steps closer to me. "Just a second, though."

Adrenaline courses through me, and fight-or-flight instinct kicks in. I take my chance and race past him, grabbing the push handle on the exit and shaking it. When it doesn't budge, I start banging on the glass, slapping it with my palms, anything I can think to do in the blur of my fear.

Darcy Wilde's words tumble through my mind. *Some of my top tips. Stay calm, make noise, know your exits.*

I spin around to face Larsen. His expression is fixed somewhere between a smirk and a scowl. Shadows are still striping his face, hollowing his cheeks.

"Why were you in the boys' locker room earlier?" he asks coolly. "Lost your way?"

"I told you, I was looking for a bathroom."

He tilts his head and runs a gloved hand over his angular chin. Then his attention lands on my wrist, and the tiny *S* charm hanging from the hair tie.

I steal another glance at the doors, catching my ghostly reflection mirrored off the glass.

"Listen, Sadie." He says my name with a bite. "Whatever you think you've figured out—"

"Quinn is my best friend, and you've been stalking her."

The muscles in his face tic. "Okay. Whatever fantastical ideas you've got brewing, I'm sorry to shut it down, but I've never met your friend."

"She told me everything," I bluff, and he falters. "She told me you've been messaging her. She knows it's you." His face falls, and my heart start beating triple-time. His expression says it all.

He moves toward me, and I think fast, taking a breath before I slip past him, edging farther into the lobby. Farther away from the exit. He closes the space between us, following me step for step.

"The police already have you on their radar," I press on. "If you don't let me out of here, they'll know that I was last seen here. *You* were last seen here. Everyone knows what you did. To Quinn, to Kai—"

He chokes out a breath.

"Because you did it, didn't you? You killed Kai. You're infatuated with Quinn, and when you saw the picture posted on Ava Kavanaugh's account, you came to the station to defend her. Because you thought Kai would hurt her. And the police are just biding their time until they've got enough evidence to tie this up."

"Oh, is that so?" His thin lips quirk. "I guess I've got nothing left to lose, then, have I?" He takes another step toward me.

But I don't move. I don't back away. Even though my every instinct is telling me to run, I can't. I'm in the perfect spot here.

"You wanna know what I think?" he whispers, leaning close enough for me to feel his hot breath on my neck. "I think you're lying." He runs a strand of my hair through his fingers, making me flinch. "I'm calling your bluff, princess. Because I think the police have got their eye on Cason, and you and him are getting antsy. I've seen you two running around together, tossing out your theories, trying to get yourselves off the chopping block. Not going to happen."

"But Quinn knows it was you messaging her, not Cason. She knows you're obsessed with her."

"Maybe. So what if I am?"

"You lied to her, pretended to be a high school student," I say, swallowing my fear. "Why? Because she's a sixteen-year-old minor? You'd lose your job, maybe end up in jail. Is that why you used the burner? Or was it because you knew she'd never be interested in someone like you?"

He grimaces, so I keep going. "You killed Kai, didn't you?"

"Did I?" he says with a frown. "That's strange, because Cason left evidence all over the place. He left DNA all over the murder weapon. The police just have to find it. Maybe they'll receive an anonymous tip telling them exactly where to look."

My heart thuds slowly. "You're setting him up?"

His eyes harden. "Someone has to take the fall. Cason is believable. He's violent and impulsive, and everyone knows it."

Impulsive. "You're Darcy Wilde's source?" I whisper.

This time he doesn't answer. But his lips twitch.

"Cason doesn't deserve this," I murmur.

His expression pulls into a sneer, hateful. "Oh yeah? He starts fights, breaks my rules, makes it seem like I can't control my own team." His chest heaves with frustration, and I shrink back. "He reminds me of this guy I played with in high school. Total asshole. Made it to the NHL and stole my shot. That should have been me." He scowls, like he's lost in the past, haunted by a memory. "That guy caught my leg with his stick right before a major game, screwed everything for me, then went on to have *my* career."

"I'm sorry that happened to you," I say weakly. "But that wasn't Cason."

He whips around, punching the vending machine beside us, rattling the glass and making me jump. "It might as well be," he spits. "Guys like that are all the same, they deserve to get humbled. Better him than Quinn, anyway."

All I can do is stare back at him, stunned.

In that split-second pause, he snatches my phone out of my hand. "Oh, look at that," he says, laughing to himself. "Your boy's texted. 'I'm on the train. I can't find you,'" he reads aloud from my screen. "We'd better write him back, let him know you're home safe and sound." He dangles my phone over my head, just out of reach, then he pulls it close to his chest, slips off his glove, and starts typing. "'I'm at home, call you tomorrow.' How does that sound? When the police check this, they're going to think he sent it himself to cover his ass. Just like he sent all those messages to Quinn on an unregistered cell. Tracks, right?"

My stomach turns. "Why did you kill Kai?"

"For Quinn," he says, shadows twisting his expression into a cruel grin. "Unfortunately, though, I've got to deal with the clean-up."

He swipes the phone across his sleeve, erasing the fingerprints before tossing it aside. Then, pulling on his glove, he lunges forward and grabs my arm, his grip so tight that I wince in pain.

And the words keep spinning through my mind. *Stay calm, make noise, know your exits—and guys, if you're going into a potentially unsafe environment alone, just make sure you let people know where you are.*

Friday, March 7

CASON

"IT'S LARSEN!" I'M SHOUTING, TELLING anyone who'll listen. "Larsen killed Kai Harrison."

Michel's up on his feet too, following me along the aisle. We're nearing the Hailing stop, and the train is slowing. Even before it's reached a standstill, I'm hitting the exit button, trying to get the doors to open. "We've got to get back to Raleigh's."

The guys are all looking at each other like they're checking if they're supposed to jump up with me, or if it's just me, if I'm losing it.

The electric doors click open, and I'm out on the platform. Rain hammers the shelter and the Hailing Station signpost creaks in the wet gale.

Michel follows after me, with Finley and Ruben close behind. Some of the other guys hover for a minute, waiting, and some just keep walking.

"So we're going back to Arcadia?" Michel asks, glancing at his watch. "To find Larsen? You think he's still there?"

"Sadie's still there." My phone buzzes in my hand, and I use my sleeve to scrub the raindrops off the screen.

I'm at home, call you tomorrow.

I frown at the text. "Wait. She's home."

Ruben musses his hair, shaking off the rain. "So we're not going back to Arcadia, or we are?"

I read the message again, then glance between them. "I don't know."

Ruben rolls his eyes, and Finley twitches. The guys who'd made a half-hearted attempt at hanging around have started to fall away, until it's just the four of us left. Us again, just like on the night of the fight.

The downpour is getting heavier, and the wind is getting wilder, bowing the trees and tearing through the platform.

"Hang on," Michel says, squinting in the rain. "I'm confused. Why do you think it's Larsen?"

"Because it is."

They side-eye each other.

"He had Quinn McKinley's hair tie thing on his wrist," I add. "Should I call the cops?"

"I don't know, man," Ruben says, rubbing his forehead. "What, you're going tell them that our coach was wearing some girl's hair thing on his wrist? I don't think the cops need to be involved in that."

"Not *some girl's*. Quinn's."

"Is it possible you're getting paranoid?" Michel asks.

Ruben's eyebrows shoot up. "Wait. Are we pinning this on Larsen now? Because I could be down with that." He's grinning like this is a joke, like I just feel like pinning a murder on Larsen.

I fumble with my phone, trying Sadie's number again, but it rings out. "She's not picking up."

"Maybe she's trying to swerve all of this," Ruben says, waving his hand in my direction. "I would."

"So we're *not* going back to Arcadia?" Michel checks, shielding his face from the rain.

I can't answer.

Ruben flips his hood. "Okay, I'm out." He starts walking away, holding up a peace sign. "Call the cops about the hair thing tomorrow, Case!" he hollers over his shoulder. "Later, boys."

Finley shrugs at me before following Ruben.

"And then there were two," Michel says, watching them leave. He brings his focus back to me. "Call it. Are we going home?"

I know I have to answer this time. "Yeah." My voice sounds scratchy. "Yeah, okay."

Michel hitches his backpack and starts walking.

I follow him down the steps and onto the sidewalk. My eyes stray to Sadie's place across the street. All the lights are out, and her dad's car isn't in the driveway.

I clap Michel's shoulder. "I'll catch up with you later. I'm going to swing by Sadie's place."

He nods. "Drop me a text tomorrow. We can watch out for Larsen, okay?"

"Yeah."

He jogs down the lamplit street, rain misting the pools of light. Alone, I make my way to Sadie's house and rap on the door.

Nothing. No lights, no sound of footsteps on the other side.

But she texted me. *I'm at home, call you tomorrow.*

I try her cell again.

No answer.

Okay, so maybe I am too much, people tell me that all the time. She's probably trying to sleep, and I'm not getting the hint. But across the road, a train rumbles in the distance. The last train to Arcadia.

I rub the nape of my neck, my eyes jumping between the dark house and the glaring light of the train careering along the tracks toward the platform.

If she isn't home, then where is she?

Friday, March 7

SADIE

STAY CALM AND MAKE NOISE.

Zach Larsen's grip tightens on my arm, his gloved fingers digging into my flesh.

"Help!" I scream as he yanks me farther into Raleigh's hallway, away from the lobby and exit.

"There's no point calling for help," he spits through his teeth. "Everyone's gone. No one's going to hear you from in here."

I stumble as he tries to pull me toward the rink. "What are you going to do to me?"

"*I'm* not going to do anything. It's Cason, remember? You're probably going to have a little slip on the ice, that's all. Nothing too complicated."

The realization knocks the breath from me. He's going to kill me and frame Cason.

"Y-You'll get caught," I stammer.

"It's the chance I've got to take. I can't let you leave here tonight and run your mouth."

"I won't tell anyone. Please, you can't do this."

But he just laughs, sharp and humorless.

Stay calm, make noise, know your exits.

My eyes move fast, scanning the low-lit corridor and the lobby that he's dragging me away from. And the glistening red fire extinguisher attached to the wall.

In a snap decision, I drive the heel of my hand into Larsen's throat, and he coughs and splutters, gripping his neck. The moment he releases his hold on my arm, I run, bolting toward the lobby. My heart gallops in my chest as I reach for the heavy fire extinguisher and wrench it from the wall.

With one last effort, I launch the fire extinguisher as hard as I can at the locked exit doors. Glass shatters, exploding into glistening fragments, and I cover my face with my arms. The building alarm starts to wail, shrieking in my ears.

Everything blurs as I race for the shattered door and clamber through the open space into the wild night.

Rain lashes down on me, sweeping through the lot, and someone grabs me, pulls me against their solid body.

I scream at the top of my lungs. I scream until my throat hurts.

"It's okay, it's okay." The familiar voice reaches me.

Cason.

I collapse into him, shaking, and he holds me close. Leaning against his chest, I can hear his heart racing.

"What happened? Was it Larsen?"

“Yes. He’s behind me. He’s . . .” My breath is ragged as I scan the lot, searching the darkness. “Where is he?”

Beyond the smashed glass, the dim lobby is empty.

“Larsen,” I say, gripping Cason’s hand. “Where is he?”

Friday, March 7

SADIE

THE BACK OF THE POLICE van is cold, and the wet gale is streaming through the wide-open doors. I adjust the blanket draped over my shoulders and lean into Cason.

In silence, we watch Detective Alanis approach from across Raleigh's parking lot, with a navy umbrella popped open above her.

"Are your parents on their way?" she asks, coming to a stop at the van.

I swallow and nod. "My dad should be here any minute."

"And my uncle," Cason says. "He's on his way too."

Alanis holds up a clear plastic baggie with a cell phone contained inside. "Is this yours?" she asks me, and I nod. "We found it in the building. Forensics will take a look and return it to you soon. Hopefully we can pin this guy from his prints."

"He was wearing gloves," I answer weakly.

If she's worried, she doesn't show it. Her expression stays neutral. "Let's just wait and see what Forensics can get from this."

"Raleigh's has a security camera," I tell her, my voice hoarse. "It covers the lobby. It picks up sound too." I'm glad I'd asked Maya if the building's security would have caught the fight. I've just got to hope that *our* voices were clear enough, loud enough, to be used as evidence.

Alanis's eyes stay on mine. "And is that where the exchange between you and Zach Larsen took place?"

"Yes. I mean, I hope so. I tried to get him to stand at the back of the foyer, I led him that way, but I don't know for sure. I just hope . . ."

Alanis signals to one of her team.

"I hope it counts for something," I murmur, and Cason folds his hand around mine. "Zach Larsen has been stalking Quinn, and he killed Kai Harrison."

The lights from an oncoming squad car blink over Alanis's face, pulsing blue.

"He said he planted evidence to frame Cason for Kai's murder," I add.

"Then we need to hope that footage has been caught on camera," she says.

Across the lot, I notice Dad's car pulling up. He jumps out, keys in hand, frantically searching the crowd. When his focus lands on me in the police van, I wave him over.

He sprints toward us. "Are you okay?" His words sound panicked, fraught. "What's going on?"

Cason's arm slips away from me.

"I'm okay," I tell Dad. Then, before he can ask, I add, "This is Cason."

Cason offers his hand, and Dad accepts it.

Not exactly the perfectly perfect introduction I'd imagined. But it's a start.

TIKTOK

DARCY WILDE

@WILDEONCRIME

Season 19, Episode 6 #truecrime #forensic #fyp #HailingNY #JusticeforKai

So you might have heard the news that a suspect has been arrested in connection to the Kai Harrison case.

Zach Larsen was detained, and the affidavit has been released. It's been documented that Larsen assaulted a seventeen-year-old girl in Raleigh's Rec Center and was caught on security. Some of the footage has been leaked, and I've stitched it here. You can actually hear him talking in this clip, and it's picked up some words implicating him in the murder and conspiracy to pervert the course of justice.

I understand Zach Larsen is pleading guilty in an attempt to reduce his sentence. I don't think any jury will go lightly on him, though.

Okay, I know a lot of you have been commenting on this news, speculating that there's more to this. I'm actually with you on that. But from my experience, if there are missing pieces here, they could easily get overlooked with Zach Larsen's guilty plea. No one's going to be digging on this if it appears cut-and-dried.

Who knows, though, right? Maybe one day the whole truth will come out.

Until then, we've got our guy. Thanks for following along with me, and hit the like button if you want more content like this.

Friday, March 14

SADIE

IT'S BEEN A WEEK. A full week that sometimes feels as though it's passed in a blink, and other times feels like a lifetime.

The police caught Larsen trying to leave the state. He slipped out of Raleigh's that night and attempted to run. But after the authorities reviewed the security footage, he was arrested and denied bail while he awaits trial.

In my living room, I lean against the window ledge and take a deep breath before I press call.

My eyes stay trained on the street outside, but in my peripheral vision, I notice Dad coming in with his coffee and taking a seat on the couch.

"Sadie, hi." Mom's voice breaks the ringing tone.

"Hi, Mom," I say, switching my cell onto speaker. "Dad's here too."

"Hi, Shannon," he calls from his spot on the couch.

"Hi, Leo," she says, her voice floating through our living room. *Her* living room, once upon a time. "Family talk, huh? Long overdue, if you ask me."

"Yeah," I say, picking at a fray in the curtains. "Sorry."

"Well, now that I finally have your attention . . . ," she carries on wryly, "Sadie, you know how I feel, so I'll get straight to the point. I'd love for you to come live with me. You have your room here, the schools are fantastic, and you could finish up your junior year."

My stomach knots. I glance at Dad, and he takes a slow sip of coffee, waiting for me to make the next move.

Here goes. "Mom, I know you think I'd be better off with you, and of course I miss you, but I really don't want to leave Hailing. I'm not ready to leave school, my friends, Dad—"

He clears his throat, so I add, "I love you, Mom, and I really do miss you. I'll visit more, call more, but . . ." I trail off, and she heaves a sigh.

"Leo," she says, her voice drifting out. "What's your take on this? Wanna weigh in here?"

He sits forward in his seat. "Yes, um." He stumbles over his words, and I can't help but smile a little as he tries to recall his pitch.

I roll my hand and mouth, "Sadie and I have talked . . ."

"Sadie and I have talked seriously about a plan," he takes over. "Curfew, guidelines, check-in times."

"Leo?" The disappointment in Mom's tone is evident, and a pang of guilt hits me. "I thought we discussed this?"

Dad rubs his brow. "We did. I know, we did. But Sadie needs to be part of this conversation too. She should have a say in this."

Mom sighs on the other end of the line.

"I'm sorry," I murmur.

"No, no," she says, attempting to sound breezy. "Don't apologize. I made the decision to move away, I can't expect you to uproot your life and move with me if you don't want to. Everything you're saying makes sense. But it's your safety I'm concerned about."

"That's why we have new rules," I say. "Stricter curfews, more transparency. Not just with Dad. With you too, Mom."

"Speaking of . . ." Dad prompts. He gives me a look, and a flush of heat creeps into my cheeks. "Sadie," he says, "are you going to tell your mom about this boy?"

This boy. Dad can't quite bring himself to call him Cason yet. We're working on it.

"Yes," I forge on, mustering confidence. It's the first time I've told either of my parents about a boy. It's the first time I've ever reached this stage. "He's great, and we're dating."

Silence across the line. Then . . . "Oh."

"He's a good guy, Mom. You might remember him from middle school. Cason Tano."

I hear her take a small breath, and I freeze, waiting for her to tell me I shouldn't be dating. But she doesn't.

"I remember him," she says, and there's emotion in her voice now. Almost as though she's trying not to cry.

I frown at Dad, and he shrugs helplessly back at me. "Mom," I say softly. "It's okay. It's not like I'm going to run away and elope, we're just dating. He's nice, you'd like him. Probably."

"No, it's not that, honey." She exhales. "It's just that I knew his mom. Adrianna."

Dad sits back and presses his hand to his brow. "Cason is Adrianna's kid?"

"Yes," Mom whispers. "Do you remember, Leo? She was a pediatric nurse. She helped us when Sadie got a concussion at the carnival when she was little."

"I remember," Dad breathes.

My heart tugs. Because it comes back to me too, the memory of sitting on a step beneath the florescent lights of the Ferris wheel, Cason's mom holding a compress to my head and doing silly impressions to make me laugh.

There's a moment of silence between us, a reverence, a recognition of how lucky we are to still have each other. To wake up every morning and know that we're still here.

After everything that happened with Kai, Dad kept saying how scared he was, how afraid it made him to think that it could have been me.

I get it. It could have been any of us. Anyone.

I move to join Dad on the couch, and he gently squeezes my shoulder. Life is precious. Time is precious.

And what I do with it matters.

Saturday, March 15

CASON

THE STADIUM IS PACKED TONIGHT with supporters stomping on beat in the stands. The ice shines under the bright lights, and I squint, trying to make out familiar faces in the bleachers.

Sadie and Quinn are right at the front. I clock the scout, sitting midway up, a guy in his thirties with a buzz cut. This is it.

Only a week ago, Larsen was caught and arrested. But the shit show goes on, and school pulled in a sub for us. Coach Something, I already forgot his name. But he's okay. Better than the last guy. At least this one probably won't be trying to set me up for murder anytime soon. I'm thanking my stars in the sky that security cameras pick up sound. Otherwise, I might not be here to kick Newport's ass.

They're coming out onto the ice in their red jerseys. I never liked the color red. Too angry. And it isn't blue.

Before we start, I look for a face in the crowd, someone who can stand in for my mom tonight. Someone who, if I squint enough, I can trick myself into thinking is her.

And then I see them, faces I recognize. Two of them, and

they're waving at me. They're holding up a banner.

I choke out a laugh and wave back.

Alec and Thalia. Thalia jumps to her feet, and the banner ripples the words *Go Number 13!*

Because that's me. Lucky Number 13.

Next to them, there's another couple. The woman looks kind of like Thalia, and the man looks like money. And it hits me—they ditched their meal, all four of them. They're passing takeout boxes between them.

Something close to a laugh, or a sob, escapes me.

The whistle blows, the puck drops.

And I go for the win.

Saturday, March 15

SADIE

HALF THE CROWD ERUPTS IN cheers, stamping their feet and shaking the stands as Hailing takes the victory.

Cason unclips his helmet, and I see him, the relief in his eyes. The total euphoria. I can't help but burst with happiness for him.

Quinn is bouncing up and down on her toes, clapping her hands. Even Emma's phoning in a cheer.

"That was so intense," Quinn says breathlessly.

"Tell me about it." Up until minutes before the final whistle, the scoreboard was tied, and it really could have gone either way.

"I've got to pee," Quinn announces, clambering over Emma and me to get out of the stands. "I'll meet you guys upstairs in the diner." Quinn's patched things up with Maya since their argument, but I don't think she has any intention of getting her job back. I don't think she ever wanted it in the first place.

Emma and I stay seated, watching Quinn shove her way through the packed stands, yelling "Excuse me!" at people.

Emma's eyes stay on Quinn for a moment longer. "She seems to be doing a lot better lately."

"Yeah. Maybe now that she has closure, she can heal a little. And it helps not having everyone at school treating us like murderers."

Emma half smiles. "No one really thought that, Sadie. You know I always had your back, right?"

I nudge her arm. "I know. Thank you."

People at school have done a complete one-eighty since the news broke about Larsen. Suddenly everyone's scrambling to backtrack, rallying around Quinn and me like we're celebrities. Even Jacob Ritter is groveling.

"Hey," I add. "I just remembered—you said you wanted to talk to me about something." With everything that's happened since, I'd completely forgotten about the text Emma sent a little while back. "What did you want to tell me?"

"Right." She presses her lips. "Actually, it's something I need to show you." She slips her camera out of her bag, then powers it up and starts scrolling through her images, the soft beeping filling our silence.

"Scroll right," she directs, handing me the camera.

I focus on the screen and see photos of Raleigh's diner, filled with familiar faces from school. These images are from the night of the Arcadia-Hailing game—the night the fight broke out.

"What am I supposed to be looking at?" I ask, frowning as I study the pictures.

"Just keep scrolling," Emma says.

I swipe through the sequence of images. In one, Cason is in the background, shrugging into his blue-and-black jacket, heading for the exit. On the opposite side of the frame, Kai's hard stare is locked on him. In the next shot, Cason is halfway out the door, and Kai has risen from his seat, his expression twisted in anger. The following picture shows Kai charging toward the door, hand clenched around his hockey stick.

Emma fills in the gaps. "Kai said Cason followed him outside that night. But you were right—Cason didn't follow him. It was the other way around."

I inhale sharply. "Have you shown these to anyone else?"

"No," Emma admits. "It felt too raw, especially so soon after Kai's death, and when Cason was still a suspect. But I wanted you to see it because Cason was telling the truth. Kai started the fight, he must have."

"I always believed that," I tell her. "But thank you for showing me these."

"I'm sorry I doubted you. And I am going to share these photos with Brandon and the guys," Emma says. "This needs to be squashed."

I nod, my gaze drifting back to the screen. In the final shot, Kai is almost at the door, and the anger pours from him, even in this frozen moment. Across the frame, Quinn, still in their booth, watches him as she reaches for her jacket, preparing to leave.

I fiddle with the *Q* pendant on my hair-tie bracelet.

There's something that's been bugging me. Something that still hasn't been answered.

The bleachers have nearly emptied now, but as Emma puts away her camera and moves to stand, I stop her.

"Hey, can I ask you something?"

She tilts her head. "Sure. What's up?"

"When you spoke to Quinn on the night Kai died, did she tell you that she and Kai had been fighting because she wanted them to get back together, but he shot her down?"

Emma's brow creases. "What do you mean?"

"I mean, when she called you from the platform, what did she tell you?"

I hold my breath while I wait for her answer. What if Quinn knew something about Kai, something that she'd said on the phone to Emma in the heat of the moment but held back from telling me when she'd calmed down at my house?

But Emma just looks blankly back at me. "I didn't speak to Quinn that night. I thought she went to your house."

"No, I mean before that. She called you from the street. Right after she had that fight with Kai."

Emma shakes her head. "Nope. I think you're mistaking me for someone else, babe."

I stop dead. It feels as though the ground has disappeared from beneath me. But I was there, I saw Quinn on her cell. I heard her.

I tried to stop him, but he wouldn't listen. . . .

Those were her words. Then she noticed me at my window, and she said, *Emma, I'll call you back*, and she hung up the phone.

If it wasn't Emma, then who was it?

Larsen's words come back to me in a jumbled flood.

Why did you kill Kai? I'd asked him.

For Quinn. Unfortunately, though, I've got to deal with the clean-up.

Quinn made a phone call that night. Twenty minutes later, Larsen showed up at the station and killed Kai.

Please, just think about this—

I already have. . . . I'm done, Quinn.

You can't do this to me. *To us.*

I don't owe you anything. Not anymore.

My heart is pounding in my chest as I remember Kai and Quinn's heated words that night. The sheer panic in Quinn's eyes. The way she couldn't look at me.

We're done here, Kai had said. *It's done.*

You don't get to make that decision alone. We need to talk about this, Kai. Please.

And his final words to her: *This was you, Quinn. You did this to us.*

When I saw him in Raleigh's parking lot, not long after the fight and the hit-and-run incident, he asked after Quinn. He asked if I'd talked to her lately, if I knew what had happened. I'd thought he was messed up over their break-up. . . .

Emma's voice jolts me back. "Sadie, are you okay?"

My stomach lurches. "I've got to go. I've got to . . ."

"What's wrong?"

"I've just . . ." I can't find the words to finish my sentence.

I jump to my feet and stumble down the stands, heading for the bathroom. In the shiny hallway, I burst into the ladies' room just as Quinn is coming out of a stall.

"Hey," she says, skipping to one of the basins. All I can do is stare at her reflection in the mirror above the sink. She flips the faucet and starts washing her hands.

I catch her gaze in the mirror, her reflection. My beautiful best friend.

"Quinn," I say.

When she turns, the smile falls from her lips. "Are you okay? You look like you've seen a ghost."

"Why did you start taking the train to Arcadia? You used to drive."

Her brow knits. "I told you it weirded me out driving after the hit-and-run."

My chest tightens, like I can't get any air into my lungs. "Because you're the one who did it?"

Quinn stills, and her lips part. She glances at the stalls. The doors are all ajar, empty.

"You did it, Quinn," I murmur, barely able to speak. "You offered me a ride home that night. I was supposed to be in the car with you and Kai." She shakes her head, but I keep going. "You were driving home from Raleigh's, after that fight, and Kai was with you, in the passenger seat. That's why he broke up with you and distanced himself from you after that night. He never came back to Hailing, and the one time he did, he drank himself into a state and told Madison he couldn't get over it."

Quinn starts scrambling for words, but nothing comes out.

"It wasn't that he couldn't get over *you*," I piece together, my pulse racing. "He couldn't get over what you'd done, and he didn't understand how you could. That's why on the platform he said, 'We've been doing this for too long. I'm done.' He was going to come clean, wasn't he?"

Quinn's eyes are moving fast, darting left to right. But she still doesn't speak.

"That's why in my room you were so shaken, telling me not to believe anything Kai says, telling me that he was gaslighting you. Because you were scared that this was going to come out."

"No," she says. "This is so . . ."

My stomach turns. "You knew it was Larsen you'd been texting," I hedge. "You must have met up with him in person because Kai *saw* you together—or he saw the Hailing jacket, at least. You didn't get the wrong bag; it was always supposed to be Larsen."

"No," she whispers. "No, I . . . I thought it was Cason."

"You were with him, Quinn. Kai saw you together. And I'm guessing when Kai found out you'd betrayed him, that's why he said he didn't owe you anything anymore. He didn't have to keep your secret. Did Larsen know about the hit-and-run, or was he just scared that Kai would call him out as a predator and he'd wind up in jail? 'I tried to stop him, but he wouldn't listen.'" I echo her words from her phone call to Larsen that night. Not Emma, *Larsen.*

Quinn swallows.

"Because *Larsen* was Darcy Wilde's source," I add, feeling cold all over. Feeling ice-cold. "He told Darcy about me yelling at Kai in class over the AI picture, and she even said in her video that *her source* wasn't there in person, but he somehow knew word for word what I'd said. Because *you* were there, Quinn. You told him. Did you give him my number too? When I spoiled your plan to pretend you'd been texting Cason? Because you and Larsen were going to set Cason up for all of this and I was getting too close to the truth?"

She's breathing fast, and her eyes start to fill. "I've never even met Zach Larsen," she sobs. "This is all so . . . so out of nowhere, Sadie. Why are you doing this to me?"

My eyes smart too. "You met him that night at Raleigh's diner. You were angry because Hannah sent you that picture of Kai and Madison."

Her jaw tightens.

"Answer me, Quinn." I choke out the words, my voice rising, making her flinch.

"Okay," she backpedals. "I just thought he was cute, a distraction. Yes, I gave him my number, but he was weird about talking to me because of my age, so he got a burner, and we just started getting to know each other. I fell for him—there were real feelings there, okay? Is that what you want to hear? I liked him. I trusted him."

"I trusted *you*," I snap back at her. "I've always trusted you. And you've lied about *everything*. Larsen even sent you that message, saying if Kai wanted to talk, he'd handle it. If Kai wanted to *talk*. To come clean about the hit-and-run." My stomach turns. "You sent Larsen after Kai, and then what? You guys decided to set up Cason because he was an easy target? Because you were already messaging on a burner and Cason would just be collateral damage in an irreparable situation? Larsen already hated him, so why not?"

She blinks and tears begin to escape, leaving mascara tracks. "Sadie, you don't understand. I was scared, and I had to protect myself! That guy on the byway, it was just an accident. Kai wanted me to go to the cops, but I couldn't. My life would've been ruined."

My breath catches. "No kidding. You're a murderer, Quinn."

She recoils. "No, I'm not! How can you say that to me?"

"Because it's true! Stop lying to yourself. Stop lying to everyone." I slide the hair tie off my wrist and drop it into her hands. "This is yours."

"Wait," she cries. "You're not going to tell anyone, are you? You're my best friend, Sadie. You can't do this to me."

I turn to leave, but she grabs my arm. "Please, Sadie," she begs, her fingers pressing hard into my skin. "After everything we've been through. Please don't do this to me. We're like sisters." I can hardly understand her through her breathless sobs, but I hear her.

My heart twists as I slip free from her hold. "Turn yourself in," I say, forcing my voice to stay steady. "Don't make me be the one to do it."

"I thought you were my best friend!" she screams, her voice cracking. Before I can react, she launches herself at me, shoving me, sending me stumbling into the wall.

A bolt of fear spikes through me and I push her away. "Quinn, *stop*."

Her face contorts, teeth bared, wild with the kind of anger I never knew existed in her. "You don't get to do this to me." She lunges again, but I dodge to the side, stumbling for the exit, even as her fingers claw at me.

The bathroom door slams, and my fast footsteps echo down the empty corridor. But she's right behind me. I glance back—her face is almost unrecognizable. So much anger twisting her features. I don't know this person.

She quickens her pace as I sprint toward the lobby. The irony isn't lost on me; I was here with Larsen not long ago, and now I'm right back here with Quinn.

As she races after me, she screams into the empty corridor, "I won't let you do this, Sadie! I didn't want Kai to have to die, but we had to kill him, or he would have—"

I burst through the lobby door, exhaling as it swings open. Because as I'd hoped, a dozen or more faces are staring at me, staring into the hallway—where Quinn is now frozen, lips parted.

Cason steps up beside me, silent.

"Did you hear that?" I whisper quickly.

"Yeah," he murmurs. "We heard it."

I blink away tears as Quinn stands motionless just beyond the doorway, panting and scrambling for words—an excuse, a logical way to explain herself, another desperate lie to cover her tracks.

Faintly, I catch the sound of someone on the phone, the call to 911 crackling in the background.

Cason's friends move closer to us, Ruben, Michel, Finley, their expressions shifting from confusion to concern.

All I can do is stare into Quinn's eyes. The years of friendship and sisterhood flash before me, unraveling. I never imagined it would end like this.

But it has.

ACKNOWLEDGMENTS

I FEEL INCREDIBLY LUCKY TO have had the support of so many wonderful people throughout the journey of writing this book, and I want to take a moment to express my gratitude.

To my fantastic agent, Whitney Ross, and the team at High Line Literary—thank you for your guidance and support every step of the way. Your insight and encouragement have meant the world to me.

To my editor, Sarah Homer, and the entire publishing team, thank you for helping me shape this book into its best possible version. From editing to cover design and all the elements that bring a book to life, I am beyond grateful.

To my amazing mum and dad, my superheroes! Thank you for always encouraging me to follow my dreams, for your endless love and support, and for all the conversations, cups of tea, and time spent together.

To James, thank you for always cheering me on, supporting me unconditionally, and listening to all my ideas, even when you can't understand them!

To Sophia and Hayden, thank you for filling my days with happiness, love, and adventure. I am so lucky to have you both. You are the sweetest people and so magical in every way.

To my sister, Natalie, and brother-in-law, Rhodri, and to my fabulous niece and nephew, Emily and Tom, thank you for everything you do, always.

To the book community, and to my family and friends who have helped and supported me on this journey, heartfelt thanks. And to Beth Dilucente, thank you for sharing your invaluable insider knowledge on high school hockey and school life in Western New York State!

And finally, to you, the reader—thank you for choosing this book. I'm so glad you picked it up, and I hope it kept you guessing!